SHATTERED

THE PROTECTORS #11

SLOANE KENNEDY

CONTENTS

Copyright	v
Shattered	vii
Trademark Acknowledgements	ix
Acknowledgments	xi
Series Reading Order	xiii
Series Crossover Chart	xvii
Author Note	xix
Trigger Warning	xxi
shattered	xxiii
Prologue	1
Chapter 1	9
Chapter 2	21
Chapter 3	27
Chapter 4	38
Chapter 5	47
Chapter 6	54
Chapter 7	63
Chapter 8	74
Chapter 9	84
Chapter 10	94
Chapter 11	100
Chapter 12	114
Chapter 13	126
Chapter 14	132
Chapter 15	142
Chapter 16	148
Chapter 17	158
Chapter 18	169
Chapter 19	175
Chapter 20	181

Chapter 21	188
Chapter 22	196
Chapter 23	202
Chapter 24	215
Chapter 25	226
Chapter 26	235
Epilogue	249
Sneak Peek	255
Prologue	257
About the Author	269
Resources	271
Also by Sloane Kennedy	273

Shattered is a work of fiction. Names, characters, businesses, places, events and incidents are either the products of the author's imagination or used in a fictitious manner. Any resemblance to actual persons, living or dead, or actual events is purely coincidental.

Copyright © 2017 by Sloane Kennedy

Published in the United States by Sloane Kennedy
All rights reserved. This book or any portion thereof may not be reproduced or used in any manner whatsoever without the express written permission of the publisher except for the use of brief quotations in a book review.

Cover Images: © Wander Aguiar

Cover Design: © Jay Aheer, Simply Defined Art

Copyediting by Courtney Bassett

ISBN-13:
978-1981607341

ISBN-10:
198160734X

SHATTERED

Sloane Kennedy

TRADEMARK ACKNOWLEDGEMENTS

The author acknowledges the trademarked status and trademark owners of the following trademarks mentioned in this work of fiction:

Trademarks
Band-Aid
Starbucks
Sno Balls
Velcro
Hoover
Marvel's Avengers
Harley Davidson
Captain America
Thor
Hawkeye
Google

ACKNOWLEDGMENTS

Thank you to Claudia and Kylee for the super fast beta reads and feedback, and to Courtney for working with my crazy schedule to get the editing done on time!

A big thank you to my readers for your patience in waiting for Jace and Caleb's story. I hope I did it justice.

SERIES READING ORDER

All of my series cross over with one another so I've provided a couple of recommended reading orders for you. If you want to start with the Protectors books, use the first list. If you want to follow the books according to timing, use the second list. Note that you can skip any of the books (including M/F) as each was written to be a standalone story.

Note that some books may not be readily available on all retail sites

Recommended Reading Order (Use this list if you want to start with "The Protectors" series)
1. Absolution (m/m/m) (The Protectors, #1)
2. Salvation (m/m) (The Protectors, #2)
3. Retribution (m/m) (The Protectors, #3)
4. Gabriel's Rule (m/f) (The Escort Series, #1)
5. Shane's Fall (m/f) (The Escort Series, #2)
6. Logan's Need (m/m) (The Escort Series, #3)
7. Finding Home (m/m/m) (Finding Series, #1)
8. Finding Trust (m/m) (Finding Series, #2)
9. Loving Vin (m/f) (Barretti Security Series, #1)

10. Redeeming Rafe (m/m) (Barretti Security Series, #2)
11. Saving Ren (m/m/m) (Barretti Security Series, #3)
12. Freeing Zane (m/m) (Barretti Security Series, #4)
13. Finding Peace (m/m) (Finding Series, #3)
14. Finding Forgiveness (m/m) (Finding Series, #4)
15. Forsaken (m/m) (The Protectors, #4)
16. Vengeance (m/m/m) (The Protectors, #5)
17. A Protectors Family Christmas (The Protectors, #5.5)
18. Atonement (m/m) (The Protectors, #6)
19. Revelation (m/m) (The Protectors, #7)
20. Redemption (m/m) (The Protectors, #8)
21. Finding Hope (m/m/m) (Finding Series, #5)
22. Defiance (m/m) (The Protectors, #9)
23. Unexpected (m/m/m) (The Protectors, #10)
24. Shattered (m/m) (The Protectors, #11)

Recommended Reading Order (Use this list if you want to follow according to timing)

1. Gabriel's Rule (m/f) (The Escort Series, #1)
2. Shane's Fall (m/f) (The Escort Series, #2)
3. Logan's Need (m/m) (The Escort Series, #3)
4. Finding Home (m/m/m) (Finding Series, #1)
5. Finding Trust (m/m) (Finding Series, #2)
6. Loving Vin (m/f) (Barretti Security Series, #1)
7. Redeeming Rafe (m/m) (Barretti Security Series, #2)
8. Saving Ren (m/m/m) (Barretti Security Series, #3)
9. Freeing Zane (m/m) (Barretti Security Series, #4)
10. Finding Peace (m/m) (Finding Series, #3)
11. Finding Forgiveness (m/m) (Finding Series, #4)
12. Absolution (m/m/m) (The Protectors, #1)
13. Salvation (m/m) (The Protectors, #2)
14. Retribution (m/m) (The Protectors, #3)
15. Forsaken (m/m) (The Protectors, #4)
16. Vengeance (m/m/m) (The Protectors, #5)
17. A Protectors Family Christmas (The Protectors, #5.5)

18. Atonement (m/m) (The Protectors, #6)
19. Revelation (m/m) (The Protectors, #7)
20. Redemption (m/m) (The Protectors, #8)
21. Finding Hope (m/m/m) (Finding Series, #5)
22. Defiance (m/m) (The Protectors, #9)
23. Unexpected (m/m/m) (The Protectors, #10)
24. Shattered (m/m) (The Protectors, #11)

SERIES CROSSOVER CHART

Protectors/Barrettis/Finding Crossover Chart

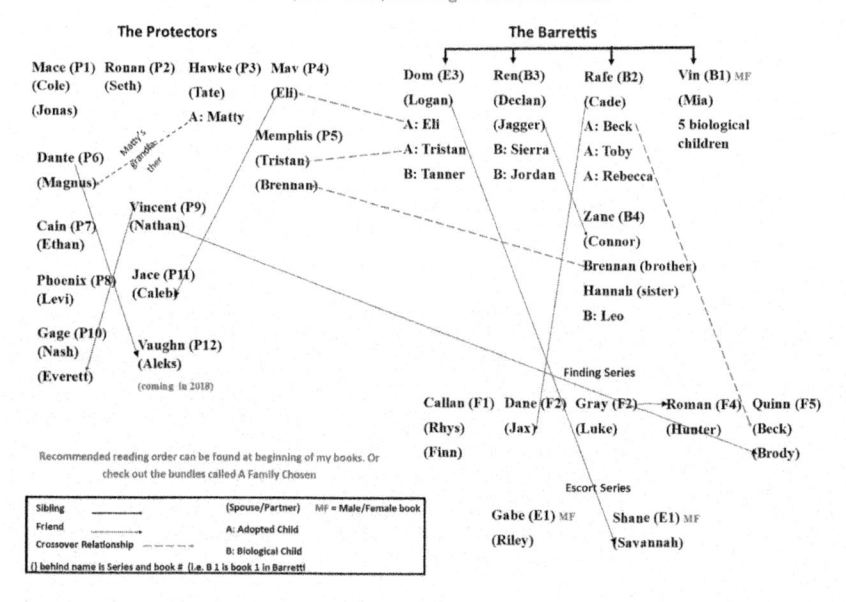

The Protectors

- Mace (P1) (Cole) (Jonas)
- Ronan (P2) (Seth)
- Hawke (P3) (Tate) — A: Matty
- Mav (P4) (Eli)
- Memphis (P5) (Tristan) (Brennan)
- Dante (P6) (Magnus) — Matty's grandfather
- Cain (P7) (Ethan)
- Vincent (P9) (Nathan)
- Phoenix (P8) (Levi)
- Jace (P11) (Caleb)
- Gage (P10) (Nash) (Everett)
- Vaughn (P12) (Aleks) (coming in 2018)

The Barrettis

- Dom (E3) (Logan) — A: Eli
- Ren (B3) (Declan) — A: Tristan, B: Sierra
- Rafe (B2) (Cade) — A: Beck, A: Toby
- Vin (B1) MF (Mia) — 5 biological children, A: Rebecca
- Memphis (P5): A: Tanner — B: Jordan
- Zane (B4) (Connor) — Brennan (brother), Hannah (sister), B: Leo

Finding Series

- Callan (F1) (Rhys) (Finn)
- Dane (F2) (Jax)
- Gray (F2) (Luke) → Roman (F4) (Hunter)
- Quinn (F5) (Beck) (Brody)

Escort Series

- Gabe (E1) MF (Riley)
- Shane (E1) MF (Savannah)

Recommended reading order can be found at beginning of my books. Or check out the bundles called A Family Chosen

Legend	
Sibling	———
Friend	·········
Crossover Relationship	— — —
(Spouse/Partner)	
A: Adopted Child	
B: Biological Child	
MF = Male/Female book	

() behind name is Series and book # (i.e. B 1 is book 1 in Barretti)

AUTHOR NOTE

While writing this book, I was faced with the dilemma of how to tackle the issue of sexual assault against a minor with the correct balance of sensitivity and realism. While a romance at heart, this book doesn't gloss over the seriousness of this issue and the other potential triggers that are listed in the next section.

While this book has all the elements of my romances including plenty of steamy times, some lighter moments and the ever-important HEA, it is a very intense read, so please, please, please proceed at your own risk.

For those of you who've had to deal with the issues raised in this book, know that you are not alone and that, like Caleb, you are worth fighting for and you will never be shattered beyond repair. I've included links for resources that can support you in your battle at the end of the book.

Please stay strong and keep fighting.

—Sloane

TRIGGER WARNING

Note: Reading these trigger warnings may cause spoilers:

Includes references to sexual assault of a minor and self-injury

SHATTERED

shat-er\

Broken into many pieces

PROLOGUE

JACE

"You've gotta be kidding me," I muttered seconds after my phone began ringing. A glance at the clock on my nightstand showed that I'd been asleep for less than twenty minutes. I was half tempted to ignore the damn thing, but something deep in my gut twisted with uncertainty. I'd learned long ago not to ignore the odd sensation. My grandmother had always assured me it was just the gypsy blood running through my veins, but I suspected it had more to do with the years I'd spent learning how to read my uncle's moods so it would be easier to dodge his fists. It had served me well in the military many years later and had saved my life on more than one occasion, so I wasn't about to cast it aside in favor of some much-needed sleep.

I fumbled for the phone as I pulled myself to an upright position and swung my legs over the side of the bed. I glanced at the caller ID and saw that it was my boss, Memphis Wheland. My plan had been to call him in the morning to let him know I was ready to be put back into the rotation, but the fact that he was calling me this late meant he likely already had a job for me.

"Yeah," I said into the phone as I searched out the light switch on my nightstand.

"Jace?"

"Yeah, what's up?" I asked as I wiped at my eyes. It had been almost thirty-six hours since I'd last slept, but the adrenaline was already kicking in as my body began to anticipate the job he'd be assigning me. Between work and my countless trips overseas, I'd been killing myself lately, but it hadn't been without purpose.

It was the only thing that helped me forget the pain-filled blue eyes that had been etched into my brain for nearly two years now.

Please... help me.

I flinched as the hoarse voice filtered through my brain.

He's fine. You got him out of there, I reminded myself.

"Caleb's gone."

My stomach dropped out at Memphis's words.

"What?" I asked, my voice sounding like I'd swallowed a handful of broken glass.

"He's been missing since yesterday morning."

"Jesus," I muttered as I climbed to my feet. "What happened?"

Memphis sighed. "I take it you haven't been watching the news."

"No," I said. "I've been... busy," I added lamely, though the word didn't even begin to describe the shit storm I'd been dealing with these last few weeks... years, actually.

"The trial against Caleb's father started last week. Eli's case."

I knew exactly what he was talking about, and I automatically sat back down on the bed as memories of the young man came flooding back to me. I'd met Eli Galvez nearly two years earlier when I'd been asked by my then-boss, Ronan Grisham, the head of the underground vigilante group I worked for, to check on Eli's stepbrother who'd been institutionalized in a psychiatric hospital. My plan had just been to make sure young Caleb Cortano was okay when I'd broken into the hospital and disguised myself as an orderly. I'd found Caleb strapped to a bed, drugged to the gills and scared to death. I'd tried to convince myself the treatment must have been necessary for whatever mental problems he'd been dealing with, but the second he'd turned his terrified blue eyes in my direction, I'd known something wasn't right. A single tear had rolled down his cheek and I'd been reaching for the restraint on his wrist before he'd even whispered the words that still haunted me.

Please... help me.

Everything had changed from that moment going forward.

Two days after I'd gotten Caleb out of there, I'd been sitting across from Eli and Maverick "Mav" James – another one of Ronan's operatives who also happened to be Eli's lover – explaining to young Eli that I'd watched several videos of him being brutally raped by his stepfather, Jack Cortano, Caleb's father. As if that hadn't been bad enough, I'd discovered multiple videos of Caleb and his older brother, Nick, being repeatedly sexually assaulted by their own father as well.

Jack had been arrested on multiple charges, but the district attorney had decided to start with Eli's case first.

"What happened?" I asked, my heart in my throat.

"The judge threw out the videos on a technicality."

I swallowed hard as I shook my head. How the fuck was that even possible? There'd been no question what had been happening in those videos and who the parties involved had been.

"Did Eli testify?" I asked. I knew that had always been the plan, though the videos alone should have been enough to prove that Jack had raped a then sixteen-year-old Eli.

"He did. It was..."

The fact that Memphis didn't finish the statement pretty much answered the question for me. My heart broke for Eli and Mav. I stiffened as I realized where Memphis was going with this.

"Jesus, Memphis, don't tell me he got off."

There was a long pause before Memphis said, "Acquitted on all the charges."

"Fucking Christ!" I yelled as I got up and began pacing the room. "How the ever-loving hell is that even fucking possible?" I shouted. "The fucker raped him! I saw the goddamn proof myself!"

I managed to calm myself as Memphis remained silent. I suspected he and the rest of the team had likely had a similar reaction to my own.

"The defense brought up Eli's history," Memphis murmured.

I shook my head in disbelief. "He was a fucking kid," I whispered. As a teenager, Eli had been forced to prostitute himself for money before someone had finally stepped in and put a stop to it. I couldn't even begin to fathom what it must have been like for him to have that shit thrown in his face in an open courtroom.

"How is he doing?" I asked.

"Not good," was all Memphis said. "That's why he and Mav didn't realize Caleb had taken off at first. They found his phone in his room and he didn't take his car. We can't find his name on any flights and we've searched everywhere we can think of. We think he might be headed to D.C. – maybe to meet up with some old friends or something. He… he hasn't contacted you, right?"

"No," I managed to get out as my worry for Caleb grew. "I've never given him my number and he doesn't know where I live."

A fact I was cursing now. The last time I'd seen Caleb had been more than a year ago at Christmas. I'd flown to Seattle after Caleb had begged me to come see him. He hadn't been doing well then either, but after spending the holiday with him, I'd hoped things would begin to turn around for him. He'd even agreed to go to therapy to start dealing with what his father had done to him.

But I hadn't had the balls to check in with him since then. I'd told myself it was for his own good, since he'd become far too attached to me, but I knew that was only half the truth.

"Is there any chance you can check out his old neighborhood… maybe stop by his friends' homes and see if they've heard from him?"

"Yeah," I said absently, though from everything I'd learned about Caleb, there hadn't been many friends left in his life. And if Caleb had left his phone and car behind and he'd avoided taking a plane, it was because he knew how easy it would have been to track him down using those things.

Fuck, why the hell hadn't I sucked it up and kept in touch with him?

"Jace," Memphis said quietly.

"Yeah."

"Caleb…he hasn't been doing well. So if you find him, don't let him out of your sight, okay?"

I could barely get my next words out. "Yeah, okay."

I said my goodbyes to Memphis and tossed the phone onto the bed. It was two in the morning, so I couldn't even start searching his old neighborhood for a few hours yet. But as I studied my bed, I knew there wasn't a chance in hell I'd be able to sleep now.

No, Caleb needed me.

I might not be able to check in with his friends for a little while yet, but I sure as hell couldn't just sit there doing nothing. There were a couple of places I could go. They were long shots, but I literally had nothing to lose.

So I grabbed my phone and my keys and told Caleb exactly what I'd told him when he'd called me just before Christmas and begged to see me.

"Hang on, Caleb, I'm coming."

It couldn't be.

That was the thought that kept running through my mind as I stared at the motel room door that had been propped open by flipping the security latch into the locked position before closing the door.

Driving to the motel in the Appalachian Mountains had been so much more than a long shot, but I'd been desperate. I'd spent the entire day scouring all the places I thought Caleb might go if he'd indeed made his way back to D.C., but to no avail. The motel had literally been my last shot.

There were absolutely no cars in the parking lot, but when I'd slipped the manager some cash, he'd confirmed that a young man with blond hair had checked into the very room Caleb and I had used nearly two years earlier while we'd been waiting for Mav and Eli to arrive.

The same room where I'd held him in my arms for the first time so he could finally find some peace in sleep.

I should have been relieved to know I'd finally found him, but I was terrified about what I might find in that room when I opened the door. Two years ago, Caleb had barely been hanging onto his sanity. From what Memphis had told me, things hadn't seemed to have gotten any better for him, despite having found some stability with Mav and Eli. At nineteen years old, Caleb should have had the world at his feet. Instead, it seemed to be crumbling around him.

I pushed open the door. The room was dark, but I could make out a slim figure lying on one of the two queen beds in the room. There was enough light seeping in from the open door to see the shock of blond hair, and I knew I'd found him. I flipped the lock so I could close the door and then made my way to the bed.

"Caleb?" I said softly.

He shifted slightly in the bed, but didn't respond or acknowledge me in any way. He was lying on top of the bedspread, his jacket and shoes still on. There was a black backpack sitting next to the bed, but no other luggage.

I went to turn on the light, but as soon as I did, he whispered, "Please, don't."

I quickly turned the light back off and sat next to him on the bed. I couldn't stop myself from running my fingers through his hair. "Are you hurt?" I asked. I had no clue how the hell he'd gotten all the way to West Virginia on his own, but I had a few thoughts and none of them were good.

Caleb shook his head.

I pulled out my phone and sent a quick text to Memphis, telling him only that I'd found Caleb and he was okay. I included a note telling him I'd call him as soon as I could, but since I knew that likely wouldn't satisfy him, I turned the phone off and then tucked it into my pocket. As hard as all this probably was on Eli and Mav, I needed to focus on Caleb right now.

There was a reason he'd picked this motel... that he'd come all the way out here, to me, even though it had been more than a year since I'd last seen him. So I carefully shrugged off my coat and tossed it on the other bed. I eased myself onto the bed and settled myself against his back. The second I wrapped my arm around him, a choked sob escaped his throat.

"Shhh, I'm here now," I murmured as I brushed my lips over the nape of his neck. He'd grown a little taller since I'd last seen him, but he hadn't filled out at all, proof that his health hadn't improved. His skin felt cold and tremors kept racking his body every few seconds.

There were so many things I needed to talk to him about, but I knew that wasn't why he'd come. I knew that wasn't why he'd searched out this motel, this room and deliberately left it unlocked for me. The thing he needed now was the same thing he'd needed that first night when I'd given in to the need I'd heard in his voice.

Giving him now what I'd given him then was just the start of what I needed to do for the young man who'd trusted me with his very life. I'd failed him once because I'd been a coward. Because I hadn't liked what holding him that night and all the others had made me feel.

But Caleb had been the one to pay the price.

Never again.

I settled my palm over the arms he had crossed protectively against his chest. When my fingers found his, he linked them with mine and a soft sigh shimmied through his lean body.

"Everything's okay, Caleb. Sleep now," I said as I brushed a kiss over his temple.

I could feel moisture on my hand and knew it was likely from the tears I couldn't see or hear Caleb shedding.

"He's coming for me, Jace," Caleb said, his voice cracking as he said my name. "He's going to get out and then he's going to find me."

I settled my mouth near his ear so I'd be sure he heard every word I said to him. "He's welcome to try, Caleb. But he'll have to get through me first. No one touches you ever again, do you hear me?"

But he didn't answer me, which was just fine with me.

Because he'd finally found the very thing that had sent him running to me in the first place… the thing he'd likely been searching a lifetime for, but that would only last for as long as sleep held him in its gentle grip.

Peace.

CHAPTER 1

JACE

He was gone when I woke up.

I didn't even know how it was possible that he'd managed to sneak out of the room with me not knowing, since I was normally a light sleeper. I could only figure my own lack of sleep had played a role.

I quickly rolled out of bed and turned my phone on. I gave myself a mental pat on the back for having had the foresight to plant a tracking device in one of the small front pockets on Caleb's backpack. It was something I'd ended up doing on a whim as I'd gotten up after just a couple of hours to send Memphis a text letting him know we were still okay and that I'd call him as soon as Caleb and I had gotten some much-needed sleep. I probably wouldn't have even planted the tracking device if I hadn't noticed how restlessly Caleb had been sleeping.

The last time I'd held him as he'd slept, the only time he'd stirred had been when he'd pressed back against my body to try and get even closer to me than he'd been. But this time around, he'd been restless the entire time. I was amazed I'd even managed to fall asleep, considering the whimpers that had kept spilling from his throat. I'd tried everything I could think of to soothe him, but nothing had worked and my tired body had finally given up the fight. He'd woken me up several more times throughout the night when he'd called out for his brother, Nick. He'd also repeated the word "no" over and over again, and I'd been sick with the fear that he was dreaming about all the times his father had hurt him.

My phone lit up with multiple missed calls and texts from Mav and Memphis, but I ignored them. I knew Mav must be going crazy with worry for Caleb, considering the role he and Eli had been playing in Caleb's life for the past two years. Mav had figured out pretty quickly that Caleb had an attachment to me that went beyond a little crush or some harmless hero worship. If that had been the only issue, I doubt Mav would've been too worried about it. Problem was, he'd noticed that Caleb wasn't the only one struggling with the connection he and I had. It was something I'd worked hard to hide from Caleb, but there'd been no fooling Mav. He'd confronted me two Christmases earlier about it when Caleb had begged me to come see him in Seattle. I'd tried to pass the whole thing off as Caleb just being overly attached to me, but Mav had seen through my act.

And he hadn't liked it.

Not that I could blame him, considering Caleb had been just seventeen at the time. The young man couldn't have been in a more vulnerable and confused state after everything he'd endured. Add in a guy like me who was not only fifteen years older than him, but also didn't exactly have a lily-white reputation when it came to relationships with other men, and it was no wonder Mav was questioning my motives.

He wasn't the only one.

I couldn't understand my fascination with Caleb Cortano. Even if he'd been closer to my age and not in such an incredibly vulnerable state, he still wasn't my type. I preferred men who matched me in size, strength and demeanor. It made things more interesting in the bedroom.

I would have liked to say my feelings for Caleb stemmed from my inherent need to protect someone weaker than me, but I knew it was more than that. First off, Caleb was just beautiful. There was no getting around that. Even though he'd lost a lot of weight in the last year and his clear skin was paler than it should be, I still found myself fighting my body's natural impulses whenever I was around him. It had taken every ounce of willpower I'd had the previous night to keep my cock from making its excitement known as Caleb had wedged his ass back against my groin. Fortunately, exhaustion had once again played in my favor.

Of course, it had also fucked me over by letting me sleep through Caleb sneaking out on me.

I bit back my anger and dismissed the messages from Mav and Memphis. I pulled up the tracking app as I snatched my keys off the nightstand. At least Caleb hadn't taken my car. Of course, that just had me wondering how the hell he'd managed to leave the motel, because the tracking app was showing he was just outside of D.C.

I tried to maintain my cool as I broke multiple traffic laws in an effort to get back to D.C. Over the few hours it took to make my way back to the city, I monitored Caleb's position. From what I could tell, whatever method of transportation he'd used, he'd had it drop him off at a house in Bethesda, Maryland. The D.C. suburb was one of the wealthier ones in the area, but I had no clue what Caleb would be doing there, since his family's home had been in Alexandria, Virginia, which was a good thirty minutes away.

I drummed my fingers on the steering wheel as I navigated my way through early morning traffic. Luckily, it was a Saturday, so the traffic wasn't as bad as it could have been. As much as I would have liked to have been comforted by the fact that Caleb's position hadn't changed, it actually made me more nervous.

As I made my way down the quiet, tree-lined street, my instincts that something was off kicked in and I parked my car around the block from the location Caleb's tracker was pinging on. As I got out of my car, I grabbed the fake license plates I often kept handy when I was working a job and quickly covered the existing plates with them. If anyone looked really close, they'd notice how I'd jimmied the fake plates to slide over the top of the legitimate ones, but I was counting on the fact that most people wouldn't be looking at my nondescript car that intently.

The houses in the area sat on large lots, which meant there wasn't a lot of traffic, either of the foot or car variety. Something that would work in my favor. What wouldn't work in my favor was the long jacket I was wearing. It was unseasonably warm for late spring, so the jacket wasn't necessary to protect against the weather.

But it was very necessary to hide the gun at my back.

As I rounded the corner of the street Caleb was on, I expected that I'd either have to knock on the door of the house he was at or find a spot and wait for him to come out, but that wasn't the case.

At all.

No, in fact, Caleb was standing right out in the open, completely impossible to miss.

Because not only was he standing on the walkway leading up to the house, he had a gun in his hand that was pointed at a man standing less than a dozen feet from him.

What the hell?

"Please," the man called faintly as he used the briefcase he was holding to shield his chest.

Caleb didn't speak or move. He had the hood of his jacket up over his head, but I knew it was him. I quickened my step as I took in our surroundings. I saw a woman with a little dog rush around the opposite corner, her phone at her ear. She kept looking over her shoulder as she ran. I had no doubt who she was on the phone with.

Which meant I had a minute, two at the most, to diffuse the situation and get Caleb out of there before the cops arrived.

My adrenaline was firing through my blood as I neared Caleb, and it took everything in me not to call his name.

"Please!" the man whispered fiercely. When Caleb didn't respond to him, just held the gun on him, the man shouted, "I can't help you!"

I was close enough to see that Caleb's arm was shaking. I couldn't see his face, but I didn't need to because everything I couldn't see, I heard in his voice as he softly said, "You promised."

He didn't yell the words, didn't cry as he said them. His tone had the same bleakness I'd heard the night before, and that scared me more than anything.

The man shook his head, then said, "I'm sorry, Caleb. I just... I can't."

He shook his head again, as if that was somehow answer enough. The fact that he knew Caleb just added another layer of *this-is-fucked-up* to the entire situation. But of course, things were only getting started because not three seconds later, the front door opened and a kid came running out. A boy, maybe twelve or thirteen years old.

"Dad!" he shouted.

"Ricky, get back inside!" the man yelled, but the kid ignored him and ran right up to him. He threw his arms around his father, who immediately tried to shield the boy from the gun being aimed at him.

"Go back inside!" the man ordered.

"No!" Ricky yelled. "Get away from us!" he cried, his terror-filled eyes on Caleb as he clung to his father. "Leave my dad alone!"

Caleb faltered at the sight of the kid and lowered his arm slightly. I was about to call out to him, when the sharp sound of squealing tires pierced the air. I was moving before the police car rounded the opposite corner, its lights flashing but its siren silent. I was just feet from Caleb when the car came to a screeching halt and a cop jumped from the passenger side.

"Drop it!" he yelled.

Several things happened in the space of the few seconds that followed.

Caleb didn't drop the gun. In fact, he did the worst thing he could have and turned to look at the cop who was shouting at him. I pulled out my own gun at that exact moment because I knew what the cop would do when he saw Caleb's gun swing his way.

Before the cop could send a barrage of bullets at Caleb, I aimed my own gun at the cop's foot, which was visible beneath the door he was using to shield himself. I ignored the screams of the man and his kid, as well as the cops, and fired. The police officer cried out and fell to the ground. It took every ounce of skill I had to shoot the gun from his hand without hitting him again. In that same instant, I reached

Caleb and yanked him behind me as I turned and shot at the second cop, who was using the hood of the vehicle for cover. I hit him in the fleshiest part of his upper arm. It was a wound I knew would cause him to lose the gun, but not potentially make him bleed out right there on the street. I took out the front tires of the car next, then I practically dragged Caleb behind me as we made our way back to my car.

The kid and his father had disappeared, probably back into the house for safety.

I shoved Caleb into the passenger seat of the car and ripped the gun from his hand. He hadn't said a word and I could tell he was going into shock. Unfortunately, I didn't have time to deal with any of that because I could hear sirens in the distance. I hurried to the driver's side, scanning the surrounding houses as I did so. I shook my head at the clusterfuck I'd just been thrust into.

I was on the phone before I even got the car started.

"Go," Daisy said. I could hear the distinctive clicking of her keyboard in the background. My team's IT girl was nothing if not efficient.

A fact I was grateful for.

"It's Jace. I'm at a house on the corner of Crescent and Maple in Bethesda. I've just wounded two cops. I need you to scrub any video footage of me and Caleb from any security cameras from the surrounding houses."

To her credit, the girl didn't react other than to say, "On it."

"Thanks," I said, and hung up on her. I knew it probably wouldn't do much good to try and hide Caleb's identity, since the guy he'd been holding the gun on had recognized him, but I'd rather get rid of as much evidence as I could before the cops could get their hands on it.

"Who is he?" I snapped at Caleb.

But he didn't answer me. He was leaning against the car door, shaking like a leaf. He had his arms around his body. He hadn't even removed his backpack.

"Caleb!" I practically shouted.

He didn't even react. It was like he didn't hear me. I focused on getting us out of the neighborhood. Several police cars raced past us from the opposite direction, but fortunately, none turned to come after us.

It meant the cops I'd shot probably hadn't gotten a look at my car.

Fuck, I'd shot cops. Yeah, I'd made sure to only wound them, but still…

"Fuck!" I bit out in frustration. I was normally someone who managed to stay calm, even in the tensest of situations, but the thought of how close Caleb had come to getting shot was making me crazy. If I'd been just a few seconds later…

"He promised," Caleb whispered. "He promised."

I looked at Caleb and saw that he'd started rocking back and forth. He just kept repeating the words over and over again.

As pissed as I was, my worry for Caleb's mental state was greater. I reached over to settle my hand on his knee. "Hey, look at me," I said.

He didn't.

"Caleb, it's going to be okay," I murmured.

It really wasn't, because we were both fucked. There was no way Caleb would ever be able to go back to his old life now, since the cops would be looking for him. Despair went through me as I considered the life he'd have – always running, always looking over his shoulder.

I considered my options as I got us onto the beltway. I couldn't risk staying in the D.C. area.

And I couldn't do this alone.

I muttered another curse and then reached for my phone. Not surprisingly, Memphis answered on the first ring.

"Where is he?" Memphis asked.

"I have him," I said. "But we need to get out of town. Far out of it," I added.

Memphis was silent for a beat and then said, "Head west and tell me where you stop. I'll meet you there."

I glanced at Caleb. He was still rocking back and forth. "We can't go for long. Caleb's not doing well."

I heard Memphis sigh just before he said, "I'll be there as soon as I can."

I hung up on him and put the phone in the cup holder. I reached for Caleb and forced him to release the hold he had on himself so that I could link my fingers with his. "Hang on, Caleb. I've got you now."

But as expected, he didn't answer.

He didn't do anything but rock back and forth, softly whispering the same two words over and over again.

He promised.

∼

I drove only long enough to get us back to the mountains, but I didn't dare head to the motel we'd stayed in the night before. There was just too great of a chance of the motel owner recognizing Caleb. I got us to the western side of the mountains and began the search for what I wanted.

I found it in the form of a remote cabin that appeared abandoned. Caleb had finally fallen asleep and while he'd looked incredibly uncomfortable pressed up against the door with his bulky backpack still strapped to his back, I hadn't even considered waking him up to urge him to take the thing off. I left him in the car as I did a quick check of the cabin and confirmed there was no one around. It took just seconds to pick the lock and get inside. I was surprised to find that the cabin wasn't as abandoned as I'd thought. It was decently furnished and had power. But there was a layer of dust on everything, so I figured the owner hadn't been back in a while.

It would have to do for the night because I needed to get Caleb settled.

I hurried back to the car and went to the passenger side. I eased open the door and used my hand to keep Caleb from falling out of the car. He jolted as his body shifted, then jerked awake.

"Don't!" he shouted as he lashed out at me.

I grabbed his wrists and said, "Caleb, it's me, Jace. You're safe."

It took him several seconds to register what I'd said before he relaxed and whispered, "Jace?"

"Yeah, baby, it's me."

I cursed myself for letting the endearment slip out, but fortunately Caleb didn't seem to notice because he began whipping his head around as the fog of sleep cleared.

"Where are we?" he asked.

I was glad he seemed a little more lucid than he had earlier.

"Someplace safe," I said. "Come on, let's get inside."

But he didn't move, and I felt a fine tremor ripple through his body as I continued to hold onto his wrists.

"He has a kid," Caleb whispered. "I didn't know he had a kid."

I figured he was talking about the guy he'd held the gun on, but as badly as I wanted to know who the man was to him, I wanted to get him inside first. The air around us was cooling quickly as the sun fell completely behind the horizon. The higher elevation meant the temperature would drop more quickly than down in the lowlands. We'd likely see freezing temperatures tonight.

"Let's get inside," I urged and then I was carefully pulling him out of the car. Caleb swayed and leaned heavily against me as he closed his eyes. The dome light from the car showed his pained expression. "Caleb, are you hurt?" I asked, terrified that I'd somehow missed him getting shot or something. I began scanning his body for blood.

He shook his head. "Just a little dizzy," he said.

"When was the last time you ate?" I asked as I closed the door and leaned him back against the side of the car.

He didn't answer me. I left him standing there and went to the trunk to get my duffel bag, which I kept stashed in the car for emergencies. I used the opportunity to remove the fake plates from the car and tossed them into the trunk. By the time I returned to Caleb's side, he'd closed his eyes again. I put my arm around his waist and said, "Lean on me if you need to."

"I'm okay," he murmured, but when I pulled him forward, he leaned against me anyway.

Once I got him into the cabin, I sat him down at the small kitchen table and began rummaging around the cabinets. I had some MREs in my bag, but I preferred to serve him something hot. Not to mention that the military style ready-to-eat meals tasted like shit. I let out a silent thank-you to whoever was listening when I spied several cans of soup. I grabbed one of the cans of chicken noodle soup and got it going on the stove, then went to the refrigerator. There was nothing in it, so I settled for some tap water in a plastic cup. Caleb was staring off into space as he sat in the chair. I worked the backpack off his back and dropped it by his feet. I didn't like that he'd gone quiet again, but my priority was getting some food into him, so I didn't try to engage him in conversation. The soup took just minutes to heat up. When I slid it in front of him, he shook his head.

As badly as I wanted to order him to eat, I could tell he was mentally on the edge and it wouldn't take much to send him over and back into the state of shock he'd been in. Between his obvious lack of sleep and food, not to mention the events of the day, I had no doubt he was at his breaking point.

"Caleb," I said softly as I covered his hand with mine where it was resting on the table. "Please eat… for me."

It was a low blow, but I was a desperate man.

His dull blue eyes lifted to meet mine. He didn't respond as he pulled his hand free of mine, but when he reached for the spoon, I stifled my sigh of relief. The cabin was eerily silent as he ate. I used the opportunity to send a text to Memphis telling him our coordinates from my satellite phone, since my regular phone didn't have reception. I'd been hoping there'd be a TV or radio in the cabin so I could see what the news was saying about the shooting, but unfortunately there wasn't either.

Caleb managed to eat about a quarter of the soup before he carefully settled the spoon on the table. He stared numbly at the bowl, as if it somehow held the answers to how his life had gone so very wrong. My heart hurt for him as I watched him, and I couldn't resist reaching out to push his hair off his face.

As badly as I needed answers from him, I needed something else more. I stood and covered his hand with mine. He let me link our fingers and when I urged him to stand, he did. I led him to the single bedroom in the cabin. When I flipped the light switch on, it turned on the small lamp on the nightstand. I left Caleb to stand next to the bed as I stripped off the dusty quilt covering the top of it. I urged him to sit and stripped off his shoes and hoodie, then murmured, "Lie down."

He did as I asked and immediately closed his eyes the second his head hit the pillow. I worked off my own jacket and shoes and went around to the other side of the bed. I put my gun on the nightstand and then got into bed with him. He didn't resist when I looped my arm over his waist. We lay there for several minutes, but I knew he wasn't asleep. I could feel it in the way he held his frame rigid against mine.

"Did you kill them?" he finally asked, his voice low and barely audible.

"No," I said, because I knew who he was talking about. "Only flesh wounds. They'll be okay."

I felt, rather than heard, his sigh of relief.

"Who is he, Caleb?" I asked.

When Caleb didn't respond, I fought back the bite of frustration that went through me. Two years earlier when I'd met him, Caleb had trusted me with anything and everything. As much as I'd known it wasn't healthy for him to put so much faith in me so soon after meeting, a part of me had wanted to nurture that emotion, to see it grow and flourish.

And I hadn't just wanted that for him.

I'd wanted it for me, too.

"I shot two cops today, Caleb. For you. We may never be able to go back to the way things were... do you understand that? As soon as that guy tells the cops who you are—"

"He won't," Caleb whispered.

"Won't what?"

"Tell them who I am."

His comment caught me off guard. "Caleb—"

"You lied to me, Jace," Caleb murmured. "You said everything would be okay."

Caleb shifted away from me, then made a move to get up. I used the hand I had at his waist to reach down and grab his right arm, which he was gripping the edge of the bed with so he could lever himself off it. As I closed my fingers around his forearm, his sleeve rode up and I automatically slid my hand farther up his arm. "Caleb," I began, but stopped abruptly when my fingers registered what I was feeling.

Raised skin.

Lots of it.

I held my breath as I moved my fingers enough so I could see what I knew had to be some kind of mistake.

It *had* to be a mistake.

It wasn't.

I was left completely dumbstruck as I stared at the dozens of scars on the inside of Caleb's forearm.

Perfectly uniform scars that couldn't have found their way onto his skin in any kind of accidental fashion.

No.

I wasn't sure if I said the word out loud or not, but it didn't matter. Caleb pulled his arm free of my hold and rubbed it against the bed so the sleeve slipped back down. He didn't look at me as he whispered a handful of words that left me feeling completely shattered.

"Everything's not okay, Jace."

CHAPTER 2

CALEB

I was so cold.

Even with Jace at my back, I was cold.

That had never happened before.

It should have been unsettling, but it actually made me feel better in a way. It meant I could not feel for a little while longer.

I liked not feeling.

It made things easier.

I'd felt a little yesterday when Jace had shown up at the motel, but that had been my own fault for going there in the first place.

For waiting for him to come, like I'd known he would. I should have just stuck to the plan.

I wanted to laugh because *plan* made it sound like I knew what the hell I was doing. Like I had some reasonable hope of finding that one magic thing that would just fix everything in my life… fix me.

For a while, I'd thought it was Jace, and I'd clung to that for a really long time.

Too long.

I'd honestly believed what he'd told me – that if I just hung in there long enough, things would get better. I'd had this ridiculous vision of getting to the point where I was a normal guy and I'd show up on

Jace's doorstep one day to show him I was worthy of someone like him. That I was no longer the kid who'd let his own father fuck him for years. That I wasn't the coward who'd watched his brother die and kept his mouth shut about the how and the why of his death.

But Jace was a liar, just like the rest of them.

Okay, so maybe liar was too harsh – but he was just like the others who kept telling me that things would get better.

Eli.

Mav.

My stepmother, Mariana.

They'd all promised me over and over again that my father would pay for what he'd done to me, to Eli... to Nick, and that I'd somehow miraculously get my life back.

But how was I supposed to get something back that I wouldn't have even recognized? My life had been watching my brother succumb to his drug addiction while I pretended to be a regular kid, even as my father found his way into my bed night after night after night. Take those things away, and who was I supposed to be? I'd hated what my father had been doing to me and I'd hated losing my brother to the drugs that had given him the same numb feeling I now craved, but I'd still had moments where I felt alive.

Moments like when my father would take me to a baseball game and high-five me as our team won, or we'd go fishing in Puget Sound and I'd reel in the first salmon.

I'd feel that little spark of energy inside of me that lit up whenever my father told me he was proud of me or when I saw glimpses of the old Nick, the one I'd practically worshipped as a little kid. There'd be those rare times where I'd feel only good things when I remembered the days before my parents had gotten divorced.

Camping trips.

Christmases with way too many presents.

Elaborate birthday celebrations.

Barbecues in the back yard.

Those were the things I wanted back. Sometimes I thought I'd even be willing to pay the high price tag that came with it. As sick as it was, I almost hated my father more for ruining everything by doing to Nick and Eli what he'd done to me. If it'd just been me, I would have found a way to live with it. But my father had been a greedy man... and an arrogant one.

I felt Jace shift behind me, and then he was getting out of bed. I didn't ask him where he was going, because I knew.

He'd felt the cuts on my arm. He'd known what they were.

Now he'd be trying to find the cause of them. I had no doubt that he thought this was something else he could fix for me.

When he returned a moment later, I didn't need to look to know he'd found what he'd been looking for. I felt him sit on the bed, but I didn't turn to look at him. The old me would have been eager to please him, but I wasn't that naïve seventeen-year-old kid who'd seen only a hero when Jace had stood over me in that psychiatric hospital and answered my whispered pleas for help.

I'd come to realize in the last year that it wasn't so much that Jace wasn't a hero, because he absolutely was. Just like Eli and Mav were heroes for everything they'd done for me.

No, the problem was that they weren't *my* heroes.

Because I was beyond saving.

I'd wanted out of that mental hospital, but the truth was, I hadn't really wanted out of my old life. Not the way I should have.

I'd wanted my father to stop hurting me, but I hadn't wanted to give him up, either. I hadn't wanted him to pay for the things he'd done to me... or my brothers.

I'd just wanted *him*... I'd wanted to go back to him just being my father and me just being his kid. I'd have gladly given up seeing him punished to get that back.

That was why I didn't deserve to be saved.

That was why Jace and Eli and Mav had been wasting their time.

And why it had been a fool's errand to come down here. That pesky *feeling* shit had reared its ugly head for a while as I'd contemplated my father coming back into my life, but only because I'd known when he did, it wouldn't be so he and I could go back to the way things had been.

No, he was going to kill me like he'd killed Nick, and despite hating every part of my current life, for some reason, my instinct to survive didn't seem to care about that fact.

It was just another sign of my cowardice.

I didn't want to live, but I was too afraid to die.

I heard the sound of something heavy being placed on the nightstand. I was surprised Jace had brought his prize into the room with him, but I guessed he figured knowing where the box cutter was would ensure I didn't use it.

I didn't bother telling him that I was too numb to need it.

"Why?" I heard Jace ask.

I hated that the despair in his voice sparked something inside of me. I'd never heard him sound like that. I also hated the little sliver of guilt that began to gnaw at my insides.

I shouldn't have gone to that motel. I shouldn't have allowed the need to feel Jace's arms around me to dictate my actions and pull him into my stupid plan. And I definitely shouldn't have believed that Richard Jennings would somehow suddenly grow a conscience and follow through on the promise he'd made to me so long ago.

"It's not your fault, Jace," I said softly, hoping that would mollify him.

But, of course, it didn't.

The bed shifted and then suddenly he was rolling me on my back. As he leaned over me, I couldn't help the spark of awareness that went through me. Jace's dark brown hair had come free of the rubber band he usually tied it back with. It wasn't long enough to actually touch me, but it fell in loose curls to just above his shoulders. I'd always secretly wished I could touch his hair, just so I could test how the strands would look and feel sliding between my fingers, but I hadn't ever been brave enough to be that forward.

The things I'd felt for Jace had gone beyond hero worship pretty much the very day I'd met him, but I hadn't known what to do about it. Despite the fact that I'd become adept at sucking a guy's cock and had been fucked more times than I could count, I was completely clueless when it came to things like interacting with a guy I was attracted to.

In truth, Jace was the first guy I'd ever really wanted. I hadn't even really been sure I was gay until I'd met the older man. And I'd been certain that the idea of any man ever touching me again would be akin to the worst kind of torture, but I'd found that Jace was most definitely the exception to that rule. Yes, the idea of him fucking me absolutely terrified me, but a part of me also wanted to feel the full weight of his body on mine. I wanted to know what his lips felt like on my skin… and more importantly, on my mouth.

Jace wasn't a huge guy, but he was well-built. His chest was broad and the collar of his T-shirt rode low enough to give me a tantalizing peek at the tattoo just above his left pectoral muscle. His body was long and rangy, and he always smelled like the outdoors with just a hint of spiciness. His skin tone was several shades darker than my own pale hue, and he had brown eyes that bordered on black. His beautifully shaped lips were framed by a sexy bit of stubble.

Jace settled some of his weight on my lower body as he braced his left arm on the bed next to my head. My body reacted to his groin brushing mine. I had no idea how I managed not to whimper as a powerful wave of sensation rolled through me.

"I left to protect you," Jace whispered, his voice cracking a bit. It almost seemed like he'd made the comment to convince himself of that fact, not me. "I stayed away because it was for the best," he practically growled.

I wasn't sure what he wanted me to say to that. Part of me wanted to rail at him that he was the biggest fool on the planet if he actually believed what he was saying, but another part of me wanted to comfort him. To let him continue to believe that what had happened hadn't had anything to do with him.

I settled for saying, "I know."

But of course, that only frustrated him more, because his mouth pulled into an even deeper frown.

"Tell me how to fix this," he murmured.

I held his gaze for a long time before saying, "Not everything can be fixed, Jace." I paused as I took in his hard expression, because the answer clearly didn't satisfy him. "You know how if something shatters when it breaks, there's no way to find all the pieces to put it back like it once was? Maybe sometimes it's better not to even try..."

I let my words hang and watched as his eyes went impossibly dark. He held me for a moment longer and then released me. Then he stared down at me like he was seeing me for the first time.

And all I could think was, *finally*.

CHAPTER 3

JACE

"Where is he?"

"Inside," I said as I took in Mav's harried expression. I wasn't at all surprised to see him, since I'd expected as soon as Memphis told him where Caleb was that Mav would want to come and see for himself that he was okay.

I'd gotten Memphis's text a few minutes earlier that they were nearby, so I'd gone outside to wait for them.

And not just because I didn't want to wake Caleb up.

Restless energy thrummed through my veins as I watched Memphis and Mav tense up at roughly the same time as they realized I wasn't going to invite them inside the cabin. Mav took a step forward, but Memphis put his hand out to stop him.

I was almost disappointed because I was itching for a fight.

Anything to get rid of the rage that was making my blood run cold.

Caleb was hurting himself.

On purpose.

I still couldn't wrap my head around it, despite having seen the proof on his arm. Despite having felt the weight of the box cutter in my hand.

I didn't know the young man who'd lain calmly beneath me last night and had told me he was too far gone already... that he wasn't worth saving anymore.

Well, fuck that shit.

After I'd climbed off Caleb, he'd turned over on his side again. I'd sat on the edge of the bed for a long time as I'd tried to figure out how I'd managed to fuck all this up so badly, but when there hadn't been any answers to find, I'd laid back down next to him and put my arm around him. He hadn't melted against me like he had the previous night in the motel. There'd been no tears of despair on my skin to prove he hadn't meant what he'd said about being beyond my or anyone's reach, and no whispered fears or pleas to take his pain away.

There'd been absolutely nothing.

Just like there'd been nothing in his beautiful eyes when he'd declared himself shattered beyond repair.

Nineteen fucking years old and acting like his life was over.

No.

Fucking.

Way.

Not on my watch.

I shifted my eyes to Mav. He looked like complete and utter shit and remembering *why* he looked like that helped tamp down some of my anger.

"How's Eli?" I asked.

"How do you think he is?" Mav asked, his own anger getting the better of him. Though I doubted it was all directed at me. "Twelve people watched and listened as he was forced to recount every single thing he had to do to survive as a kid and decided that somehow that meant he deserved to be repeatedly raped by a man twice his age who he also happened to call 'Dad.'"

Memphis put his hand on Mav's arm to calm him and Mav sucked in a deep breath. "He's coming apart," he murmured. "He's with his fathers until I can get back."

"I'm sorry," I said. And I was. I'd met Eli several times and he was a really good guy. He'd made a good life for himself, despite all his suffering, and he'd taken Caleb in when Caleb hadn't had anyone left.

"Eli needs to know his brother is safe," Memphis suggested.

"He's safe," I said.

"I don't have time for this shit," Mav snapped, then he stepped forward. He stopped abruptly when I threw the box cutter at his feet.

"He's safe," I growled. "But he's not okay. Far from it."

Mav stared at the box cutter in confusion.

"He's using that to cut his own fucking skin so he can escape all the shit inside him that he can't deal with," I bit out. Mav swallowed hard and then looked at Memphis before returning his attention to me. He began shaking his head, but I cut him off before he could speak.

"Believe it," I snapped. "I saw the scars myself. You were supposed to be taking care of him!"

Mav's expression hardened and this time when he came at me, Memphis had to step in front of him and force him back. "And where the fuck were you, Jace?" Mav yelled. "Not even one fucking phone call to see how he was doing?"

"You know why I couldn't do that," I retorted as the guilt cascaded through me.

"Yeah, I know why," Mav ground out. I knew he wasn't talking about Caleb's attachment to me as having been the issue that had kept me away. He hadn't said the words, but he knew the real reason I'd stayed away. And it wasn't just because of the bullshit I'd spouted to Caleb the night before about wanting to protect him. I'd been protecting myself too.

I forced a deep breath of air into my lungs and then looked at Memphis and said, "Who's the guy?"

Mav had calmed enough that he wasn't trying to get past Memphis anymore.

"His name is Richard Jennings. He's the headmaster at the prep school Caleb was attending. He doesn't have a record... not even a parking ticket," Memphis said. "He led a perfectly boring, quiet life until yesterday afternoon."

"I doubt that," I bit out. "Caleb wasn't gunning for him because he assigned too much homework," I said snidely. I paused and asked, "Did the cops track Caleb back to Seattle yet?"

"That's the funny thing," Memphis murmured. "Caleb's name never came up in the investigation."

"What?" I asked, completely taken aback.

"Daisy got her hands on the initial police reports. Jennings says he didn't recognize the kid who tried to mug him."

"That's impossible," I said. "I heard the guy say Caleb's name. Why wouldn't he tell the cops—" I stopped suddenly as my mind put two and two together.

"He said the guy wouldn't tell the cops who he was," I murmured, more to myself than anything else. I looked up at Memphis and Mav, expecting to find them watching me with confusion, but their eyes weren't on me.

I followed their gazes to see Caleb standing on the porch of the cabin. He was leaning against one of the half-rotted posts, his arms wrapped around his slim body. I turned and went to him. Pain slashed through my belly when he took a step back from me as I reached for him.

"Go back inside," I said. "It's too cold out here."

Caleb's eyes shifted to Mav. "Eli?" he asked.

"Hanging in there," Mav said. "He's worried about you."

Caleb was quiet for a moment before saying, "Did Jace's name come up in the investigation?"

"No," Memphis said before I could tell Caleb it didn't matter. "There's no video footage of the incident. The one security camera with a view of the front of the Jennings' house wasn't working."

Caleb looked at me. "So Jace can go back to the way things were, right?"

Irritation went through me as he threw my words back in my face. I didn't miss the fact that he didn't say anything about himself going back to the way things had been.

Caleb held my gaze for several long seconds, but unlike in the past, I couldn't tell any of what he was thinking. He finally tore his eyes from mine to look at Mav. "Tell Eli I'm sorry. For everything. But I'm not coming back with you." He let his gaze slide back to mine. "I'm not going with anyone," he said, his voice low.

I was about to protest when a flash of red on Caleb's shirt caught my eye. "Down!" I screamed as I lunged at Caleb, knocking him backwards. I had no hope of cushioning his fall as my heavier body landed on his. The soft popping sounds over my head had me wrapping myself tighter around Caleb as he gasped for air beneath me. A split second later, gunfire erupted all around us. I rolled with Caleb so we were somewhat blocked by the porch railing.

"Caleb, are you hit?" I asked as I began running my hands over his body. "Are you hit?" I practically shouted in his face.

He coughed and gasped, then began shaking his head. Since I knew I'd probably knocked the wind out of him, I didn't wait for him to confirm that he was okay with words. Instead, I grabbed my gun from where it was tucked in my waistband and turned to survey the scene.

Memphis and Mav had taken cover behind their car. They were shooting in opposite directions, so I quickly scanned our surroundings. I could still hear the distinctive popping sounds, a sure sign our attackers were using suppressors on their guns. There was no way to tell how many shooters there were, but I guessed there were at least five based on the volume of shots being fired. I forced myself to focus on the woods around us and finally zeroed in on what I was looking for. I raised my gun, slowly blew out my breath and pulled the trigger. The man who'd been about to take a shot at Memphis and Mav crumpled soundlessly to the ground.

"Get inside!" I yelled at Caleb, but just as he started to crawl for the front door, I heard glass breaking and I grabbed his leg to drag him back to me. I covered his body with mine and closed my eyes at the same time that I covered my head as best as I could. A second later, there was a deafening bang followed by a bright flash of light.

A flash grenade.

I fought through the haze of pain and confusion as my ears rang.

"Jace, go!" I heard Memphis yell. "Get him out of here!"

I grabbed Caleb by the shirt and hauled him to his feet. The flash grenade had done its job and completely disoriented him, so I leaned into his body so that I could get him over my shoulder. Despite all the weight he'd lost, he wasn't a small man and I staggered beneath his bulk as I rushed down the stairs. I managed to scan our surroundings as Mav and Memphis covered me. I was able to take out another shooter just as I reached my car. I'd had the sense to turn the car around the night before so that it was facing the path leading to the road, rather than the cabin itself. And luckily, Memphis and Mav had parked next to me instead of blocking me in.

I shoved Caleb into the car, pushing him over the driver's seat. "Move, Caleb!" I ordered. He'd recovered enough from the flash grenade that he was able to follow my order. "Get down!" I said, when he went to sit on the seat. He squeezed himself onto the floor as best he could and covered his head. Just as he did, the passenger side window blew out. I winced as flying glass hit my face, but managed to fall into the driver's seat. I sent a silent thank-you heavenward that I'd left the car keys in my pocket, rather than inside the cabin. I managed to get the car started and flew down the driveway toward the road.

"No, wait!" Caleb shouted. "We can't leave Mav and Memphis!" he yelled as he tried to get into the passenger seat.

"We're not! Stay down!" I ordered.

Thankfully, Caleb did as I said. I drove for almost half a mile before I found what I was looking for. I slammed on the brakes and said, "Stay here!"

I didn't wait to see if Caleb followed my instructions. I scanned my surroundings as I got out of the car. My gut was telling me I'd gotten us far enough away from the assailants that Caleb would be safe in the car for the few minutes I needed. I went to the trunk and practically ripped it and the long black case inside open. My fingers flew as I quickly assembled my AS50 rifle. I was running even as I attached the scope to the gun. It took less than thirty seconds to get to the small rise overlooking the cabin. It wasn't as much height as I would have liked, but it was enough.

I fell to the ground and looked through the scope. Relief flooded my system as I spied Memphis and Mav still holding off the assailants. Memphis was holding his right shoulder, even as he continued to fire his gun. There was a bloom of blood beneath his hand.

I tore my gaze from my teammates and began searching out the area. I already knew from the first guy I'd shot that the attackers were wearing army camouflage. It took just seconds to find the first assailant and with one pull of my trigger, he went down. Three more followed. I spotted another two bodies in my scope as I did a sweep of the area. The last two men were on the move, trying to flee. Presumably because they'd realized they'd come under sniper fire. I easily took them out and then spent another minute searching for any stragglers. When I swung my scope back to Memphis and Mav, I saw that Mav had his hand on Memphis's gunshot wound. I saw that Memphis was holding his hand in a thumbs-up position – it was a message to me that he was okay.

I climbed to my feet and ran down the rise. I didn't bother dissembling the gun before tossing it in the trunk.

Caleb was still huddled in the same spot, and I could hear him crying softly. I reached down and grabbed his arm. "Hey," I said. When he looked at me I said, "We're safe. Mav and Memphis too."

He let out a little sob and then nodded his head. He wiped at his tears and followed my urging to get into the seat after I swept as much of the broken glass off it as I could.

"You're not hurt, right?" I asked.

"My ears hurt... my head too."

"The ears are from the flash grenade," I explained. "They'll stop ringing soon." I reached for his head and turned it so I could see the back. I could see a little bit of blood dampening his blond hair. "Looks like you hit your head when you fell."

"I'm okay," he said.

"I'll take a look at it when we stop."

"Stop?" Caleb asked as he looked over his shoulder. "Aren't we going back to help Memphis and Mav?"

I shook my head but didn't say anything. I didn't know how to explain to him that I wasn't about to take him back into a situation that I couldn't be sure was one hundred percent safe. The attackers had been gunning for Caleb. Of that, I had no doubt, considering the first bullet had been meant for him. There was only one way those men had been able to find us, and despite Memphis and Mav being on my side, until I had some answers, we weren't going anywhere but as far away from this place as we could get.

Alone.

I reached into my pocket and pulled out my phone as I got the car moving. As soon as the phone got a signal, I located the number I wanted and hit dial.

"Jace, what's going on?" Ronan asked the second he answered. It sounded like he was on the move and I instinctively knew he'd already talked to Memphis.

"How'd they find us?" I asked. I respected Ronan like nobody's business, but I couldn't keep the accusatory note from my voice.

"We don't know," Ronan said. "The jet is at the airstrip in Monroe County. Take Caleb there and Memphis and Mav will meet you—"

"No," I cut in. "Those guys were professionals. If they'd been tracking me and Caleb, they would have hit us last night. There was only one way they found us."

Ronan was quiet for a moment and I could practically see him frowning. "Mav and Memphis would never—"

"I know that," I said. "Caleb was the target," I confirmed. "But they used Mav and Memphis to find him. I don't know if they tagged their rental car or bugged their phones or what, but Caleb stays with me until we get some answers." I paused and added, "Just me," to make sure Ronan understood I was in charge. I was likely going to end up without a job after all this, not to mention that having Ronan Grisham as an enemy wasn't going to be pretty, but Caleb's life was on the line. I wasn't messing around with protocol.

Ronan didn't speak for the longest time and I was about to hang up when he said, "Caleb's due to testify in a pre-trial hearing in three weeks. If he's not back here by then, his father will walk."

"Maybe that's not a bad thing," I said. My trigger finger practically itched at the prospect of getting Jack Cortano in the sights of my scope. Ironically, the man was safest in prison. It was one of the few places beyond Ronan's reach.

"Look at the young man sitting next to you, Jace."

I couldn't help but do as Ronan said.

"Now tell me if you think he's strong enough to carry the weight of his father's death on his shoulders."

I sighed because I didn't need to look at Caleb to know that.

"If the jury in Caleb's case pulls the same shit the one in Eli's did, then you and Mav can battle it out for which one of you gets to take the fucker out. But until then, we need to play it by the book – for Caleb's sake."

I didn't say anything because Ronan already knew I was in agreement.

"You have three weeks of radio silence," Ronan murmured. "But just remember that you're not the only one who's worried about Caleb, okay?"

"Yeah," I muttered.

"If you get anything out of him, fuck radio silence and reach out, do you hear me? I don't care if you have to use goddamn carrier pigeons, you get word to me so we can figure out what the fuck is going on."

I smiled at that. "I will." Ronan and I were on the same page – the chances that Caleb knew something about who was after him was high. Even if he didn't know exactly who it was, he'd clearly been hiding secrets. The encounter with Jennings had been proof of that.

"Mav and Memphis will clean the scene at the cabin," Ronan said.

"Memphis was hurt," I said.

"He says it's a flesh wound. I'm already working to find someone to treat it before he and Mav fly home."

Ronan's words made sense. If Memphis went to a hospital, they'd have to report the gunshot wound to the authorities. As for the cabin, it had seemed remote enough that the gunshots wouldn't have alerted any neighbors, but there was always the possibility of a hunter or hiker having heard something. Which meant Mav and Memphis would have to work fast to get rid of the evidence that Caleb and I had been there.

"Take care of yourself, Jace," Ronan murmured, then he hung up. I didn't waste any time in powering the phone off so it was no longer traceable.

"What *was* that back there?" Caleb asked. I turned to see that he was hunched over like he was in pain.

"A hit," I said, not wanting to pull any punches with him. If I wanted his cooperation with what would happen next, I needed him to understand the full weight of the situation.

"A hit?" he said, shaking his head. "No, that's not possible."

"Those men were there to kill you, Caleb. The flash grenade, the suppressors—"

"The what?"

"Silencers," I clarified.

I didn't think it possible, but he paled even more. He was quiet for a moment before saying, "I thought he'd do it himself."

"Who?" I asked as I tried to keep my focus on the winding road as we began heading down the mountain.

"My dad."

"You think your dad put the hit out on you?"

"He hired those guys to hurt Eli," he murmured.

I knew who he was talking about, of course. I'd been with Caleb when we'd joined Mav and Eli on the journey to Seattle after I'd gotten Caleb out of the psychiatric hospital. The plan had been to go to Eli's apartment to get his dog, but the scene we'd walked in on had been pure chaos. Two men had broken into the apartment to find the flash drive that'd had proof of Jack Cortano's crimes against his sons and Eli on it. Eli's friend had been at the apartment instead and had ended up getting shot. Fortunately, the young man had survived the incident. The men Jack had hired had been ex-military... mercenaries. They'd likely been contacts he'd made through his work in both the army and at the Department of Defense.

I knew Caleb's theory had some merit to it. While it seemed odd that Jack would wait two years to finally take out one of the witnesses to his crime, the fact that he'd been acquitted in Eli's case could have been the catalyst. It would have been too risky to take out both Eli and Caleb before the trials, but with only Caleb left, maybe he'd gotten nervous. Especially since he didn't have anything from Caleb's past to use against him, like he'd had with Eli. Not to mention the added charge of murder that Jack was facing in Virginia for killing Nick. The prosecutors were planning on going after him for first-degree murder there, a charge that could potentially carry the death penalty. If Jack had had someone monitoring Caleb and had discovered his son had disappeared, it would have been the perfect time to eliminate him. If those men had succeeded in taking us all out, they would have likely done what Memphis and Mav were going to do – burn the cabin and the bodies to get rid of as much evidence as possible and make it virtually impossible to identify the men. If it'd been our bodies burned beyond recognition in that cabin, our identities likely never would have been discovered. It would have just appeared that Caleb had up and vanished, and Jack would have walked away a free man.

"Have you been in contact with your father since he was arrested?" I asked.

When Caleb didn't answer right away, it was answer enough.

"When?" I asked.

But Caleb just shook his head. As much as I wanted to press him, I knew I needed to stick to my plan and take care of step one.

Getting us good and lost.

CHAPTER 4

CALEB

I was happy to stay in the car as ordered because my anxiety was through the roof. I could still see Jace through the windshield as he talked to the man in front of a small red house just yards from the water's edge. As I watched him nod his head at something the man said, I fought back the emotions that were threatening to bubble to the surface. The timing couldn't be worse. I tried slowing my breathing in the hopes that would calm me down, but I knew it wouldn't.

There was only one thing that would take away the burning need to get out of the car and walk straight into Jace's arms.

I kept my eyes on Jace as best I could as I dropped my hand to the floor of the car and began searching out what I wanted. A mix of shame and relief went through me when I closed my fingers around one of the larger pieces of glass from the shattered window. I didn't even stop to think about what I was doing as I slipped the sleeve of my shirt up on my right arm. Fear of discovery had me keeping my eyes on Jace, even as I drew the edge of the glass over my skin. And just like that, the pain took away everything.

The fear.

The anger.

The hope.

I couldn't enjoy the moment because I could tell from Jace's body language that he and the man were saying their goodbyes. I quickly dropped the glass between my seat and the console of the car, then reached into my pocket for the small scrap of fabric I kept there specifically for moments like these. I applied pressure to the cuts and was relieved when blood didn't instantly seep through the cloth – it meant I hadn't cut deep enough that I couldn't easily control the bleeding. I spied the hair tie Jace had removed from his hair and left in the cup holder. I grabbed it and looped it around my arm so that it held the fabric in place. It was a little tight, but that was a good thing. I quickly dropped my sleeve back down, then scanned our surroundings.

I had no clue where we were because I'd fallen asleep after Jace had pulled over long enough to look at my head and to make a phone call from a payphone at a convenience store at the base of the mountains. My head was throbbing, but he'd been right that the ringing in my ears had stopped shortly after we'd left the cabin.

It was late afternoon by the time we'd reached our destination, but now that the anxiety was gone, I was so tired it felt like we'd been driving for days. I couldn't make sense of the fact that despite all the terror I'd lived through in the last thirty-six hours, I could barely keep my eyes open. Why was my body deciding to catch up on sleep now, after nearly two years of not being able to sleep for more than a few hours a night?

I was still struggling to process the events of the morning. One minute I'd been trying to figure out how to make it clear to Jace and Mav that nothing they could say would make me return to Seattle, and the next minute Jace's big body had slammed into mine and I'd felt like all the oxygen had been sucked out of my lungs. I was terrified for Mav and Memphis, but I had to believe what Jace had said – that they were okay.

I watched as Jace shook the man's hand, then walked back toward the car. I hated the sight of the smeared blood on his face. The flying glass had left several small cuts on his skin. I'd wanted to stop long enough so I could make sure there wasn't any glass in any of them, but he'd said there wasn't time and had merely wiped at the blood with the sleeve of his shirt. The idea that he'd been hurt protecting me made the tension I'd just gotten rid of start to roll around in my belly again.

Jace didn't say anything as he started the car up. It wasn't lost on me that I was completely reliant on him at that point. I'd promised myself just that morning when I'd woken up that I wouldn't lean on him again, but that was exactly what I was doing. Of course, it wasn't like I had a lot of choices. It was one thing to try and just disappear… to start over. But to do it with killers on your trail? Nope, I wasn't down for that. That pesky will to survive was still kicking in.

I wanted to laugh at the sense of betrayal I couldn't shake as I tried to accept the fact that my father had hired people to kill me. After all he'd done to me, not to mention that I'd fully accepted that he would kill me himself when he got out of jail, here I was, hurt that he'd decided to not even waste his time getting his hands dirty by killing me himself.

God, I really was a fucked-up mess.

Jace drove the car around the back of the property and pulled it into an old barn. "You can get out," he said to me as he climbed out of the car. I did as he said and then watched as he worked to disassemble the rifle he'd used earlier after we'd driven away from the cabin. He placed the gun in a case, then grabbed it and a small bag from the trunk.

"Can you help me?" he asked as he put the things on the ground and then reached for a tarp. I helped him spread it over the car. Just before he covered it completely, he removed the license plates from the car and tucked them in the bag.

I followed him from the barn and back toward the front of the house. I thought we were just switching cars, but realized I was wrong when we began heading toward the large dock.

"Where are we?" I finally asked.

"Elkton, Maryland."

It was an answer, but not really the one I wanted. "I thought we were headed west," I said.

"We need to get more lost than originally planned," Jace responded. "Water's as good a place as any." He pointed at a large boat bobbing gently on the water at the end of the dock.

"Is that your boat?"

Jace shook his head. "My friend's," he said as he motioned to the man watching us from the front of the house.

"How do you know him?"

"He was my spotter."

"Spotter? What's that?"

"He monitored things like wind, trajectory, and temperature and helped identify targets for me."

It took me a moment to understand what he was saying. "What, you mean like for a sniper? Is that what you were?" I remembered the big gun and the scope on the top of it.

"Yeah," was all Jace said. From his tone, I gathered it wasn't his favorite thing to talk about. "Dalton," – he motioned to the guy – "got out about a year after I did. He bought this place a few years back. I come out here sometimes when I need to decompress."

I glanced back at Dalton. He was about the same age as Jace and had black hair that was a little longer on top and shorter on the sides. His stance was rigid while his eyes stayed on Jace as we made our way toward the dock, and I couldn't help but wonder why. Did the two men have a history that went beyond their time in the military?

I hated the burn of jealousy that went through me.

"So, what, he's agreed to let you use his boat? Just like that?"

Jace glanced at me, then at Dalton. "Just like that," he agreed.

I fell silent as I followed Jace onto the dock. The boat was big, but not like the fancy yachts I'd seen at the marina my father had kept his own fishing boat in. Jace helped me climb aboard and while he got the engine started, I explored the boat. It was surprisingly well appointed with a small kitchen, bedroom, and bathroom. The bedroom had a full-sized bed in it, as well as a television and a DVD player. Several plastic bags sat on top of the bed. Curiosity got the best of me and I looked through a couple. There was an assortment of new clothes in the bags, in two different sizes. There were toiletries too. A glance in the kitchen showed the fridge was full, as were the few cabinets.

I went above deck in time to see Jace throwing off the lines securing the boat to the dock. Jace gave Dalton a final wave before maneuvering the boat out into open water. I knew we were likely on Chesapeake Bay. My father, Nick, and I had spent a lot of time fishing in Chesapeake Bay. It was only later that the fishing trips had stopped being about fishing.

I felt a wave of cold go through me and I automatically wrapped my arms around myself as I made my way to the front of the boat. It was late spring so the weather wasn't particularly cold, but as the boat picked up speed, the wind bit at my skin.

I wasn't sure where on the bay we were at, but I felt some of the anxiety start to ease as we got farther out onto the water. There were other boats around, but it wasn't particularly busy, and seeing regular people just going about their day as they fished or just explored all the little inlets made things feel a little bit more normal. It was easier to pretend that the events of the morning had just been some hellish nightmare.

We traveled for a good twenty minutes before the boat slowed enough so that there was barely any wake as we cut through the water. I lost myself in the sensation of the sun trying to warm my body as the sounds of seagulls and passing boats filled the air around us. I nearly jumped out of my skin a moment later when I felt something at my back. A hand came out to grab my arm.

"It's just me," Jace murmured softly from behind me.

I felt like a fool. We were alone on the boat, for God's sake.

Something warm was placed over my shoulders. Jace's hands appeared in my vision as he wrapped the small blanket around me from behind. Since the boat was still moving, I had to assume he'd made use of the autopilot feature, which would keep us traveling in a straight line.

I grabbed the corners of the blanket with my hands to hold it in place, but to my surprise, Jace's hands lingered on my waist. And was he...?

God, he was.

I closed my eyes as Jace's stubble scraped over the skin along the back of my neck for the briefest of moments as he nuzzled me. My body reacted to the contact and it was all I could do not to lean back against him.

It was the stinging sensation from my arm that reminded me that I couldn't lean into him.

Or on him.

I'd done that once before.

Never again.

It took every ounce of willpower I possessed to step forward just a little. I felt the fingers at my waist press into me just a little bit before completely falling away. I risked turning around and saw him staring at me, his expression shuttered. As he turned to walk away, I grabbed his wrist. I didn't say anything as I pulled him to the back of the boat. Before we went below deck, I quietly asked, "Will the boat be okay for a few minutes?"

Jace scanned the horizon, then nodded.

He didn't resist me as I tugged him down the stairs with me. I released his hand, but he continued to follow me. I led him past the kitchen, then motioned to the bed. I waited until he sat down before I went back to the kitchen and found what I was looking for beneath the sink. I'd spied the first aid kit earlier when I'd been checking things out.

I returned to the bedroom and felt something clench deep inside of me at the sight of Jace sitting on the bed. As I approached him, I wondered what he'd do if instead of slowing when I reached him, I just kept moving forward until I was pushing him back on the bed. Would he go pliant beneath me? Would he finally kiss me? Would he roll me so I could know what it was like to feel the full weight of his body on top of me? He'd given me a hint of that last night when he'd hovered over me, but I wanted more.

I shouldn't, but I did.

I forced myself to sit next to him on the bed. When I turned to face him, he did the same. I searched out some antiseptic wipes. It was comfortably quiet, with just the gentle slap of water against the hull of the boat to keep us company. Jace barely reacted as I began cleaning his cuts with the antiseptic. I knew it had to hurt, but I might as well have been using water for all the reaction he showed. I was both disappointed and envious.

Disappointed because while he appeared perfectly relaxed, my insides were bouncing around like someone was playing ping pong in my gut. And envious because I would have given anything to be able to not feel like he did.

Most of the cuts weren't bad enough to need any kind of dressing, but there was one near his eyebrow that was deeper than the rest. I had to shift closer to him to make sure there weren't any bits of glass in it. The position had us practically nose to nose. Once again, I could barely breathe because of the sheer temptation of having his mouth so close to mine, but Jace didn't react at all.

"So, what's the plan?" I asked, since I needed something to distract me from my thoughts.

"We keep moving and we keep monitoring the news for a while to make sure your name doesn't come up anywhere. Ronan and his guys will try to figure out if your dad really is behind all this."

I nodded. Being trapped on a boat for the foreseeable future with Jace Christenson seemed like the worst kind of hell… and a little bit of heaven too.

"And Caleb?"

I was in the middle of placing a bandage over the cut by his eyebrow when he said my name. I looked at him and got caught up in the firm set of his jaw and dark eyes. They looked black this close up.

"We're going to talk. About what happened this morning and yesterday. And this…"

Before I could stop him, he closed his hand around my forearm. Even though I managed not to wince at the contact, it didn't matter, because I knew Jace could feel the unevenness beneath the fabric.

"Jace, don't," I said when he reached for the end of my sleeve.

He ignored me, of course.

I closed my eyes so I wouldn't have to look at him as he carefully pushed my sleeve up.

But it didn't matter because I heard his reaction. I wanted to laugh out loud because a couple of minutes ago I would have killed to get some kind of response out of him. Now I just wanted to sink into the floor.

I forced my eyes open and watched Jace work his hair tie and the swatch of fabric free. He shook his head when his gaze fell on the three cuts that were still seeping blood. He rested his hand and mine in his lap as he closed his eyes.

"I'm sorry, Jace," slipped out before I could stop myself. I had no idea why I was apologizing, because I didn't owe him anything. I hadn't since he'd turned his back on me.

Liar.

I ignored the inner voice and turned to look out one of the little circular windows. I kept my eyes averted even as I felt Jace begin cleaning the cuts with an antiseptic wipe. I flinched as pain stung my arm at the contact. Despite sometimes craving pain, I had no interest in it if I couldn't control it.

And right now, I felt like there was absolutely nothing in my control anymore.

I was sure it was over when Jace put a large, square Band-Aid over the cuts, but he didn't release my wrist. Instead, he took his free hand and cupped the back of my neck with it. I waited for him to tell me to look at him, or to ask me why I'd done what I'd done, but he didn't do any of that.

Instead, he pulled me forward and then pressed his forehead against mine. I was stunned to hear his voice break when he whispered, "Caleb." He paused and sucked in a breath. "Please, please don't do this anymore. I'm fucking begging you."

I closed my eyes and felt a tear trying to escape my clenched lids. I failed to hold it back.

"I'll try," I lied, because I couldn't stand the hitch I'd heard in his voice as he'd whispered the plea.

How in the world had I ever thought he didn't feel?

He didn't respond to my words and I wondered if it was because he knew what he was asking was impossible.

We sat like that for a few more precious seconds before Jace released me and stood. "I need to go check things out," he muttered, then he was gone.

I took my time cleaning up the stuff from the first aid kit and returned it to the kitchen. When I was done, I went back to the bedroom instead of going above deck. I grabbed the blanket Jace had put around my shoulders and covered myself with it as I laid down on the bed.

My exhaustion didn't make any damned sense, but hell if I didn't welcome the shit out of it.

CHAPTER 5

JACE

"You bedding down for the night?" Dalton asked.

"Yeah, we're by Poole's Island," I said. I was using the burner phone Dalton had purchased for me after I'd called him from a payphone earlier in the day to let him know what supplies I'd need. He'd bought one for himself too, so there'd be no chance of anyone tracing the calls. The fact that no one, not even Ronan, knew about my friendship with Dalton made me comfortable enough to keep the lines of communication open with him. It would come in handy in more ways than one.

But as helpful as the phone was to have, it didn't have the best reception and I wasn't about to waste my time trying to search out anything on the internet about the attack this morning.

"You find anything?" I asked.

"I found mention of a cabin burning in the local paper, but it didn't make the wire yet. Either your guys didn't stash the bodies in the cabin or some idiot at the fire department's not doing their job."

"My guys probably made sure there wasn't much left to discover. *They* are good at their jobs," I said.

Dalton snorted, then said, "No news about the shooting either. Really like to know how you pulled that off."

"Can't take credit for that one," I said. I hadn't told Dalton the full details of the Jennings encounter, other than I'd been involved in a shooting at the man's house and to let me know if my name or Caleb's came up at any point. It was driving me crazy to still have no idea how Caleb had known Jennings wouldn't give his name to the cops. My gut was telling me it was bad, whatever it was. It was the only explanation as to why Jennings wouldn't want the cops finding Caleb.

Because Caleb had something on him.

"Well, you guys take it easy, you hear?"

"Yeah," I said. "You too."

I'd been fortunate enough to walk away from the military with only a giant chip on my shoulder, considering all the bullshit I'd seen and been forced to do during my four deployments. Dalton hadn't been as lucky. In addition to having sustained injuries in a roadside bombing that had not only left him scarred but in constant pain, he'd also walked away with a hefty case of PTSD. It was one of the reasons he'd holed himself up in his little house by the water and had spent a good chunk of his savings on the cabin cruiser that he spent most of his days on. I felt guilty for asking him to let me borrow the boat for so long, considering it was one of the few things that brought him any measure of comfort as he fought the demons war had left behind, but he'd assured me he could use the time to work on his house.

And the reality was, I'd been desperate.

I spent a few minutes checking that everything was locked down for the night. I'd picked a quiet place near a small, uninhabited island for us to moor overnight. My plan was to play it by ear in terms of how far down the Chesapeake we traveled. I wouldn't make the decision to leave the bay for the open ocean until I absolutely had to. In truth, I was floundering a bit, both with my plan and with my charge. I'd gotten used to working alone, so being without Ronan's team to back me up wasn't a new thing, but the stakes were higher than they'd ever been. If I'd just been protecting some average joe, I wouldn't have felt so off-balance.

But there was nothing average about any of this.

God, he'd cut himself again.

Under my own goddamned nose.

Even now as I thought about the three almost perfectly uniform cuts, I wanted to throw up. On the one hand, I just wanted to shake Caleb and tell him to wake the fuck up from the zombie-like state he was in and just come back to me. But the other part of me knew I had this one chance to make things right and if I pushed too hard, I'd just drive him further away. I had a little bit of hope that the old Caleb wasn't completely gone yet, because I'd seen glimpses of him when he'd taken care of the cuts on my face. His touch had been gentle, but his reaction to the close proximity of our bodies had been anything but. I'd heard his ticked-up breathing as he'd practically been pressed nose to nose with me. I'd felt his warm breath coming in quick bursts against my skin and I'd seen the slight tremor in his hand as he'd tended to my injuries.

It would have been so easy to turn my head at any time and just capture his mouth with mine.

But the same things that had held me back from taking what I'd wanted two years ago were the same things keeping me from storming into the bedroom below deck and covering his body with mine as I sought out his perfect mouth.

He was still just so damn young.

And the vulnerability was a thousand times greater than it'd been when I'd first met him.

But worst of all, I'd joined the list of those who'd betrayed him.

I had no illusions about what would have happened today if we hadn't come under attack. Caleb had said as much right before the first shot had been fired.

He'd had no intention of going home with Mav... or coming anywhere with me. And at nineteen, there'd have been no way to force him except to *actually* force him.

Which I absolutely would have done, Mav and Memphis be damned. So if there was a silver lining to the events of the morning, it was that Caleb was once again reliant on me. But unlike the last time that had happened, I wasn't going to squander the opportunity.

As I made my way below deck, I stopped in the kitchen and

checked the microwave to see if Caleb had eaten the plate of food I'd left for him. I'd kept things simple with dinner by just heating up the leftover lasagna Dalton had included for us when he'd stocked the fridge. I wasn't surprised to see the food was sitting untouched. I sighed and found some plastic wrap to cover the food with, then put it back in the fridge. I searched out the small containers of milk I knew would be in the fridge and took two into the bedroom. I flipped on the small light right above the bed and then sat down on the edge of it.

"Caleb, wake up," I said as I settled my hand on his shoulder.

He barely stirred.

His exhaustion was starting to worry me. It wasn't normal for someone to sleep so much after having been sleep-deprived for so long. As much as I would have liked to believe being around me made him feel safe enough to lose himself so deeply to sleep, the fact that he'd chosen to cut his own skin during the few minutes I hadn't had my eyes on him was telling. That peace I'd found so much pleasure in being able to give him was a thing of the past. If anything, being around me now was the reason he'd taken something sharp to his arm in the first place.

I set the milk down on the shelf that was built into the headboard of the bed and then climbed in next to him. I drew the blanket off his body and scooted up behind him until our bodies were pressed together. I let my fingers toy with the soft skin just behind his ear. "Caleb, I need you to wake up," I urged as I let my hand skim down his shoulder and along his arm until it came to a stop at his waist.

"Mmmm," was all Caleb said, then he was turning over and pressing his face against my chest. He kept moving until I shifted my arm beneath his shoulders and cuddled him closer to me. He let out a breathy sigh against my neck. I managed to position a pillow beneath my head so I was a little more comfortable and then just held him for a while, relishing the way his breath fanned over my skin. His left hand was wrapped around my upper arm as if he was afraid I was going to try and get away from him. I played with his hair for a while, then pressed a kiss to the top of his head before I said his name again.

He let out a little groan of protest when I began tickling his ear.

When it became too much, he frowned and swatted at my hand. His eyes opened and for the briefest of moments, they were completely clear as he looked up at me. A small smile graced his pretty mouth as he muttered, "What are you doing?"

Before I could even answer, his eyes shuttered themselves again and he righted himself so that he was no longer pressed against my body.

I immediately missed the contact, despite what having his lithe body practically draped across mine had been doing to my libido.

He looked around the cabin. "What time is it?" he asked.

"Just after ten."

"Oh."

Caleb sat up, so I did the same.

"Are you hungry?" I asked.

Not surprisingly, he shook his head. I reached behind me and grabbed one of the milks and handed it to him. "Would you please drink this? You need to get something into your system."

I was amazed when he didn't argue with me.

"Strawberry milk?" he said with a smile. He worked to rip the straw free of the small container, then got it out of the plastic. "I haven't had this in… God, I don't even know how long."

I reached for my own container of milk. "It's a weakness of mine," I admitted. "One that Dalton indulges me in every time I come up here."

I swore I saw Caleb tense when I said Dalton's name, but the moment was fleeting.

"I wouldn't have pictured that," he murmured.

I shrugged my shoulders. "My father had a hopeless sweet tooth that he passed on to me and my sister, so my mother had to come up with ways to feed our need for sugar while still keeping it somewhat healthy. She'd let us have a treat every night before bed and it was always strawberry milk for me. Can't explain it," I admitted with a smile as I tugged the straw free of the packaging. "But knowing there's strawberry milk waiting in the fridge for me just makes everything look better, you know?"

Caleb smiled. He was quiet for a moment before he said, "Sno Balls."

When I looked at him in confusion, he said, "You know, those round pink coconut-covered cakes?"

I laughed and nodded. "Oh yeah, I remember those. They were nasty."

"They were awesome," Caleb countered, his grin growing wider. It did funny things to my insides to see him smile. I'd seen it a few times when he'd shown me around Seattle once a couple of years earlier at Christmas, but I hadn't thought I'd see it again anytime soon.

See, Caleb, not shattered beyond repair, I wanted to say.

"I'd eat them any chance I got. I even used to ride my bike down to the store after school every day to buy some when my mom stopped getting them for me. She had to go down there and tell the manager to tell his cashiers not to sell me more than two a week." Caleb chuckled and said, "As soon as I walked in the door, the cashiers would call out to each other and say if they'd sold to me already that week or not."

I laughed and asked, "How old were you?"

"Nine or ten, I guess." I saw his smile falter, then he dropped his eyes. I had no doubt he was thinking about how his life had changed so drastically just a few years later, since he had been only thirteen when his father had touched him for the first time.

I gripped my milk hard enough that some of it spurted up the straw and dripped onto my hand.

"I haven't had one of those things in a while," he murmured. He lifted his eyes again and managed a half-smile. "Guess we all have to grow up sometime, huh?"

I lifted the milk and said, "Not completely, no."

He nodded and took a sip of his milk. "You have a sister?" he asked.

I automatically flinched at the question, though I'd known it would eventually come up, since I'd let it slip earlier when talking about my father's sweet tooth.

I nodded.

Something must have clued Caleb in because he fell silent, then began to fiddle with the straw. I knew he wouldn't ask me what he obviously wanted to, so I bit the bullet and said, "I don't know where she is. She's been missing for almost two years."

CHAPTER 6

CALEB

I hadn't been expecting him to tell me anything after he'd tensed up when I'd mentioned his sister, so I was momentarily shocked into silence at his admission.

"What happened?" I finally asked. I knew it wasn't any of my business, but I was desperate to know more about Jace, and while it wasn't exactly the best topic, I'd take anything he gave me. In the two years since he'd gotten me out of the psychiatric hospital, he'd never once talked about himself.

"She and her boyfriend went to Europe a couple years ago for a long backpacking trip. Everything was going fine until they got to Germany. She used to call me like clockwork every week to check in. Just like that, the calls stopped. There were no more posts to her social media pages, either. Her boyfriend's parents didn't hear anything either. The German authorities said they'd likely just run away together... decided to cut ties and just not come home. They refused to even consider her missing until about three months later when her boyfriend's body was discovered in a field outside Berlin."

Although Jace's voice was even as he spoke, I could see the tightness in his jaw and the spark of pain in his eyes.

"There was no word of your sister?" I asked.

Jace shook his head. "It was like she just disappeared off the face of the earth."

"How old is she?" I asked, careful not to use past tense.

"She'd be twenty-four now. Her name is Maggie."

"I'm sorry, Jace," I murmured. "I can't even imagine," I began, but then shook my head. I understood the pain of losing a loved one, but knowing Nick was dead was somehow easier than imagining him being out in the world and not knowing if he was okay or not. "Your parents? How are they dealing with it?"

"Our parents died when I was fifteen and Maggie was five. She and I were sent to live with an uncle, then later my grandmother."

I could tell by the tone of his voice that there was more to that particular part of the story, but I refrained from asking about it. "Is your grandmother still—"

"No," Jace cut in. "She died a few months before Maggie left for her trip. Maggie used her part of the inheritance our grandmother left us to pay for it."

"God, I don't even know what to say," I managed to get out. I looked at him and said, "No, scratch that, I do know what to say. It fucking sucks, Jace. I can't even imagine how hard all that's been on you."

Jace sent me a small smile, but he didn't say anything.

"Are the police still looking for Maggie?"

"Not really. Once the news of a pretty young American girl going missing dies down, so does the interest in finding her. I go over there every time I get a new lead, but they're few and far between."

"Lead?" I asked in confusion. "Do you... do you know who took her?"

"I don't know who," Jace responded. "But I do know why."

When he didn't elaborate, I debated whether I should just let the terrible conversation die a natural death. If he'd been anyone else, I would have. But he wasn't just anyone – he was the one person who'd been there for me when I'd been at my most vulnerable. Just hearing his voice as I'd been strapped to that hospital bed, my brain addled by countless drugs, had helped me feel a little less alone.

"Why was she taken?" I asked.

Jace hesitated, then pulled in a deep breath. "Have you heard of sex trafficking, Caleb?"

My throat threatened to close up as I nodded. I'd seen stories about it on the news every now and then. But it also hit closer to home.

"I heard Eli and Mav talking about it once... that's what happened to Dante's younger brother. He was taken when he was just a little boy and... and sold..."

I hadn't actually met Aleks, but I'd occasionally met his brother, Dante, who worked with Mav and Memphis. Dante and his fiancé, Magnus, had found Aleks a couple of years earlier and had managed to rescue him from the man who'd been holding him captive. From everything I'd heard, Aleks was still struggling to find some sense of normalcy in his life. To think Jace's sister had been taken to be used like that...

I felt like I was going to be sick. "No," I whispered. I'd wanted to be strong for Jace, but I was failing miserably. He was holding himself together just fine, but I felt like I was going to come apart.

"Are you sure?" I asked. Jace looked blurry through my watery eyes.

"I'm sure," Jace said. "I've managed to find things here and there about her, but every time I think I'm getting close, the trail goes cold. I was there a few weeks ago, but the lead I was given didn't pan out."

I wanted to say something meaningful, something that would give him strength or hope, but I couldn't manage to say anything at all, because my tears chose that moment to start streaking down my face. Jace's sister had to be so damned scared, and the suffering she endured every single day of her life...

"Hey," Jace said as he leaned into me and then drew me forward. I felt the milk get plucked from my fingers and then I was being drawn against Jace's chest.

"I'm sorry," I blurted.

"For what?"

"For not saying the right thing... for not making it better somehow. Because it can't be better. I can't even imagine how scared you must be but you're so strong—"

"Not strong," Jace murmured with a shake of his head before he pressed his lips against the top of my head. "Just really good at faking it."

I wouldn't have believed him if it hadn't been for the fine tremor that I felt go through his body. And the way he was holding me... so okay, maybe I couldn't give him the right words, but maybe this moment was enough for now.

But he was wrong about one thing... he *was* strong. I would have given anything for even an ounce of whatever it was that kept him moving forward, despite the inevitable hopelessness he must have felt every time he'd had another lead on his sister dry up.

"And Caleb?"

"Yeah?"

His arms closed around me even tighter. "This helps," he said gruffly.

I didn't resist when Jace maneuvered us so that we were lying down. Unlike the previous times he'd held me as we'd slept, this time I was pressed up against his chest, my head tucked right beneath his chin. His fingers sifted through my hair and I found myself sinking more of my weight down onto him, even as my brain tried to warn me that I was getting too close.

"Make me understand, Caleb," Jace said softly.

It didn't take a genius to know what he was really asking me. I suspected he had a million questions for me, but the surprise would have been if he'd led with anything that *wasn't* related to the scars on my arm.

"I don't understand it myself sometimes," I admitted.

"When did it start? I don't remember... I don't..." His voice dropped off, but I didn't need him to continue. He didn't remember seeing the scars on me when we'd first met two years earlier or the one Christmas we'd spent together.

"About six months ago," I said. I could feel my anxiety building, so I began toying with the material of his shirt. "This kid from school told me about it. I walked in on him when he was doing it in the bathroom. I saw the blood in the sink and the razor blade in his hand and I thought he was trying to kill himself. I told him I'd get help, but he just laughed at me. Said help was already there and then he lifted the razor blade. I couldn't stop thinking about it – he was so… relaxed. Almost… happy."

I was still playing with Jace's shirt when his hand settled over mine. I smiled against his chest when he began to thrum our fingers together. I wondered how he knew I needed to keep some part of me moving at that point. Most people needed quiet to focus.

I wasn't most people.

Quiet and I didn't do well together.

"I'd been getting into trouble with Mav and Eli the past year because they caught me drinking a lot. The alcohol made it so I didn't have to feel anything, but it was too hard to hide. I didn't want to risk messing around with drugs, since I'd seen what they'd done to Nick."

I felt Jace tense beneath me and his fingers stilled for a moment, but I continued. I wasn't interested in dragging this whole thing out.

"Then I remembered the kid's expression from that day in the bathroom and I decided to try it. I've never felt more in control than when I have that blade in my hand, Jace," I admitted. "I know that sounds fucked up—"

"It doesn't," Jace interjected. "But you know it's not real, right?"

I sighed because I did know that. "I know," I murmured. "I don't control it. It controls me." I hesitated and said, "I'd still rather have the illusion, though."

Jace sighed. "What happened to going to therapy? You told Eli you'd try."

"I did," I said softly. I pulled my fingers from Jace's and let them rest on his chest. "Tell me how I was supposed to tell a complete stranger the truth, Jace. That not only did I let my father fuck me, but that I actually got jealous when he'd pretend I was someone else."

Shame curled through me and I wasn't surprised when Jace shifted us until we were both sitting upright. He grabbed my chin and forced me to look at him. "Don't you dare try to take any of what that man did to you on yourself."

I willed myself to remain quiet, but giving voice to that particular secret was like punching a tiny hole in the dam that was holding back all the shit that was threatening to drown me. "I hated him so much, Jace."

"Of course you did, Caleb. The things your father did to you—"

"Not him," I whispered. "Eli."

Jace stilled. "What do you mean?" he asked carefully.

"Sometimes when Dad and I were together and he'd be... he'd be behind me, he'd cover my head with a pillow and he'd say Eli's name." A sob got caught in my throat, but I forced it back. "The things he said... they were disgusting. Afterwards, he'd whisper things in my ear... things meant for Eli. It made me sick. But then things would go back to normal and he'd take me to a baseball game or fishing or whatever. And I'd think it wasn't so bad – that it had all been worth it. After a while he'd start talking about how he wished Eli was around more and the whole thing would start all over again and I just..."

I shook my head and automatically reached for my arm and began digging my nails into my skin as I slid back from Jace. Why the hell had I said anything? And why couldn't I stop talking?

"How was I supposed to tell the same therapist that Eli was seeing the truth – that I was jealous that that sick fuck liked Eli more than me? That it felt like he was cutting me open with a knife every time he fucked me and whispered Eli's name instead of mine. Tell me what that doctor could have said to me to make the shit that goes through my head okay!"

I tried to escape the bed, but Jace caught me just as I was scooting off the edge of the raised platform. His arm went around my waist and he pulled me back against his chest.

"Don't!" I shouted. "Don't touch me!"

I ripped the Band-Aid off my arm and dug my fingers into the cuts. The pain helped, but it wasn't enough to stem the agony that tore me open inside. Jace grabbed my wrist to stop me and pinned my arms at my sides. His arms were like iron bands around me that I had no hope of escaping.

"Shhh, just take deep breaths for me," he whispered in my ear.

"No! Let me the fuck go, Jace!" I screamed, not caring who heard me at that point.

Jace ignored my demand and continued to murmur into my ear, but I was too far gone to hear anything. I was so angry that he'd asked me the question in the first place. I'd heard so many times from Eli and Mav and my stepmother that talking to someone would help, but it was all bullshit.

So I took my rage out on Jace. I ranted, I raved and I called him every name in the book, but those soft words never let up.

The ones reminding me to breathe.

And telling me it was okay to let go.

And promising he was there and he wasn't going anywhere ever again.

That was harder to hear than anything else. That whispered vow was what kept me fighting, even when my body told me to give it up. By the time my muscles gave out, I could barely breathe. My throat hurt from screaming and crying and I couldn't see because of the tears that continued to seep from my pained eyes. Snot was coming from my nose, but I didn't care about that either.

I just wanted to call back my admission.

And I wanted to see my blood flow so that I had some shred of proof that I was still human.

Because I didn't know what I was anymore.

I had no idea how much time passed before I felt like I could breathe again. I expected Jace to release me, since I'd calmed enough that I wasn't fighting him anymore. But he didn't. He just kept holding me until I slumped back against him. When I did, he said, "I think that doctor would have told you that what happened to you and Nick and Eli was beyond comprehension. I think she would have told you that your mind had to cope with that level of depravity in the only way it could and that there is no making sense of any of it. And she would have told you the same things she's probably had to tell Eli over and over again."

Jace paused before whispering his next words one agonizingly slow syllable at a time.

"It's. Not. Your. Fault."

He gave me a little shake. "Do you hear me? It's. Not. Your. Fault."

I sucked in lungsful of air as the anxiety in my belly began to grow every time he spoke.

It was too much.

It was just too fucking much.

Jace's mouth pressed against my ear and I heard him let out an almost agonizing sounding whimper. "Please, Caleb. Even if you don't believe me, say you hear me. Please."

I didn't believe him.

I couldn't.

But I wanted him to not hurt anymore.

And I knew he had to be hurting.

A man like Jace didn't beg – unless maybe he was desperate.

I didn't answer him out loud. I didn't have the strength for that.

But I did nod.

Just once.

It appeared to be enough for Jace, because his hold eased on me just a little bit. He held me there like that for several more seconds before he said, "Come back to bed, Caleb. Let me hold you."

There were no platitudes about how things would look better in the morning or requests asking me to believe him. All he'd asked was for me to hear him and to hold me.

And it was probably me stretching things, but I wanted to believe he'd asked to hold me not just for me, but for him too.

I wasn't sure how Jace knew it was safe to release me and urge me back into bed, but he did. We ended up in our regular position, with him pressed up against my back, his arm around my waist. I hadn't noticed, but at some point, he'd grabbed some tissues. I didn't resist as he worked my sleeve up and mopped up the blood that had started flowing from the three small cuts after I'd gouged at them with my fingers. He held the tissues against my skin for several minutes until the bleeding stopped.

We didn't speak, because there was nothing to say.

Nothing had changed. I wasn't magically fixed and the urge to cut hadn't gone away. I'd done it all for nothing. I hadn't even managed to drive Jace away with the humiliating admission that I was so much more than a freak who sliced up his own skin to feel better.

So if nothing had changed, why did I feel different?

Not better, exactly.

Just… different.

Emptier maybe, but not in the way I liked.

It wasn't until my eyes drifted closed and the edge of sleep crept in that I realized what was different. I wasn't emptier. No, that definitely wasn't the right word.

Jace's muscled arm tightened around my midsection as his breath fanned over the back of my neck, and I wanted to smile. Did he think I would float away from him while we were sleeping?

And that was when it hit me.

That different feeling… I wasn't feeling emptier, but something else entirely. Something I hadn't felt in a really long time.

Lighter.

CHAPTER 7

JACE

He was gone when I woke up and the panic that went through me was complete and absolute. That was twice in three days that he'd managed to get away from me without me even so much as stirring.

I practically fell out of bed as I tried to get my bearings. I darted toward the upper deck but came to a sudden stop when I caught sight of him standing in front of the small stove, carefully cracking an egg into a skillet. He looked up at me in surprise, the empty eggshell dangling in his fingers above the crackling pan.

"You're still here," I said dumbly.

I saw a smile ghost across his mouth. "We're in the middle of Chesapeake Bay, Jace. Where am I going to go?" He dropped his eyes to what he was doing, but the smile didn't leave his face.

I'd take it.

After the hell of last night, I'd pretty much take anything at this point.

"How do you like your eggs?"

"Um, scrambled," I said. My stomach growled as my senses finally caught up to my brain. Not only could I smell bacon, but the sweetness of syrup pervaded the air too. One glance proved that Caleb was cooking pancakes, in addition to the bacon and eggs.

"There's coffee," Caleb said as he motioned to the full coffee pot.

"Thanks," I said as I searched for a mug and filled it up. "Do you want some?" I asked.

Caleb shook his head. "Never did get a taste for it," he said. "Two years in Seattle and I still haven't been inside of a Starbucks."

"I think that might be a crime out there," I said as I returned the coffee pot to its place.

"Probably," Caleb responded with a soft laugh.

His laugh was a balm on my battered soul. I knew the events of last night hadn't fixed anything for him, but maybe it was the start of something. Even as that flicker of hope flared inside of me, my eyes fell to his right arm. He'd put on one of the shirts Dalton had bought him. It was the only long-sleeved shirt in the bunch. It made me wonder if he was hiding any new cuts beneath the fabric. I hadn't even thought about all the knives that were in the kitchen. There was probably even a utility knife in the tackle box.

As I lifted my eyes, I saw that Caleb was watching me. His smile was gone and I cursed myself for my stupidity.

An awkward silence filled the small cabin, so I used the time to set the small table against the opposite wall. I was certain I'd fucked up enough that Caleb would make some excuse about being tired and not wanting to eat, but he surprised me when he began serving food on both of the plates I'd put out. Once we were seated, we each began picking at the food.

"It's really good, thanks," I said.

Caleb nodded but didn't say anything else.

"I can't cook to save my life," I admitted, hoping to break up some of the tension.

It was several beats before Caleb said, "My grandmother taught me how when I was little. My mom and dad were too busy to cook, so my grandmother did most of it. She was living with us." His eyes lifted to meet mine briefly before he lowered them again and began digging into his food with a little more gusto.

"My grandmother tried to teach me, but after I set the kitchen on fire that third time, she gave up and started collecting take-out menus for me. By the time I got out of the military, she'd amassed like a hundred of them."

It felt like a small victory when Caleb smiled, and I felt myself relax.

"Have you always lived in the D.C. area?"

I shook my head. "No, I moved down here after my grandmother died. Maggie is planning to go to school at Georgetown University. She got accepted into their graduate program for art and museum studies. She was supposed to start right after she got back from the backpacking trip."

I refused to let my thoughts linger on Maggie. It was a coping strategy I'd come to rely on after I'd learned of her disappearance. If I gave myself even a few minutes to think of the things she was enduring, quite possibly even at this very moment, I'd lose it completely. Fortunately, like the night before, Caleb seemed to sense my need not to go into too many details about my sister.

"Where did you used to live? You said you moved in with your grandmother when you were a kid?"

I nodded. "We lived in Vermont. When my grandparents emigrated from Romania, they opened a little gift shop near this ski resort. When my mom was a kid, they managed to scrape together enough money to also buy one of the lodges and fix it up. My mom and dad ran the lodge after my grandfather died."

"Do you still have it?"

I shook my head. "No, my uncle – my father's brother – and his wife inherited the lodge. They ended up running it into the ground and had to file for bankruptcy. My grandmother had managed to hang onto the gift shop she and my grandfather had started, so that kept us afloat until I was old enough to enlist. When our grandmother died, she left the gift shop to me and Maggie. Since neither of us wanted to run it, we sold it and Maggie used some of the money to go on that backpacking trip. The rest was for her tuition at Georgetown."

"So you must love the slopes," Caleb ventured.

"Um, no, not exactly."

My response had Caleb perking up. He must have sensed my embarrassment because he said, "Why not?"

I studied him for a moment, then crooked my finger at him to motion him closer to me. "Can you keep a secret?" I asked.

Another smile split his gorgeous lips. "For the right price," he said.

I'd only seen this side of Caleb once before. It'd been when I'd spent Christmas with him and Mav and Eli. While Eli and Mav had attended a wedding, Caleb and I had gone sightseeing in Seattle and it was like he'd become a different person. We'd laughed and joked as we'd explored the marketplace, aquarium, and Space Needle. Under all the pain was a bright, charming, kindhearted young man with a melodic laugh and sparkling eyes.

I eyed him and said, "Okay, what is this going to cost me?"

He studied me for a moment, then said, "I'll let you know when I'm ready to cash in my chips."

There was something about the way he said the words that had my insides heating and my cock reacting. We'd somehow wandered into dangerous territory, but I couldn't find it in me to object.

"Fair enough," I murmured. I paused and then admitted my shameful secret. "I can't ski."

"Lots of people can't ski," he said.

"No, I mean, I *really* can't. When I was a kid, my parents paid for me to take lessons with an Olympic gold medalist who lived in the area. I broke her skis... and her arm."

Caleb sat there for a moment, his fork halfway to his mouth, before he laughed. "What?"

I nodded. "She was trying to guide me down the bunny hill and by the time we reached the bottom, I was lying on top of her. She was only the first in a long line of many. I ended up giving another instructor two black eyes and a broken nose when my skis got away from me as I was getting them out of the car. I broke my own leg once and sprained more joints than I can count. Even after almost four years of lessons, I never made it off the bunny hill."

Caleb began to laugh so hard he had to put his fork down. He covered his mouth with his arm, but I was glad when he was unable to muffle the sound.

"Nice," I said, feigning irritation.

"I'm sorry, I just can't picture it. You're so… so…"

He shook his head.

"So what?" I asked.

"Put together… untouchable," Caleb finally said after settling. "I'd have thought you'd be good at everything."

I shook my head. "Nope, I was such an awkward kid… you wouldn't have even recognized me."

"Do you have a picture?"

"Maybe," I said as I began eating again.

"Can I see it?"

"Maybe."

"How do I turn the maybe into definitely?" Caleb asked, his eyes dancing with amusement.

I pretended to study him for a long time before saying, "I'll let you know when I'm ready to cash in my chips."

Caleb chuckled. I grabbed my wallet and searched out the picture I kept in it. It was an old, wrinkled photograph of me, my sister, my parents, and my grandparents standing in front of a Christmas tree. I handed it to him.

"Wow," he said as his eyes scanned the picture. "How old were you here?"

"Fourteen. It was the last Christmas we had together. My grandfather died a couple of months later and we lost my parents the following summer."

"I'm sorry, that must have been hard."

I nodded. "What about you? Is your grandmother still alive? The one who taught you to cook?"

Caleb shook his head. "She died about a month after my mom did. I think losing my mom broke her heart, you know? She kept saying no parent should outlive their child. My mom's dad died when she was a little girl and my dad's parents were both gone by the time I was born, so Nana was the only grandparent I had. No aunts or uncles, either."

I'd figured there hadn't been any other relatives, since it was his stepmother, Eli's mother, Mariana, who'd had to take Caleb in after his father had been arrested.

"How were things with Mariana?" I asked. "Before you moved in with Mav and Eli."

Caleb began to pick at what little food was left on his plate. "She was always really nice. We got along well from the time she married my dad. But that made things worse, you know?"

"How so?"

"I could tell she really loved my dad. It was hard to be a part of the secret he was keeping from her. And since I knew what Eli and my dad were doing, it felt like I was lying to her about that too." Caleb lifted his eyes and quickly said, "I mean, what I *thought* Eli and my dad were doing at the time – I didn't know Eli wasn't into it."

I reached out to cover his hand on the table. "I know, Caleb. Your father was really good at making people believe what he wanted them to." It was a polite way of saying the man was a lying bag of shit who deserved a bullet to the brain like no one's business. I'd seen the proof myself that Eli had been led to believe for years that he'd drunkenly instigated the first sexual encounter between him and his stepfather. The fucker had gone so far as to doctor a video of the brutal rape to make it look like Eli had not only been a willing participant, but that he'd started it. The reality was that he had, in fact, been drugged. I had no doubt Jack Cortano had played the same kind of mind games with his sons.

"Anyway, Mariana did her best, but I didn't make it easy for her," Caleb admitted. He settled his fork on his plate.

I didn't want him to stop talking, since I'd finally made some progress in getting him to open up, so I said, "Things didn't improve with Mav and Eli?"

He shook his head. "They tried really hard. I know they only asked me to move in so I wouldn't get into so much trouble—"

"That's not true," I interrupted. "Yeah, they were worried about you, but they love you, Caleb. They wanted you to feel like a part of their family because that's what you are."

Caleb didn't say anything for a long time. When he did, his voice was uneven. "I tried, Jace. I really did."

He just sounded so lost that I couldn't stop myself from linking my fingers with his on the table and saying, "I know you did, baby."

This time, he noticed the endearment.

And I found that I wasn't particularly upset by that fact.

"I went to the therapist, I tried to focus on my grades, I helped around the house," Caleb began. "But it wasn't real. I was still that same disgusting freak who let his dad do that shit to him."

"Caleb—"

"Some of the kids at school found out about me. The guy prosecuting my dad said that my name wouldn't be made public because I was a minor, but it still got out. First it was the kids, then the reporters..."

"Did Eli and Mav know?" I asked. My heart broke for him as I considered all the cruel things the other kids would have said to him.

"About the reporters, but I never told them about what the kids were saying... and doing."

I tensed at that. "What did they do?"

"It doesn't matter now."

"It matters to me," I said firmly. I reached for his chin to force his head up. "Please, Caleb, I need to know."

He closed his eyes and then looked in the direction of the stove. Probably so he wouldn't have to look me in the eye as he spoke. "Just stupid stuff. They'd call me names when I walked by, write stuff on the bathroom walls about me, put things in my locker."

"What kinds of things?"

"Jace—" Caleb whispered with a shake of his head. His fingers went to his arm and he began scratching at it. I doubted he was even aware he was doing it.

I got up and then reached for his hand. I pulled him along behind me as I snagged a throw from a cubbyhole by the stairs leading above deck. The air was crisp around us. There were only a few boats out and about, but I knew that would change as the sun rose higher in the sky. I tugged Caleb to one of the benches at the back of the boat. I sat down and then pulled him down to sit next to me. I maneuvered him until we were facing the back of the boat and he was sitting between my outstretched legs, his back against my chest. The position gave us both an unencumbered view of the water. I wrapped the blanket around both of us and said, "For every question of mine that you answer, I'll do the same for you. I'm not untouchable, Caleb. I bleed on the inside just like you do. I've just found different ways than you to not feel."

"Like how?" Caleb asked. His fingers were digging into the hands I had wrapped around his upper body.

"I push people away when they try to get close. I never offer trust or respect, it has to be earned. I can count on one finger how many friends I have."

"Dalton?" Caleb asked.

"Yes. What things did the kids put in your locker, Caleb?"

It took him a long time to answer, but when he did, I felt a measure of relief. At least he was talking, even though I knew I wasn't going to like hearing what he had to say.

"Drawings, mostly. More like a comic strip, I guess. It was of a father and son. Different sexual acts, the father asking the son if he liked it, the son saying yes, stuff like that."

I suspected he was glossing over the worst of it, but I didn't make him expound on the subject. I was already itching to hunt down the kid or kids who'd tormented him and make them feel just an ounce of the pain they'd inflicted on Caleb.

"Why don't you have any friends besides Dalton?" Caleb asked.

"Because losing them is too fucking hard. I watched men I considered my brothers get blown to bits for eight long years over four deployments. I'd have to watch some high-ranking official say fancy words about men I considered blood having sacrificed their lives for something greater. They've been saying the same shit for years now, and guess what? We're no closer to winning. Those men are still dead and their widows and kids are still trying to figure out how to go on without them. What things did the kids do to you, besides the drawings and the name-calling?"

Caleb shook his head. I leaned down to press my lips to his ear. "It's okay, Caleb. You can tell me anything. It's just between us."

He hesitated, then said, "Some guys cornered me in the shower after gym class one day. They... they forced me to face the wall and started asking if I liked any dick up my ass or if it had to be my daddy's dick. Then they started to wonder if it even had to be a dick."

I felt my blood run cold at his words. I closed my eyes and sent a silent prayer heavenward that I could hang onto my control, no matter what he told me.

"One of them went and got one of the bats from the room where all the sports equipment was kept."

No.

I managed to keep the word in my head, even though all I wanted to do was yell it out loud. But Caleb must have picked up on my distress because he turned and looked over his shoulder at me. "Nothing happened," he said quickly. "The gym teacher saw him taking the bat into the shower and yelled at him. The guys let me go and pretended like nothing was going on, then got out of there when the teacher told them to get to their next class."

"Did you tell anyone?" I asked.

Caleb returned his gaze to the water and shook his head. "I started skipping gym class after that, then my other classes. That's when the drinking intensified. I was failing most of my classes and since there was no way I could get my grades back up in time to graduate this spring, they started talking about holding me back another year. I ended up dropping out. Mav and Eli were so disappointed."

Jesus fucking Christ. How had I not known things had gotten so bad for him?

You didn't know because you didn't ask, you fucking coward.

"Are you and Dalton together?"

Caleb's question pulled me from my thoughts. "What?" I asked, completely thrown.

"Is he your boyfriend?"

"No," I said. "He and I have never been together like that."

"But he's gay, right?"

"He is," I confirmed. "How did you know?"

"The way he looks at you," was all Caleb said. "Why weren't you ever together?"

I sighed because the conversation had taken a turn I hadn't been expecting. But I'd promised him that I'd answer his questions. "Because I'm not what Dalton needs. And he's not what I need, either."

"What do you need?"

Yeah, this was definitely not the direction I'd wanted this to go. I debated how to phrase my response so I wouldn't scare the hell out of him. "Caleb, when the pain gets to be too much for you, you cut to let some of it out, right?"

"You didn't answer my question—"

"I'm going to," I assured him. "Just answer mine first, please."

"Yes. Most of the time I'm just numb, but when things get to be too much, I… I need to get it out. I'm afraid of what will happen if I don't."

"I use sex to accomplish the same things, Caleb. I don't hurt my partners, but I'm aggressive with them. I turn everything I'm feeling on them. I always make sure they get off, but that's really all it's about. There's no emotion when I touch them. I never see them again, never talk to them again. I control the encounter, their reactions, my own…"

"It's not real," Caleb murmured.

Humiliation went through me as he repeated my own words back to me. "And just like you, I'd rather have the illusion," I said.

Caleb let out a heavy breath but didn't say anything. After all, what could he say?

"Jace?"

"Yeah?" I said. It was funny because I suddenly felt wiped out. I'd gone into this thing in the hopes of drawing out some of the shit that was festering inside of Caleb, but somehow, he'd turned the tables on me without even trying.

"I know what I want now for keeping your secret about your complete and utter lack of grace on the ski slope."

I smiled despite myself. "Okay," I responded.

I was surprised when he turned around so that he was facing me. He sat Indian-style between my outstretched legs. There was a little color in his cheeks, but I wasn't sure if it was because of the cold morning air or the emotion that had come with the admissions he'd made. But none of that mattered the second he gave voice to his request and whispered, "I want to kiss you."

CHAPTER 8

CALEB

I was sure he wasn't going to go for it. Not with the way his jaw went tight and his fingers dug into where they were resting on his thighs. But he surprised me by nodding his head. I wanted to laugh because I couldn't tell if he was pissed or worried or excited.

Since I didn't want to give him a chance to change his mind, I quickly shifted my weight so that I was on my knees in front of him. It made me a little taller than him. When I reached for his face, I felt his hands come up to my waist to steady me.

"Caleb—"

"I know, Jace," I interrupted. "It won't mean anything." I'd heard him loud and clear when he'd talked about his view of sex. Admittedly, it had been hard to hear, especially since I'd been holding out hope that there might be some part of him that wanted me that way. But even if there was, he and I both knew I wouldn't be any kind of match for him. The idea of sex, even with him, terrified me even as it intrigued me. But aggressive sex and being used to get off? No, I wasn't capable of handling that. No matter how much a part of me wished I was.

With me being higher than him, Jace was forced to look up at me just a little. I waited until his eyes met mine and then quietly said, "It means something to me, Jace." Then I pressed my lips against his cheek. I relished how warm his skin felt through the scratchy stubble on his face and the way his fingers dug into my waist just a little bit. He clearly hadn't been expecting the move, because when I pulled back, his eyes were closed and he looked like he was in pain.

"Jace," I breathed.

He opened his eyes. It seemed to take him a moment to look at me. Our faces were just inches apart. It would've been so easy to lean in and taste his lips next.

"Thank you," I said softly, then I let my fingers do what my lips couldn't. They skimmed his warm, firm lips. I hung there for a moment, long enough to let the memory of touching him take root deep inside of me in a place where I'd be able to find it later. Then I pulled out of his reach and stood. I left him sitting there and headed back to the kitchen to clean up the breakfast dishes.

I didn't look back at him.

I'd told him more than I'd ever planned. He'd made it possible to do so by giving me something in return. As open as he'd been with me, I suspected he'd only scratched the surface. He was so much more complicated than I'd ever imagined. Of course, I'd seen him through the rose-colored glasses of a victim worshipping his rescuer. Never in a million years would I have guessed he was so very... human.

I heard the engine of the boat kick in and a few moments later we began moving. After the dishes were done, I pulled up my sleeve and began to clean up the dried blood on my arm from the night before when I'd gouged at the wounds with my fingernails. I hadn't missed the way Jace had looked at me this morning – he'd been wondering if I'd hurt myself while he'd still been asleep. I supposed it was a look I'd have to get used to. I didn't really have the right to be upset that he didn't trust me.

He shouldn't.

The cuts had already scabbed over, so I left them alone. Although I was still physically exhausted, I felt mentally restless, so I gave up on the idea of going back to bed and returned above deck. Jace had gotten us headed south again, though we weren't moving very fast. I grabbed the blanket still sitting on the back bench and took it up to the front of the boat with me. The boat was designed so that the driver sat a little higher than the front of the boat, so I knew Jace could see me as I sat close to the edge to watch the hull slice cleanly through the water. We traveled for about a half an hour before Jace stopped the boat, then dropped anchor. I could see the Chesapeake Bay Bridge, which meant we were near Annapolis, which was where my father had kept his own boat.

The boat swayed as Jace came around to the front. He sat down next to me and said, "So, any chance you have a recipe in your repertoire for striped bass?" He cracked a smile at me and I was instantly glad that I hadn't ruined things with the kiss I'd given him.

"I think I can pull something together. Are you planning on bringing the little woman home some fish to fry up?" I joked.

"Hell, no," Jace said as he gave me a gentle slap on the back. "I can't fish for shit. Dalton's the one who has to bait my hook and cast my rod. No clue how to clean a fish, either."

I laughed. "So what exactly *can* you do?"

He waggled his eyebrows at me. It was so ridiculous that I couldn't help but laugh. "I mean, what can you do when it comes to fishing?"

"Not a damn thing."

"So is this you cashing in your chips?"

I'd meant the comment as a joke, but the humor slipped from Jace's face and something flashed in his eyes. His voice was sultry as he said, "No, I'm gonna save that for a bit."

My dick responded to both his words and the way he'd said them. Not to mention how he couldn't seem to take his eyes off me.

Or I him.

A boat overloaded with several twenty-somethings flew past us, breaking the moment. Jace jerked back, as if remembering where we were. He recovered quickly and stood as he said, "So, what do you say?"

"I say I should probably get moving because if I don't, we're surely going to starve to death on this trip."

Jace let out one of his growly little chuckles that I felt in my bones as he reached his hand down to help me up. The first wave from the passing boat hit our boat at the exact moment I got to my feet, pitching me into Jace's arms. My entire body lit up with expectation as Jace steadied me. I could barely breathe as my eyes met his. Then his gaze was dropping to my mouth.

Despite everything he'd said about sex earlier, I wanted his kiss more than anything in the world. I'd tried to be mature by not kissing him like I'd wanted when I'd had the chance, but now I was thinking I'd squandered the opportunity.

God, it was all just so complicated.

But as he held me there in his arms, all I could think was, *Fuck complicated – I want to know what it's like to have a man's mouth moving over mine. This man's mouth.*

So much for my promise to myself to keep my distance from him. I couldn't afford to need him like I had for so very long. But just because it wasn't good for me didn't mean I didn't crave it just the same.

"Is this a good spot?" Jace asked.

"What?" I asked. I didn't give a shit where we were when he kissed me. I was pretty certain the second his lips touched mine, the rest of the world would cease to exist.

"Maybe something closer to the bridge? Or one of the inlets?"

God, he was talking about fishing.

"Oh, um, yeah, an inlet might be better. It's quieter."

Jace released me and stepped aside so I could walk ahead of him. It took a few minutes to get the boat in position and go through all of Dalton's fishing gear.

"I think he left some bait for us in the fridge," Jace said. He disappeared below deck and returned a few minutes later with a plastic container.

"Clams… nice," I said as I took it from him. "We'll start by just casting and see how it goes. If we don't get any bites, we can try trolling."

Jace looked at me blankly, and I couldn't help but laugh. He hadn't been kidding. The man was completely clueless when it came to fishing.

"I'll take care of you," I said with another laugh.

Jace's eyes held mine for a moment and we once again got lost in that place where it seemed like only the two of us existed.

"I have no doubt you will," he finally said.

I wanted to say a lot of things to him in that moment, but then I remembered who I was and who he was, and that was enough to have me turning away from him so I could focus on the task at hand.

Anything to keep from reaching for Jace and begging him not to leave me again.

"Son of a bitch!"

"Again?" I said in disbelief as I turned to look over my shoulder at Jace. I stifled a laugh at the sight of Jace caught in the awkward position of holding his rod over his head, the line stuck behind him somewhere. I quickly put my own rod in the holder and then hurried to his side.

"God, you weren't kidding," I said as I eyed the hook that had gotten caught on one of the loops of Jace's jeans. Fortunately, the sharp tip hadn't penetrated the material and reached his skin. "You really do suck."

"You going to help me out?" Jace growled, though there was no true anger behind his words.

I dropped to my knees so I could get a better look at the hook and work it free of the thick denim. "Okay, got it," I said after a minute of working it loose. Jace carefully maneuvered the rod and then turned to face me.

That was when I realized I was still on my knees.

In front of him.

Tantalizingly close to…

I stumbled to my feet. Jace grabbed my elbow to steady me, but I quickly pulled free of him. My body felt like it was on fire. "I'll… I'll re-bait your hook," I stuttered. I avoided Jace's gaze as I worked. "Do you want to try casting again?" I asked when I was finished. Jace's eyes were still on me, but I couldn't tell what he was thinking.

"No, not sure my ass can take a second hit."

His attempt to lighten the tension worked and I found myself smiling. I took the rod from him, avoiding touching him as I did so, then quickly re-baited the hook and cast the line into the water. I returned to my seat and Jace did the same. The silence between us grew, causing my anxiety to build.

"So, um, you can't ski, cook, or fish," I blurted. "What can you do? Besides save my life and stuff," I added, flashing him a slight smile.

"I can juggle," he said with a grin.

I chuckled at that.

Jace sobered and said, "There was never one thing I was particularly good at when I was a kid. I got mediocre grades, I wasn't popular or good-looking, I did okay in sports but I wasn't any kind of standout. I eventually just accepted I was average."

"I find that hard to believe," I admitted.

"It's true," he said. "At first it was hard for me to be okay with it. My parents, they were amazing – they always encouraged me to try things, but never pressured me to succeed – it was always more about me doing things that I enjoyed. The skiing was my idea because I just wanted to find that one thing I was really good at – that thing that would make me *me*."

"And did you?" I asked.

"Yeah, it's just not something I can say I'm particularly proud of. I mean, I was at the time, because I thought it was really cool that I could do what only a handful of people could. I mean, suddenly I was being noticed for something."

"You were good with a gun," I said softly, as it dawned on me what he was referring to. The tone in his voice suggested it wasn't a topic he enjoyed talking about.

"No, lots of guys in the military can shoot. But they can't take out a moving target from a mile and a half away." Jace took a sip from his bottle of water.

"You hated it," I murmured. On the one hand, I hated having brought him down with the unpleasant conversation, but on the other, I wanted to understand what made him tick.

"Sometimes," he said. "I didn't know shit about the men and women I saw through my scope. I was told who to take out and that was it. I didn't ask if the person on the other end deserved it. I was a good little soldier and followed orders."

When he fell silent, I instinctively knew there was more. "What happened?" I asked quietly.

"Over two hundred kills in ten years. Didn't hesitate even once. Final mission, final deployment. Order comes in, I find my target... it's a woman and a kid approaching a checkpoint. She ignores orders to stay back. Soldiers on the ground can't get a good shot – too many civilians around. She was acting suspicious enough that they were worried she had an IED and was using the kid to blend in. I knew something was wrong because she was drawing too much attention to herself," Jace said with a shake of his head.

"Did you take the shot?" I asked. My heart was in my throat because I already knew the answer.

"Had to follow orders," Jace said quietly. "I didn't have a clean shot, not with the way she was holding her kid. Baby couldn't have been more than a year old. But I did what I was told."

"I'm sorry, Jace," I offered.

He shook his head. "Turned out she was just trying to get some help for her kid, but she was deaf. Couldn't understand the orders the soldiers were calling out to her. The baby had been sick for a few days, but she'd been afraid to take him to the hospital because the city had been overrun by insurgents. When we showed up, she thought we were her kid's salvation."

"You couldn't have known," I said.

"But I did. In my gut, I knew. But all that discipline that had been drilled into me when I enlisted, that I'd *needed*, had me pulling that trigger anyway. There's a husband out there who no longer has his wife or youngest son. There are four other kids who don't have a mother anymore. And what did I get out of the whole thing? A medal. An actual fucking medal."

Jace took another sip of his water, then motioned to the bay. "That fucker's out here. Hopefully buried under twenty feet of fish shit where it belongs."

I took that to mean he'd tossed the medal overboard at some point after he'd returned to the States.

"What about you, Caleb Cortano?" Jace asked with a loud sigh. "What are you good at?"

Besides fucking my father?

I shoved the errant thought away and began reeling in my line, more so I'd have something to occupy my hands while I spoke than anything else.

"Everything," I admitted. "Well, I was, anyway." I cast him a glance. "Straight-A student, captain of the football team, basketball team, baseball team, soccer team… you get my drift," I said with a shrug. "I made friends wherever I went and grown-ups loved me because I was respectful and well-behaved. Perfect kid," I muttered. I looked over at him and said, "So to answer your question… nothing important."

I expected him to argue with me and he did.

But not in the way I was expecting.

"Not true… you're a much better hook-from-ass remover than Dalton, and I've never seen anyone bait a hook so gracefully."

I couldn't help the smile that drifted across my mouth.

"And the lengths you went to just to feed your Sno Balls habit? Impressive," Jace said in all seriousness.

"Shut up," I growled. "At least I don't still need a cup of warm milk at bedtime."

"Hey," Jace said loudly. He pointed at me with mock irritation. "That's *pink* milk, not warm milk. Because that shit's just nasty."

I chuckled and we both fell into a more comfortable silence. I cast my line back out.

"Jace," I said as I kept my eyes on the water.

"Yeah?"

"If it helps, I don't think there's anything average about you."

He was quiet for a really long time. "Caleb?"

"Yeah?"

"It helps."

I found myself smiling wide, but I kept from looking at him.

"Caleb?"

"Yeah?"

"Do you want to know what you're good at?"

I didn't answer him. I heard him shift his weight and then sensed him behind me, but I didn't turn to look at him, though I really wanted to. I shivered when his fingers briefly drifted over the back of my neck. Then his lips were dropping to the top of my head and his fingers curled around my throat until they were resting on my thrumming pulse.

"All the stuff that really matters. Don't forget that, okay?"

He didn't wait for an answer. Instead, he reached past me to grab my nearly empty water bottle. The move put his face precariously close to mine. "Will you watch my line for a second?"

I swallowed around the knot of anticipation in my throat. "Yeah," I choked out.

Then he was gone and I finally managed to take in a deep breath. Seconds later I heard a clanging sound behind me. I looked over my shoulder just in time to see Jace's fishing pole bounce along the bench and then disappear over the side of the boat and splash into the water below. I let out a bark of laughter as I realized Jace had forgotten to put his rod in one of the holders to keep the pole from going overboard in case a fish took the bait.

I began laughing.

And laughing.

And laughing.

And that was how Jace found me.

Bent over my own rod, tears of laughter streaming down my face.

"What?" he asked. "What happened?"

I managed to point at the place his pole had been.

"Oh hell," he muttered. "Not again. Dalton's going to fucking kill me."

That just sent more peals of laughter bursting from my throat.

Jace had been right.

He couldn't fish for shit.

And it was in that exact moment that I lost the first little bit of my heart to Jace Christenson, and I just knew it would only be a matter of time before the rest followed.

CHAPTER 9

JACE

"Favorite color?"

"Black," I responded between bites.

"Nuh-uh, no one's favorite color is black."

"Not how this works," I reminded Caleb. "Favorite movie?"

He sent me a dirty look, then said, "*Lord of the Rings*. Favorite celebrity?"

"Martha Stewart."

"No way!" Caleb practically yelled.

"Favorite holiday?" I asked.

"Nope, we're going back to the Martha Stewart thing." I nearly chuckled at his look of outrage. "Martha Stewart is *not* your favorite celebrity."

"She is," I said. "Scout's honor."

"Were you even a scout?"

"You answer my question first."

"Halloween," Caleb said. "Were you really a scout?"

"I was… most of my merit badges were the pity ones, but—"

"Wait, wait, wait," Caleb said as he put his hands up in the universal time-out sign. "Time out. Martha Stewart? *Martha Stewart*? What… how… *what*?"

I felt my insides warm as I watched Caleb. He was so animated and... free. It was the first time in the six days since we'd been on the boat that he'd finally let his guard completely down and was just himself.

"Why Halloween?" I asked. Predictably, Caleb sent me an annoyed look.

"Because..."

When I arched my eyebrows at him, he sighed and said, "Because I got to go as my favorite character from *Harry Potter*."

I nodded. "Harry," I said knowingly.

Caleb dropped his eyes and picked at his food.

"Ron?" I queried.

Color stained Caleb's cheeks and I chuckled. "You did not go as Hermione Granger," I said.

"Shut up, Martha-Stewart-lover."

"Hermione?" I asked. "Really?"

"What? She was the smartest of the three of them!" Caleb declared. I smiled as he began spouting off all of Hermione's many attributes.

I waited until he was finished to say, "Not buying it."

Caleb frowned, then deflated. "Fine," he bit out. "My brother used to go as Ron Weasley and his friend, Pete, went as Harry."

I smiled and said, "Someone was crushing hard on Pete, huh?" I sent Caleb a wink and he immediately threw one of the leftover dinner rolls at me. "Shut up. I was eight!" He paused and then smiled. "Fine. Pete was the one who suggested it because he thought Hermione was awesome and we'd look cool as the trio. But I do think Hermione was the smartest," he added with a waggle of his finger.

"My mother loved Martha Stewart. We used to watch her show all the time and we constantly tried out her recipes and crafty shit. My sister wasn't into that stuff. But even though I sucked at most of it, I really liked spending time with my mom. She idolized Martha and modeled the lodge after Martha's designs. After my parents died, I still found myself watching the show and reading the magazine. I have a subscription."

Caleb stared at me for the longest time. "You couldn't have just said you have a freakishly weird obsession with her?" he groused. "You had to go and say something sweet like that while I'm admitting to dressing up as a girl for five years straight because I was perving on my brother's friend."

I smiled and grabbed the roll he'd tossed at me. I started picking at it, but stopped when I replayed his words. "Wait, five years straight? Weren't your brother and his friend older than you? Wouldn't they have stopped trick-or-treating a couple of years before you?"

"Shut up," was all Caleb said.

I laughed, but refrained from poking the bear by pointing out that Caleb had been free to dress as something besides Hermione Granger for a couple of years.

"Favorite hobby?" I said as I searched out the butter.

Caleb was silent for a long time. His gaze drifted to the small window on the opposite side of the small kitchen. "That's a hard one," he murmured.

"Why?" I asked.

He shrugged. "Because I'm not sure if you want the before answer or the after one."

"I know it's hard to see it right now, Caleb. But you're still one person. What happened to you is only a piece of you, but there are so many other pieces. I think you just need time to put some of those pieces together."

"Can I get back to you on the hobby thing?" he asked.

I didn't like how quiet he'd gone. Something had changed between us after that first day on the boat. We'd found this comfortable rhythm with one another and had started engaging in conversations much like the one we'd just had. It'd been Caleb who'd decided to keep our mutual question thing going. I knew it was his way of sharing things about himself that were easy. As badly as I'd wanted to push him to talk to me about the Jennings encounter, I'd made too much progress with him to blow it by pressuring him. I still had two weeks before I had to get him back to Seattle for the pre-trial hearing. I needed to make use of every minute I had with him. I wanted him to tell me the truth about Jennings, but I wanted him to start to feel like himself even more.

I'd somehow managed to limit how much physical contact I was having with him, despite my growing attraction to him. It wasn't easy, though, because my mind was no longer seeing him as that scared, vulnerable teenager and that seemed to have given my body permission to react accordingly. I was almost always half-hard around him and it didn't take much to have my dick standing at full attention. What was worse, though, was there was absolutely nothing I could do about it. With the close quarters we were sharing, I couldn't even jack off in the small bathroom. Add in the fact that we were sleeping in the same bed each night and Caleb usually ended up sprawled half on top of me come morning time, and I was barely keeping it together. He was still very much off-limits, since nothing had changed. Even if I could get past his age, I couldn't overlook the fact that what he needed in a lover was something I couldn't offer him.

"Sure," I said.

"What about you?" Caleb asked. "What's your favorite hobby?"

"You mean besides reading Martha Stewart's *Living* cover to cover the moment it arrives in my mailbox?"

Caleb chuckled. "Yeah."

"The basics, I guess. Watching TV, reading. But if I had to pick just one thing, it'd be woodworking."

That got Caleb's attention. He had his mouth full, so he covered it with his hand as he said, "Really?"

I nodded. "I'm not great at it or anything, but I've managed to not lose a limb yet, so I think in my case that makes me a semi-professional."

"Wow. So what do you build?"

"Furniture, mostly." I nodded at the kitchen. "I did those cabinets. And that shelf in the bedroom. The headboard too."

Caleb's eyes shifted to the cabinets. "You made those?"

I nodded. "I learned from my grandfather when I was a kid. I inherited all his tools and equipment when he died. Martha Stewart is how I stayed connected with my mom, and woodworking kept me close to my grandfather."

"What about your father and grandmother?" Caleb asked.

"My father always wanted me to join the military, since he, his father, and his grandfather had all been enlisted. As for my grandmother, I have this habit of collecting take-out menus. Doesn't matter if I'm just in the area for a job or something, I'll keep any take-out menus I order from. I have drawers full of them at home."

Caleb smiled. "And your sister?" He blanched almost instantly and dropped his fork. "Oh God, Jace, I'm so sorry… that was… that was…"

He made a move to get up, so I quickly grabbed his hand. "It's all right, Caleb. I do have something of hers that I keep with me."

He settled, though he still looked flustered and embarrassed. "Maggie has always been an amazing artist. She never wanted to actually sell her art, which is why she's planning to go to Georgetown for their art and museum studies program. She's hoping to get a job working at the National Gallery of Art in D.C. when she graduates. When she was about seventeen or so, instead of buying me a birthday present that year, she drew this butterfly for me – butterflies were kind of her thing. I kept that drawing with me no matter where I was. But after she disappeared, it wasn't enough… I felt like to get her back, I had to keep her even closer to my heart."

I let Caleb's hand go and then stood up. I peeled my T-shirt off and watched as Caleb's eyes went wide.

"Oh my God," he whispered, then he was climbing to his feet. I wasn't surprised when he reached for the tattoo on my chest. "It looks alive," he murmured as he drew his finger along the edge of one of the wings of the butterfly that was tattooed to the left of my heart. The design spread out across most of my pectoral muscle.

"It's a 3-D tattoo," I explained. I smiled as he shook his head in disbelief. I'd had the same reaction the first time I'd seen the completed tattoo in the mirror. It was made to look like the delicate creature had merely landed on my chest and could fly off at any moment. The tattoo artist had done an amazing job of capturing Maggie's design.

"It's beautiful. Your sister is so talented."

I tried to focus on Caleb's words, but admittedly, it got more difficult as he continued to trail his fingers all over the butterfly. He clearly had no clue what he was doing to me, because he stepped even closer to me and dropped his face so close to my skin that I could feel his warm breath. "So beautiful," he repeated. He was so lost in studying the tattoo, that his fingers slid unnoticed to my nipple. I wasn't able to successfully hold back a rush of air when the pad of his finger slid over my sensitive flesh. The sound caught Caleb's attention, but instead of jerking back, he held there for a moment, then slowly looked at his own fingers.

And then, God, he started playing with me.

I trembled as pleasure spiked throughout my entire body. From the way Caleb's lips parted and his thumb stilled over my nipple, I knew he knew what was happening to me.

"Caleb," I breathed, though I wasn't sure what I wanted to tell him.

I knew what I was *supposed* to tell him – that he needed to stop.

But my traitorous brain just had me repeating his name in a voice I barely recognized as my own.

Caleb's hand slid down my body and settled on my waist as his gaze stayed on my nipple, which had tightened under his touch. I knew what he was going to do, but I didn't even try to stop him.

His moves were slow and deliberate, but held a hint of uncertainty in them. As his lips landed in a gentle kiss just to the right of my nipple, his hand slid around to my back. His other was resting on my hip. I told myself not to do it, but I dropped my hand to the back of his head anyway. Caleb chose that moment to lift his eyes.

But he left his mouth where it was.

I was caught in the snare of his gaze. My dick was straining against the fabric of my jeans and it took everything in me not to just grab him and toss him down on the small table we'd just been sitting at.

Neither of us spoke in the few seconds that passed. I held my breath when Caleb moved his mouth, but it was impossible to look away.

Because he never stopped looking at me.

Not as he licked my skin.

Or when he closed his mouth over my nipple.

"Fuck," I muttered as I tightened my grip in his hair. "Yes," I whispered. Caleb's sinful tongue flattened over my nipple as he licked me, then continued up my chest. I wrapped my free arm around his waist and pulled him flush against my body as he began placing kisses along my collarbone. I still had my hand in his hair, but I refrained from forcing his head back so I could take the kiss that I really wanted.

My ringing phone split the silence of the air around us and Caleb jerked out of my hold. He looked at me with wide eyes, then at the burner phone, which was sitting on the kitchen counter. I wanted to ignore the damn thing, but I knew I couldn't.

"It's Dalton," I said. "He might have an update."

Caleb nodded shakily. "I, uh, should go make sure we didn't leave the bait above deck... it'll spoil."

I'd brought the bait down and put it in the refrigerator myself, but I didn't say that. I merely nodded and watched Caleb flee. My body was tight with lust as I snatched up the phone.

"What?" I practically barked.

There was a beat, then Dalton said, "Dude, if you're suffering from cabin fever after only six days—"

"Sorry," I cut in. "It's not that."

It's the fact that if you'd have waited five more goddamn minutes, I would have had Caleb beneath me on your bed and I wouldn't have given two shits about answering your call.

"Just tired," I lied.

Dalton didn't respond at first, probably because he knew I was lying.

"Any updates?" I asked.

"No. But there's a storm coming up fast from the south. You might want to head further inland if you aren't already."

"We're by Barren Island. I'll put us north of the island and that will hopefully shelter us from the worst of it. We'll be close enough to shore that we can head in if things get bad."

"Should be all clear by tomorrow."

"Good," I murmured. "There's a general store on Hooper's Island, right?"

"Yeah. You going to stock up there?"

"That's the plan."

"Call me in the morning to let me know you're good," Dalton said. I could hear the worry in his voice.

"I will. We'll be okay, Dalton."

I sensed I was no longer alone and turned to see Caleb sitting on the steps leading into the cabin from above deck. His expression was unreadable. I said my goodbyes and hung up the phone.

"Dalton said there's a storm coming."

Caleb nodded. "I saw some lightning."

"You okay?" I asked.

"Don't like storms," he murmured.

"Why don't you stay down here while I get the boat moved to the northern side of the island?"

"I'll do the dishes," Caleb offered. We were forced to pass one another as I headed above deck. The close proximity as we nearly brushed chests was akin to torture. It was all I could do not to grab him.

It took just a few minutes to get the boat moved and anchored in the small inlet at the northernmost part of the little island, but in those minutes, several peals of thunder rattled the air around us. The heavens opened up just as I stepped below deck and closed the door. Darkness had already fallen so the lightning lit up the interior of the boat with every flash. The wind had kicked up the waves enough so the boat was swaying back and forth, but nothing bad enough to warrant seeking shelter closer to the shore.

Caleb wasn't in the kitchen and the dishes, while now in the sink, weren't done. Concern had me hurrying to the bedroom. I found him sitting on the edge of the bed, his knees drawn up so that his feet were resting on the lip of the platform. His arms were around his legs and he was rocking back and forth slightly. It took everything in me not to automatically look at his arm. He was wearing short sleeves, so it would have been easy to check to see if he'd cut himself in the few minutes I'd been above deck, but I didn't want to do that to him. I wanted to build trust with Caleb and I couldn't do that if his condition was always at the forefront of my mind.

Caleb had turned on all the lights in the bedroom and had drawn the curtain on the one window that had one, but the flashes of lightning through the other windows were impossible to miss. Not to mention the cracks of thunder that followed just moments later.

"You okay?" I asked, more to start the conversation than anything, since I could tell he wasn't.

"Stupid, huh," he said. "Someone my age afraid of storms."

"Nope," I said as I sat down next to him. "Everybody's afraid of something."

He didn't need to speak for me to know what was on his mind. "Clowns, for starters," I said. "And those troll doll things... with the hair... my sister had a whole bunch of those and they creeped me the fuck out. Not a fan of geese, either. Those fuckers are just mean."

Caleb laughed and buried his face in his knees. "What did I do to deserve you?" He turned so he could look at me, but kept his cheek resting on his knees. "Why did you do it? Why did you get me out of the hospital that day?"

I lifted my own legs so my position was mirroring his and then rested my arms on my knees. "I just knew," I said. "I could see it in your eyes."

"See what?"

"That you didn't belong there. That you weren't broken like the others. At least not in any kind of way that those doctors could put you back together again."

Caleb jumped when more thunder rumbled above us. I shifted closer to him and he automatically leaned into me.

"And *this* is why I keep coming back," I murmured.

He looked up at me in confusion.

"The trust you show me, Caleb. After all you've been through, you're still willing to trust. I wish I had that kind of strength."

"I'm not strong. I'm so fucking scared, Jace. I know I made a big deal about me just going off on my own and disappearing, but the me who still feels shit knows I wouldn't last five minutes."

I put my arm around him.

"Being scared doesn't make you weak. Neither does asking for help. Leaning on people again, even after everything that was done to you, that takes a kind of courage most of us could only dream of having."

Caleb pressed his head against my shoulder. "Why did you stop talking to me, Jace? It wasn't really to protect me, was it?"

"It was," I murmured.

"I don't understand. What were you protecting me from?"

"Not what," I said. "Who."

"Okay, *who* were you protecting me from?" Caleb asked.

"Me."

CHAPTER 10

CALEB

"I don't understand," I admitted. I tried not to flinch when I felt the next clap of thunder in my very bones.

"I would've thought what just happened between us would make it pretty clear," Jace said softly, then he was putting some space between us. I missed his heat instantly.

A tremor went through my body as I remembered what I'd done to him in the kitchen. I had no clue what had even possessed me to do it, but if that phone hadn't rung...

"I don't believe you," I said. "Even if you were attracted to me back then—"

"No ifs about it, Caleb. I was... I am."

At any other time, I would have been freaking out at his admission, but strangely enough, I wasn't satisfied.

"You didn't pick up the phone. No emails. You didn't even ask Mav how I was doing."

Jace scrubbed his hand over his face and I almost regretted starting the conversation.

Almost.

But not quite.

"Something happened when I was a kid, Caleb... I did something.

It scared the people around me and they never... they never looked at me the same. I knew they still loved me, but I also knew there was this part of them that was afraid of me, and probably always would be. You've never looked at me like that. Even after everything you went through, even knowing you probably *should* be afraid of me, you weren't."

Jace paused and said, "I didn't know how badly I needed that until you gave it to me. And once I had it, it was really hard to let go of it again."

"Then why did you?" I asked bluntly. "I would have given you anything, Jace."

"*That's* why I left," he responded. "I would have taken it all, Caleb. And you wouldn't have gotten anything back. I don't do relationships. I'm not interested in being a part of that family thing Ronan and Mav and them have going on out there. I can't... I can't have that day come where you look at me and that trust is gone and all I see is fear. You're nineteen years old. You have your entire life ahead of you—"

"That's just an excuse," I muttered. "Don't use my age against me. If you think I'm too immature or too naïve or inexperienced or whatever, just say it. But don't turn what I feel into a fucking number... like that somehow makes the things I think and feel *less*."

"You're right, I'm sorry," Jace said on a sigh. "I don't want you to waste even a second of everything that's good about you on me, Caleb. You might be willing to give me everything, but I have nothing to give you."

I felt like he was talking in riddles, but I didn't call him on it. I understood enough. He wasn't interested in seeing if there could be something between us. He only saw me as a troubled kid who he had the unfortunate luck of being attracted to.

"What did you do?" I asked. "That scared the people in your life?"

Lightning flashed in my periphery, but surprisingly, I didn't jerk in response to it. Somehow the violent storm had been moved inside this very room.

Jace didn't answer right away. When I was certain he *wouldn't* answer, I started to climb to my feet.

"I killed my uncle," he finally said, his voice so low I barely heard him. "Why did you go after Richard Jennings?"

I stilled at that, because I knew what he was doing. If I wanted him to share something painful with me, I'd have to do the same with him. I was reeling from his blunt admission about killing his uncle, but as desperate as I was to know more, I really didn't want to tell him my own truths. He'd pretty much told me that anything between us was dead in the water, so what was the point of learning all of the things that made him who he was? I'd only just end up falling even more in love with him. And as soon as he found out that I was still hiding more shameful secrets, he'd look at me with disgust.

I had no clue how long we sat there for as I tried to come to terms with what he wanted.

"Caleb—" he began, but I put my hand up.

"I can't do this face to face," I said.

Jace hesitated and then reached behind him to turn the lights off. "Come here," he murmured as he reached for my hand. I kicked off my shoes and then followed him as he lay down on the bed. I settled my back against his front and breathed in a sigh of relief when his arms came around me in a frighteningly familiar hold.

How the hell would I ever be able to go back to sleeping by myself after all this?

We lay there for a while as the storm quieted. Lightning occasionally illuminated the room, but the thunder had moved off into the distance and the boat was rocking gently back and forth, proof that the winds had started to die down. Jace didn't rush me, for which I was grateful.

Since I needed a few more minutes to gather my courage, I took a risk and asked, "Why did you kill your uncle?"

Jace didn't call me out on the fact that it was my turn to answer his question. Instead, he said, "Remember how I told you my sister and I were sent to live with him and my aunt when our parents died?"

I nodded. "Before you went to live with your grandmother."

"That's right. I'd just turned fifteen and Maggie was five. My uncle and aunt moved into the house my parents had built on the same plot of land where the lodge was located. I thought it was because they wanted to make things easier on us, but I learned later they'd lost their own house to foreclosure a few weeks before my parents died. My uncle had lost a lot of his money in risky investments in the stock market. I don't think my father ever realized how low my uncle had fallen. The will had been written several years earlier when my father and my uncle were still on good terms and I'm sure, like most parents, they never thought they'd actually need any of that stuff, you know?"

"Yeah," I said in agreement.

"My uncle was a mean son of a bitch, even before he got custody of us. But it got really bad when he moved in. He didn't stop at just calling us names or saying mean shit to us. He was particularly hard on Maggie, probably because she was so little and just kept asking for her mom and dad."

"What about your aunt?" I asked.

"She wasn't any better. She wasn't gutsy enough to hit me, but she'd slap Maggie if Maggie did something she didn't like. I did my best to take the brunt of both their anger, but I couldn't be with Maggie twenty-four seven. She hadn't started kindergarten, so she was stuck at home with my aunt during the day when they first came to live with us. It wasn't unusual to come home and find her hiding in her closet in tears."

My heart broke for Jace and his sister. "Did your grandmother know?" I asked.

"No, my uncle was smart and used my love for my grandmother to keep me in line. One of the reasons my grandmother hadn't fought my uncle and aunt for custody had been because she was showing early signs of dementia. It wasn't bad, but there was no way to know how quickly she'd go downhill. My uncle constantly threatened to have her put away in one of those places that just tied the patients to the bed and left them there all day in their own filth. I knew he'd do it, so I never said anything. When kids and teachers at school would ask about the bruises, I'd pass them off as a result of my natural klutziness and they'd laugh it off."

Jace took a beat and then said, "It all changed about a month before I turned seventeen. I came home from school and found my uncle hitting Maggie. She'd spilled some paint on the couch. I pulled him off her and he turned on me. I don't know what made that time so different, but it was. I could see it in his eyes. He began beating the shit out of me. At some point, my grandmother and aunt arrived home – my aunt had taken my grandmother to a doctor's appointment and she was joining us for dinner that night. Anyway, I didn't even know they were there. I guess that they were screaming at him to stop, but he wouldn't. His hands were on my throat. I couldn't breathe, I couldn't see because of the blood pouring into my eyes from where he'd split my head open. I started to lose consciousness and I knew I was going to die. My grandmother tried to grab him to pull him off me, but he pushed her away. She fell and hit her arm on the edge of the fireplace. She was screaming in agony because the fall had broken her wrist."

I could feel Jace trembling behind me as he spoke, so I began rubbing my fingers over his where they were resting on my chest.

"I lost it. I don't know how, but I found the strength to fight back. I managed to reach the fire poker and I hit him with it. He let me go. He was on his hands and knees, yelling at me that he was going to kill me. My grandmother was crying, Maggie was in her arms, her lip bloodied and her face covered in bruises. My aunt was just screaming at the top of her lungs. All that and he *still* kept saying he was going to kill me... us."

Jace's voice began to crack. I pulled his fingers up to my lips and pressed a kiss against them. "It's okay, Jace. You're safe now," I reminded him.

He sucked in several deep breaths. When he'd calmed, he continued. "I just started hitting him with the fire poker over and over again. Even after he stopped moving, I kept hitting him with it. His blood went everywhere. On me, my grandmother and Maggie, the walls, the floor. And I just kept going. Even when I fell to my knees because I couldn't stand any longer, I still kept hitting him. When the cops showed up and took the poker from me, I kept swinging my arms like I still had it. I only stopped when they put me in cuffs."

"You were arrested?" I asked, completely sickened by what he'd been forced to endure... and do.

"No charges were pressed. It was a clear case of self-defense. Maggie and I went to live with my grandmother. My aunt left the state – we never saw her again."

Thank God for small favors.

"All three of us – me, my sister, and my grandmother – went to counseling, but it wasn't like any of us could unsee that night."

"You really think your grandmother and sister were afraid of you after that?" I asked.

"Not all the time. But if I lost my temper or raised my voice, I could see it in their eyes. Just this brief flash and then it was gone. But I knew in that moment they were remembering that night. I couldn't blame them. Before the fight, I wouldn't have thought it possible that I could do something like that to another human being."

"You had no choice," I said. "He would have killed you."

"Yes, he would have," Jace agreed.

"I'm sorry, Jace. You shouldn't have been put in that position, but I'm glad you're still here."

Jace's lips pressed against the top of my head. It was another move I was becoming far too dependent on.

"Me too," he murmured.

We fell silent for a while as I tried to work up the courage to be even half as brave as he'd been in telling me his story. Shame curled through me as I sucked in the oxygen I would need to say the words that I'd never spoken to another living soul.

"My father let Richard Jennings have sex with me."

CHAPTER 11

JACE

I'd tried to prepare myself for whatever Caleb had to tell me, but truthfully, I hadn't been ready for the admission.

I wasn't sure there was any way to be ready to hear something like that.

I found myself holding him tighter and dropping my face to the back of his neck as I squeezed my eyes shut. I managed to quell the sob that was bubbling up from my throat.

Caleb had said "have sex with" but I knew what that really meant.

"It happened on a camping trip. It was me, my dad, Mr. Jennings, and this guy who worked with my dad. He called him Rush, but I'm not sure if that was his real name or not."

"How old were you?" I asked.

Caleb hesitated, then answered, "Fifteen." He paused for a moment, then said, "They were drinking and playing poker... they kept getting louder and louder, so I stayed in my tent and read." His voice cracked when he whispered, *"Harry Potter."*

"Oh God, Caleb, I'm sorry," I bit out. I wanted to tell him he didn't have to continue, but I also wanted him to get it out... to lance that wound so that it would...

It would what?

Heal?

Was that even possible? Could someone ever truly heal from that kind of brutality? Maybe I was making things worse by making him relive it. Before I could even consider that, Caleb continued on his own.

"My dad called for me. They were sitting around the campfire. It was this spot we used to go to all the time. Most of the time, Nick would come with, but by then he'd started to use more so he wasn't around as much. My dad had me sit down next to him on this log and he put his hand on my thigh. I couldn't believe he was doing it – I was afraid Mr. Jennings and Rush would figure out our secret. He started telling me how Rush really liked me and told me to go sit next to him. Rush was… he was a really big guy. He made me uncomfortable because he'd been looking at me weird all weekend. I told my dad I didn't want to sit by Rush, but he got upset and told me to do it."

My stomach dropped out because I knew what was coming.

"I did what he said. Rush started touching me and saying how pretty I was. He made me put my hand on his… his groin. I looked at my dad…"

Caleb's voice broke and he sucked in a harsh sob. "I actually thought he'd stop it. When Rush forced me to my knees in front of him, I called out for my dad. He… he told me to show Rush how good I sucked cock."

Caleb began sucking in deep breaths of air. I turned him around so he was facing me and pulled him up against my chest. "You're safe, Caleb. They can't hurt you anymore. I'll never let anyone hurt you ever again, do you hear me?" My words were harsh, but I couldn't help it. Tears blurred my vision. I felt Caleb nod against my chest.

"I thought it would just be the blow job, but then Rush made me get on my hands and knees. I thought my dad would stop it… it was… it was our thing. He used to say that to me – that it was our special secret and no one could ever know because they wouldn't understand just how much he loved me. But when he let Rush do that to me…"

Caleb shook his head. "I cried the whole time. When Rush was finished, he just left me lying there in the dirt. I heard him and my dad talking about how Rush knew my dad was bluffing. I... I didn't get it at first." Caleb choked back a sob and whispered, "He lost me in a bet."

"What?" I asked, because I was certain I'd heard him wrong.

"My dad ran out of money while they were playing poker so he bet me. And lost."

"Fucking son of a bitch!" I snarled. I slammed my fist into the headboard. The wood held and pain radiated throughout my hand and arm. But it wasn't enough.

I got up and began grabbing whatever I could reach and throwing it against the walls. I ripped at fabric that found its way into my hands. Books hit the floor, glass shattered.

The lights flipped on, and I found myself staring at the remnants of a broken picture frame. Glass was all over the floor.

In a million pieces.

Beyond repair.

Oh God.

Despair curled through me as I turned to face Caleb. He'd needed me to support him through this, and I'd lost my temper instead. I'd gone on a rampage when he'd needed me to just listen, to hold him.

What the fuck is wrong with me?

I expected to find him cowering in one of the far corners of the bed, but instead, he was standing next to it, one arm crossed over his chest and holding the other arm.

"I'm sorry," I said. A bitter taste filled my mouth and I wondered if I'd actually throw up right there in front of him. God knew I was feeling sick enough for that.

"Come back to bed," Caleb said as he held out his hand to me. "Watch the glass," he added. There was absolutely no fear in his eyes as he waited patiently for me to take his hand.

"I'm sorry," I repeated. My skin felt like it was on fire and the last thing I wanted to do was remain still. I needed to move – to run or hit or *something*. I needed... I needed... God, I needed to not feel.

Disgust filtered through every cell and nerve ending. Caleb had needed me to be strong and I'd done this. When Caleb took a step forward, I reached out and grabbed his hand so he wouldn't step into the glass. I moved back toward the bed and sat down, but Caleb wasn't satisfied. "Move up toward the headboard," he murmured.

I did as he said. I leaned my back against the headboard and stretched my legs out in front of me. I was expecting him to do the same thing next to me, but he surprised me when he carefully straddled my lap. His knees came to rest next to my hips and his groin was pressed against my abdomen. His arms wrapped around my neck and he pressed his forehead against mine.

In any other scenario, the position would have turned me on. But sex was the very last thing on my mind, and I knew it wasn't on Caleb's either.

No, he'd picked this position for a reason. Maybe so he could be as close to me as possible. Maybe because he knew I needed the same thing while he finished his story. I didn't know and I didn't care. He was in my arms where I could keep him safe.

"My plan was to go back to my tent," Caleb began, and I closed my eyes and willed the nausea rolling violently around in my belly to settle.

"My dad told me not to move. Then he and Mr. Jennings started talking. I could tell Mr. Jennings was shocked by what had happened."

"He was the headmaster at your school, right?"

Caleb nodded. "He and my dad had gone to high school together or something, I think. That's how they knew each other. The school he worked for was very exclusive and I think he helped get me and Nick admitted."

I nodded in understanding.

"I was kind of out of it, so I missed some of what my dad said to Mr. Jennings. But then my dad started yelling at him and telling him he needed to take his turn so he'd be more inclined to keep his mouth shut. I... I didn't understand what he meant at first."

"He wanted Jennings to be just as culpable so he wouldn't tell anyone what your dad and Rush did," I murmured.

Caleb nodded. He let out a brutal sob. "I didn't think he'd do it."

"I'm sorry, I'm so fucking sorry," I whispered over and over again until he settled. He tucked his face against my neck and I could feel the warmth of his tears sliding down my skin.

"He kept saying he was sorry," Caleb said. "Even as he grabbed my arm and forced me over this log. When he pushed inside of me, when I began to cry, when I begged him to stop... *I'm sorry, Caleb...* he just kept repeating it. When he was finished, I heard him yelling at my dad. He was upset because he saw that my dad had recorded the whole thing with his phone. Collateral, my dad called it." Caleb managed to pull in a few breaths. "When I saw Mr. Jennings at school the next Monday, he pulled me into his office. I was so scared he was going to do it again. But he began sobbing and then got on his knees in front of me and begged me to forgive him. That he'd done it only because my father had made him and that he cared about me and hadn't meant to hurt me. He... he threatened to kill himself because he felt so terrible. I believed him," Caleb murmured.

I had no doubt the sick fuck had put on quite a show to convince Caleb to keep quiet.

"I told him I forgave him. He said he'd find a way to help me – to make my father stop hurting me. He just kept promising over and over again that he'd fix it."

Caleb's whispered words as we'd fled from the shooting at the Jennings' house rang in my ears.

He promised.

"I believed him," Caleb said. "I kept waiting for it to stop. I was foolish enough to believe Mr. Jennings could somehow make it so my dad would stop what he was doing, but still be my dad. But it didn't stop and every time I confronted Mr. Jennings, he said he was still working on it."

Caleb sat up enough so he could look at me. I automatically wiped at his tears and was stunned when he did the same to me.

When the fuck had I started crying?

Caleb dropped his eyes. "This kid I used to sometimes drink with told me that someone had managed to record Eli's testimony during my dad's trial. Cameras weren't allowed in the courtroom, but I guess someone used their phone to secretly tape everything. He gave me the link and I listened to some of the testimony." Caleb dashed at his eyes. "It was brutal," he whispered. "The things the defense attorney said to Eli, accused him of, it was sick. I've never heard Eli sound like that – so scared and confused. It was like… it was like he was being assaulted all over again. When they announced that my father had been acquitted, I lost it. I knew I'd be next and my only thought was to run. But I knew when he got out, he'd kill me. I had this weird thought that Mr. Jennings would help me now. He was the only one besides Nick who knew what my father had been doing to me. I thought…"

Caleb laughed harshly, then looked up at me. "I thought he'd finally keep his promise."

"But you went to the motel first," I said.

He nodded. "I knew Mav would call you as soon as he found out I was gone. It was stupid, but…"

"But what?" I asked as I ran my hand up and down his back.

"I just wanted to sleep," he said so softly, I barely heard him. "I just wanted to sleep, Jace."

"I know, baby," I said softly. I stroked his cheek. "What happened when you went to see Jennings?" I asked. "Before I got there," I clarified.

"I waited until he came out of his house. He recognized me right away. I just wanted to talk to him. I asked him to come to Seattle and tell the D.A. what he knew about my dad. I told him he didn't have to say the part about him and Rush… you know."

I nodded. I wasn't about to make him say the words. He knew he'd been raped, but saying that word out loud was the last thing he needed at the moment.

"He started making excuses, then flat-out said no and told me to leave and never come back. That's when I got the gun out."

"Where did you get it from?"

"From the kid who told me about the secret recording of Eli's testimony. His older brother sold it to me. I wanted to be able to protect myself if they let my father out of jail on bail or something." He hesitated and said, "Mr. Jennings' kid… he wasn't much younger than me when Mr. Jennings… how could he do something like that?

He was a father. He *knew* me. He was always nice to me in school – said I was a good kid and he was proud of me. But out in those woods, he treated me like…"

Caleb fell silent and just shook his head. I didn't know what to say because Caleb was looking for something more insightful than just hearing the guy was a sick fuck.

"Did you ever see Rush again?" I asked.

Caleb shook his head.

I clasped his face in my hands and forced him to look up at me. "Thank you for telling me. Your father won't get away with what he did, and so help me God, neither will those other two fuckers. You're safe now, Caleb. No one will ever touch you again. Not while there's blood still running through my veins."

"Don't make me promises you can't keep, Jace," Caleb murmured. He began to climb off my lap, but I grabbed him by the waist to stop him.

I straightened, which forced Caleb to loop his arms around my neck so he could maintain his balance. The need to kiss him was profound and my lips were just inches from his when I managed to catch myself. I rolled Caleb beneath me and then settled my weight fully on top of him. I was glad when he didn't react with fear.

"If I could give this to anyone, it would be you," I murmured.

Caleb's sapphire eyes held mine for the longest time. "I know," he finally said. Then his fingers were pushing my hair behind my ear. He didn't say anything else and I ended up just holding him like that for the longest time. It wasn't until he fell asleep that I forced myself to lever off him and lay down next to him. The second I did, he was rolling into my embrace again, his nose tucked up against my neck. His hand came to rest on my chest. I reached up to turn the lights off, then just lay there for a while, willing sleep to claim me.

But it didn't.

And part of me was glad, because I had no doubt I would have dreamed of Caleb.

Alone in those woods with his abusers, waiting for help to come, even knowing it never would.

I was restless as I waited for the line to move forward. The warm weather had brought lots of boats out, so the general store on Hooper's Island was busy. I'd already bought and paid for gas for the boat, so I just had my groceries to pay for. Dalton's boat was sitting in a quieter part of the marina, but that meant it was also out of sight and that was making me nervous. Caleb had promised he'd stay below deck no matter what, but not being able to have eyes on him was causing my tension to build with every passing minute.

I scanned the store as I waited, then noticed the television over the clerk's shoulder. It was turned to one of the early morning national news channels, but I couldn't hear anything. Dalton had a television on the boat and while Caleb and I hadn't made use of it in the first few days of our trip, we'd started to watch it more recently, but mostly just to watch some of the DVDs Dalton had. I'd watched the news a few times after Caleb had gone to sleep to make sure there was no mention of the Jennings' shooting, but I'd been reliant on Dalton to keep me in the loop the rest of the time.

As I finally neared the counter, something pink caught my eye and I smiled. I reached out to grab a couple of the packages and added them to my pile. I'd just handed my cash over to the clerk when I chanced another look at the television. The sound was turned off, but it didn't matter. I recognized the face of the man staring back at me.

Caleb's father.

"Can you turn that up?" I asked as nonchalantly as I could. The clerk looked over his shoulder, then reached for the volume.

"...it does lead many to wonder if Mr. Cortano isn't being railroaded by these kids," a commentator said off-screen. My eyes fell to the tagline beneath Jack's picture.

Son Sends Letter of Apology to Father Accused of Abuse.

"Your change."

It took me a moment to realize the clerk was talking to me, because I was focused on what the news anchor was saying.

"*The Seattle District Attorney is refusing to comment on this latest bomb-*

shell. Again, for those of you just joining us, there's been a new development in the case of Jack Cortano, a former Department of Defense employee, who is charged with multiple counts of felony sexual assault against his youngest son. Several news agencies received a copy of a letter Mr. Cortano's son allegedly wrote him in prison in which he apologizes to his father for lying to authorities. This comes on the heels of Mr. Cortano being acquitted of similar charges against his stepson, Eli Galvez, earlier this month. The defense is claiming the letter is proof that Mr. Galvez convinced Mr. Cortano's son to lie about being assaulted by his father. Possible motives include a personal vendetta on the part of Mr. Galvez or an attempt to bring a civil suit against Mr. Cortano in the hopes of reaching a financial settlement—"

My phone rang at that moment and I ignored the money the man was holding out to me. I grabbed my bags and snatched up my phone.

"I just saw," I said bitterly before Dalton could even say anything. I hurried from the store.

"I'm sorry, Jace. I'm not sure what time the reports started... I had a bad night..."

I knew what that meant and I quickly softened my voice. "It's okay, Dalton. Thanks for letting me know."

I barely listened as Dalton said his goodbyes and hung up.

Jesus, how the hell was I going to tell Caleb about this? Thank fuck he'd gone back to sleep after I'd woken him up to tell him I was taking the boat to shore to get gas and supplies. After his admission the night before, I wanted him to get as much rest as he could. Not to mention that I was still trying to figure out what to say to him this morning. I hadn't meant to push him into telling me about Richard Jennings, but when he'd asked me about my uncle, I'd selfishly seen an opportunity to get the information I'd needed so badly in exchange for sharing something I never talked about... to anyone.

I returned to the boat as fast as I could without attracting attention to myself. All was quiet, so I quickly got the boat started and headed back to the inlet where we'd spent the night. It would hopefully be quiet enough that Caleb could sleep a little longer and I could get my shit together and figure out what to do next.

I dropped the anchor and then grabbed the groceries and went below deck. I'd just reached the last step when I saw one of the drawers from the kitchen lying on the floor, the contents inside of it strewn all over the place. My heart leapt into my throat as I dropped the bags.

"Caleb!" I shouted and then I was running to the bedroom. It took just seconds to reach the room and rip open the narrow door.

What I saw chilled my blood.

Caleb was standing by the bed, right arm extended next to his body. There was a large knife in his left hand – it was the single butcher knife that Dalton kept on board.

The television was blaring in the background. It was turned to the same news program I'd just been watching. The anchors and commentators were still discussing Caleb's case.

"Caleb," I said softly as I put my hands out. Despite not seeing any blood on Caleb's arm or on the blade of the knife, I was more scared than I'd ever been.

Tears streamed down Caleb's face. "I didn't lie!" he shouted. "I didn't, Jace!"

"I know you didn't, Caleb. Please put the knife down."

He looked at the blade as if just then realizing he had it. "It hurts too much," he whispered. "It's too much."

"Baby, look at me," I urged, even as I took another step toward him. Caleb raised his eyes.

"I promised you I wouldn't do it again," Caleb said softly. "I... I lied about that, but I... I don't want to let you down."

"Nothing you say or do could ever let me down. And I knew it would be hard for you to promise me that for real. But look at yourself, Caleb. You had the chance, but you stopped yourself. I don't care why you did, I just care *that* you did."

He seemed confused and I had no doubt it was because there was just too much going through him at the moment. "Tell me about the letter," I said as I closed the distance between us.

Caleb shook his head. "He... he called me. From prison. Six months ago. I don't know how he got my number, but he told me he missed me and that he wasn't mad and that he loved me more than anything. He sounded like..."

"Your dad?" I offered.

Caleb nodded. "He started to cry and tell me he was sorry and that he didn't understand why I wanted to hurt him. He thought I hated him, but... but I didn't. I *did* write him a letter and I told him I was sorry, but I didn't say anything about lying to the police."

Caleb's voice kept going higher and higher as the desperation took over. He was waving the knife around.

"I was sorry he was in jail! I was sorry I put him there, but I just wanted him to stop!"

"People believe you, Caleb," I offered.

"They don't!" he shouted. "That reporter said Eli and I made all this up to get back at my dad! She didn't mention the videos! Or Nick!"

Caleb suddenly took several steps back from me, but I got the feeling it wasn't to escape me. More because he needed to move.

"I shouldn't have said anything!" he yelled. "I should have destroyed that flash drive."

I knew he was talking about the flash drive his brother had copied some of the videos of Jack assaulting all three boys onto. The videos that had gotten thrown out of court on a technicality.

"No—"

"Things could have gone back to normal! Maybe Nick would still be alive if he hadn't... if he hadn't..."

"What, Caleb? Hadn't what?"

"Tried to protect me," he whispered.

"You think that's why Nick copied the videos?" I asked.

Caleb nodded. "He kept asking me if my dad was doing that shit to me and I kept telling him no. I promised I'd tell him if my dad ever touched me. I think he used the threat of leaking the videos to keep my dad from messing with me. But it didn't stop him and I was too ashamed to tell Nick that I couldn't say no."

"What happened to Nick isn't your fault," I said.

"He's dead because he walked in on me and my dad. If I'd just told him the truth—"

"There's no way to know what would have happened, Caleb," I said.

He'd calmed considerably, but it didn't bring me any kind of relief. It was like he was sliding a completely different direction – like he was shutting down before my very eyes.

"Eli would have been okay... he had Mav." Caleb continued as if I hadn't spoken. "Nick was planning to move in to the dorms at school. I could have... I could have found a way to live with it."

"It would have destroyed you, Caleb."

His eyes lifted to meet mine. "It did anyway, Jace." He looked at the knife in his hand. "Nick is dead and twelve people looked Eli in the eye and basically told him he deserved what happened to him. How are any of us better off from telling the truth?"

"I know it doesn't seem like it, but things will get—"

"Don't," Caleb cut in. "Don't tell me it will get better."

Frustration coursed through me because I really didn't know what to tell him. Platitudes about him having a bright future meant shit at this point. He was hurting *now*. His efforts to do the right thing were being thrown back in his face *now*.

He didn't need promises about the future. He needed them for now.

And I had no fucking clue how to give him that.

I watched in silence as Caleb carefully put the knife on the bed. "I need some air," he whispered.

"Caleb," I began, but he pushed me away when I reached for him and stepped past me. I followed and stopped in the doorway between the bedroom and kitchen when I saw him start picking up the contents of the drawer he'd spilled in an effort to get to the knife. I was about to go help him when he stilled in the process of reaching for a spoon. I followed the path of his gaze and knew instantly what he was looking at.

I felt my insides twist as he ignored the spoon and went to where the plastic bags were sitting discarded by the steps leading above deck.

One of them had spilled and the shock of bright pink was hard to miss against the backdrop of white plastic.

Caleb reached for the package. He had his back to me, but I didn't miss his next words.

"Sno Balls," he whispered.

I'd bought the treats to put a smile on his face, but instead, he began sobbing.

And I knew this time it wasn't about his father and the terrible events of the morning.

"Why?" Caleb cried between sobs. He turned to face me, the package of Sno Balls clenched between his fingers.

But I didn't have an answer for him.

I was completely clueless to understand why I had to keep him at arm's length, but I couldn't let him go, either. All I knew was that I was a piece of shit for doing this to him again. I'd done it when I'd first gotten him out of the hospital and again at Christmas later that year. I'd been a selfish asshole who'd wanted to relish how good being around him made me feel, even though I'd known I wouldn't be sticking around. And I'd done it again the previous week when I'd all but forced him to come with me after the attack at the cabin.

He would have been safe with Mav and Memphis and his extended family back home, but I'd selfishly wanted the old Caleb back. *I'd* wanted to be the one who made him feel safe and warm and protected. *I'd* wanted to benefit from his kind heart and guileless laugh. *I'd* wanted to have a little bit of that rightness back in my life that I'd only ever felt around him.

When I didn't answer him, he shook his head. "I can't do this," he managed to get out. "It hurts worse."

His words sliced me open. The fact that my actions could hurt him even more deeply than all the shit he was going through was threatening to make me violently ill.

"I need to go home," he said, his voice an odd mix of hurt and resolve.

I needed to agree with him. I needed to do what was best for him and let him go. I needed to find the words to tell him I was sorry for not being able to keep my promise and make things better for him. But the reality that I would likely never see him again was strangling me.

There were a lot of things I *needed* to do, but I didn't do any of them. I didn't say the right thing and I didn't tell him it was okay and that I was sorry. No, what came out of my mouth as I strode toward him was a sign of my complete and utter desperation... and my cruelty.

"I need to cash in my chips." The words sounded strangled and I wondered if I'd even said them out loud. I knew I must have when Caleb's eyes went wide. He backed up several steps until his back hit the wall next to the steps leading above deck.

I didn't stop until I had him crowded up against the unforgiving wood. I clasped his face with my hands. I searched his eyes for fear, but there was none.

Only a hint of confusion and...

Trust.

That goddamn unflappable trust.

"Please, Caleb, tell me it's okay."

His skin felt wonderfully warm beneath my hands. His hands had come up to grab my wrists, but he wasn't trying to push me away. His lips parted deliciously, but he didn't speak.

He didn't need to.

The fervent nod he gave me was answer enough.

CHAPTER 12

CALEB

I was expecting his kiss to be rough and overwhelming.
It was definitely overwhelming,
But there wasn't anything rough about it.

I had no clue if he somehow knew it was my first kiss or not, but I didn't really care when his mouth settled on mine. At first, his lips seemed to just be teasing mine as he brushed his mouth over mine with little to almost no pressure at all. The effect was no less devastating, though. Excitement shot to my very bones and I had to lock my knees to keep from collapsing to the floor.

Over and over, he kissed me. Sometimes it was just my upper lip that got the attention, sometimes it was the lower, sometimes it was both. But each contact had my need spiraling higher. When I opened my mouth to tell him so, he took advantage and eased his tongue into it. He swallowed my gasp of surprise and then he started all over again with the teasing, playful contact that was so very much and still not enough. His hands slid from my face, down my neck and eventually ended up around my waist. As our tongues met and I tried to figure out how to kiss him back, he drew me forward and I had no choice but to wrap my arms around his neck. When I finally got the nerve to slide my tongue against his, I heard him let out a deep groan.

So I did it again.

And that was when something switched inside of him.

And me.

Gentle exploration turned into rough and needy. Tongues dueled and lips clashed. I was grateful for whatever instinct kicked in deep inside of me, because it somehow made it possible for me to keep up. And by keeping up, it meant Jace let go even more.

"Caleb," he ground against my mouth. "Tell me you're okay," he said harshly.

"Okay," was all I managed to get out as I followed his mouth when he tried to draw back from me a little. "Very okay," I repeated and then I slid my hands into his long hair to keep him still. I took a chance and let my tongue slip into the cavern of his mouth. Jace let me have the moment, then he took over again and I was shoved hard against the wall behind me. His hands grabbed my wrists so he could pin them next to the wall against my head. I thought it was his way of trying to stop or slow down what was happening, but if anything, the move just ratcheted things up even higher.

He consumed me after that.

I didn't know how else to describe it.

I managed to keep up with his greedy mouth, but when I needed to come up for air, his lips would find their way to my jaw, my neck, even my shoulders. His five-o'clock shadow scraped deliciously over my skin as he licked, sucked and nipped at my skin, and the second I drew in a couple of deep breaths, he'd latch onto my mouth again. We were both panting by the time he released my hands. I used the opportunity to do some of my own exploring. My body was on fire and my dick was pressing painfully against my jeans. I'd masturbated plenty of times, but I'd never felt such a raging level of need before.

"Jace," I whispered as my panic began to build. I'd orgasmed on occasion and it had felt good, but nothing like this. What if whatever he was doing to me would end up hurting? There'd been a few times during sex where my body had reacted beyond my control and I'd wanted to die from the shame afterwards. What if that was what this ended up being? Or worse, what if I was a freak whose body only reacted normally to someone else when it was against my will?

"Breathe, baby," Jace murmured against my mouth. "Tell me how it feels."

I sucked in a long draw of oxygen. "Hurts," I admitted. "But... but not all bad," I managed to get out. I shook my head because I didn't know how to explain it. "Don't want you to stop."

I was shaking like a leaf. Jace was pressed up against me from head to toe. One of his legs was wedged between mine and shame curled through me as I began riding his muscled thigh in the hopes that I could find some relief. Sparks of energy danced just beneath the surface of my skin and I cried out at how good it felt.

"God, so responsive," Jace muttered. He laid a searing kiss on me, then slid his hand down my chest. He rubbed my dick through my pants.

"Let me take care of you," he urged.

I nodded because that was all I was capable of. I'd already started humping his hand. I'd do anything to make the ache inside of me go away.

It did.

The second his hand closed over my cock through the denim and began rubbing. His mouth found mine again just as I let out a little shout of relief. But when he stopped moments later, I shook my head violently. "No, Jace, please don't stop, please!"

I felt like my body was no longer my own.

"Fuck," Jace muttered against my mouth and suddenly both his hands were at my waist. They ripped and tugged until my jeans were open, the zipper drawn all the way down. I pressed my open mouth against Jace's shoulder when his bare hand closed around my dick. I let out a raw shout as he began pumping me.

"Look, baby," he said as he nuzzled my ear. "Look how badly I want you."

I forced my eyes open and kept my forehead pressed against Jace's collarbone as I looked between our writhing bodies. Jace had freed his own dick from his pants and was stroking it with his free hand. His other hand pulled my shaft from my pants and I watched in awe as he mashed our dicks together and began using one hand to stroke us at the same time. His skin was so hot and soft, even though his cock was hard as a rock.

"Oh God," I moaned as pure pleasure began to radiate out to my limbs. It felt like there was a coil inside of me that kept getting tighter and tighter.

Jace's mouth searched out mine and I eagerly kissed him back. His free hand closed around my throat, but only to hold me in place. His thumb gently massaged my hammering pulse. I began bumping my hips forward.

"That's it, baby, fuck my hand. Imagine it's my ass wrapped around you."

I stilled at that and looked at him in surprise. He kissed me gently. "I'd be at your mercy, Caleb," he murmured. "I'd be begging you to make me feel every inch of this gorgeous cock of yours."

The mental imagery alone could have made me come, but the fact that he was talking like he'd really let me do that to him... it was actually slowing me down. "You'd let me do that?" I whispered in disbelief.

"You'd be the first," he said as he nipped at my lips. "If I thought I could last a few more minutes..."

He let the statement hang.

I wanted to question him further, because never in a million years would I have thought such a thing was possible. I'd always assumed another guy would look at me and see a hole to fuck and nothing more. I wasn't assertive or confident or built...

But my questions about all that would have to wait because my body had no interest in anything other than finding relief.

Jace's hand began to frantically stroke us both. He slapped his other hand on the wall next to my head and closed his eyes, his brows drawn up as if in pain. "Fuck, so close," he muttered. "Fuck my hand again, Caleb," he demanded. His hand slid down long enough to cup my balls. His lips latched onto my neck before searching out my mouth again. "Fuck me hard," he ordered.

I cried out and did as he said. His hand was slickened from our combined juices so I easily slid through his grip. He countered my thrusts with his own body and my mind returned to thoughts of what it would be like to push inside of him. He'd probably be even tighter than the grip he currently had on both of us. He'd whisper my name as he pleaded with me to fuck him harder and harder. His body would writhe beneath mine as he begged me to give him what only I could.

The orgasm hit me like a freight train coming out of nowhere. One second I was still climbing impossibly high, the next second something inside of me snapped and I exploded. I screamed Jace's name as I came. I felt his forehead press against mine.

"That's it, Caleb," he urged as he continued to stroke me. I clung to him as I tried to fight the wave that was threatening to take me under, to steal all awareness from me.

"Don't fight it, baby. I've got you… always, Caleb."

I began sobbing as I welcomed his words and gave in to my body's need. Everything went white behind my closed lids and I felt my knees give out as I emptied into Jace's hand. Jace still had his leg between mine, so he held me up. My entire body thrashed as spasms overtook it, but Jace's weight held me against the wall so I could do nothing but dig my fingers into his upper arms. It seemed to go on forever, but Jace's muffled shout against my neck as he came, followed by hot liquid hitting the sensitive skin of my dick, brought me back to earth. I struggled to draw in breath after breath as Jace's body jerked against mine. I couldn't have come up with any kind of guess as to how long we stayed like that for, but when the cum between us started to cool, reality began to intrude. I waited for Jace to jerk away from me and tell me what had happened was a mistake, but he didn't say anything at all.

Maybe I was supposed to say something?

I wasn't sure.

What I *was* sure of was that I could have died happy there in his arms, his hot breath sliding over my skin, the fingers of his free hand buried in my hair as he held me against his trembling body.

"Caleb," he whispered.

God, here it comes.

I closed my eyes to try and stem the tears that threatened. Moments ago, I'd been strong enough to walk away, but how was I supposed to do that now?

"Please don't leave," Jace murmured.

His words caught me off guard and I was sure I'd heard him wrong. He pulled back and pressed his forehead against mine. "I'll figure it out," he whispered. "I just need a little more time."

I wasn't sure what it was that he was going to figure out, but I didn't really care. He'd done what I hadn't been able to do for myself these past two years, and he'd done it long before he'd kissed me.

He'd made me hope.

If I had to risk my heart to hang onto that for just a little while longer, was it even a choice?

Who was I kidding? I'd already lost my heart to him, so no, it wasn't a choice. It was already far too late for that.

"Yes," I whispered. "Yes," I repeated over and over, relishing his sigh of relief and the way he held me just a little tighter every time I said it.

~

"No, don't add that yet," I cried out as I snatched the plate of fish from Jace before he could put the filets into the skillet. "You need to add more butter."

"Fuck," Jace muttered as he searched out the butter.

I smiled and took another bite of my Sno Ball. The sugary goodness melted on my tongue and I barely suppressed a moan.

"Jesus, if you keep doing that I'm definitely going to end up burning this boat to the ground," Jace sniped.

"Water," I said as I swallowed what was in my mouth. Jace was watching me hungrily.

"What?" he asked. The butter was still in his hand.

"I think you mean you'll burn the boat to the water," I said. He didn't appear to be listening at all because his eyes were on my mouth.

I took another bite of the Sno Ball, making sure to get some of the frosting on my lips.

When I went to lick it off, Jace snapped, "Fuck it," and dropped the entire stick of butter into the pan. His mouth crashed down on mine. I groaned as his tongue swept between my lips and when he pulled me against him, I eagerly went, not caring that the Sno Ball ended up mashed between our bodies.

Sno Balls be damned, Jace's mouth was my new addiction.

I'd expected him to come to his senses at some point today, especially since he'd been careful not to touch me again after we'd gotten ourselves and the kitchen cleaned up this morning. There'd been some awkward silence between us as we'd worked, but when Jace had suggested we try our luck at catching our lunch, some of the tension between us had broken. We hadn't talked anymore about the letter I'd sent to my father or my mini-breakdown, but I knew it was just a matter of time before we had to deal with the fallout. I had no doubt the district attorney in Seattle was probably freaking out over the letter, because I'd never mentioned it to him or anyone else. I wasn't sure what it meant for my case, or if there even was a case anymore. I was trying very hard not to think about it, because I didn't want reality to intrude on my life just yet.

I had sex with Jace.

Okay, maybe not actual sex, but I couldn't imagine the actual act being better than what Jace had done to me.

And I seemed to be on track to experience all that pleasure all over again, because Jace's mouth was doing sinful things to me.

Not to mention his hands.

Which were currently sliding over my ass. I should have been scared, but I was too preoccupied with what his tongue was doing. I gasped when Jace suddenly lifted me and settled me on the counter. It was barely big enough for my ass, but Jace didn't seem to notice because he tipped me back as he pulled my legs up around his waist. I'd changed into sweats after getting cleaned up this morning, so my dick wasn't as constricted as it could have been. But it still ached like a son of a bitch.

Jace's hands roamed up my body, sliding my shirt up in the process. His mouth slid down my neck, over my chest and settled on my abdomen. The mashed-up Sno Ball had left pink frosting all over me and him, so when he nuzzled my abdomen, it was covered in frosting. I knew he'd done the move on purpose, because he looked up at me and held my gaze as he slowly licked up every little bit of it. His mouth returned to mine. I moaned at how good the combination of Jace's sweet flavor and the frosting mixed together tasted.

I reached for the hem of Jace's shirt so I could feel his skin, but before I could lift it, a loud, blaring sound shattered the stillness of the cabin. Jace and I jerked apart. It wasn't until that moment that I noticed both the smoke and the burning smell.

"Shit!" Jace snapped as he reached for the pan and burner dial at the same time. The butter in the pan had gone completely black and had started to crust along the sides of the pan. Jace deposited the pan into the sink and got the water running over it as I hurried to silence the smoke detector.

We were both breathing hard by the time I got it turned off.

"That's four," Jace muttered.

"To be fair, there wasn't an actual fire," I pointed out as I opened the windows to air out the room.

My body was still simmering with need as I took in Jace's appearance. At some point during our make-out session, his hair tie had come out, so his hair was loose around his face. There was a smattering of frosting along his chin and his shirt was covered in the remnants of my Sno Ball. The rest of the cake was all over the floor.

Jace's eyes were sweeping my body, probably because I looked much the same as him. "I, ah, guess we need to clean up again," I murmured.

"Yeah," Jace agreed. I didn't like how quiet he'd gotten. "Why don't you go change and I'll clean this up?" he suggested as he motioned to the cake on the floor.

Disappointment flared as I nodded. I'd kind of hoped we'd pick up where we'd left off.

I went to the bedroom and stripped off my shirt, then began

searching for another one. My pants were okay, though my arousal was obvious. It was probably a good idea to change into jeans, since being around Jace going forward was likely going to make it impossible to keep my dick in check.

I was in the process of pulling out one of the drawers that was built into the platform of the bed when I felt a shiver go through me. I turned to find Jace watching me from the doorway, his eyes burning. He had his arms braced on the doorframe, like he was trying to support himself. I could see that his fingers were digging into the wood. If I hadn't known any better, I would have thought he was angry.

And maybe he was.

But not at me.

I wasn't afraid of him, but admittedly I was a little nervous. Not that he'd hurt me, but that I wouldn't be able to keep up with him... that my mind would confuse him with those who'd used me in the past.

"I was just going to change my pants," I said, my words stumbling over one another.

The hunger in his eyes was undeniable and the way he was watching me should have creeped me out. But all it did was make my already hard cock even harder. He wasn't even touching me and I could feel my body reacting like it had this morning – like it was no longer *my* body, but his.

His to command.

His to find pleasure in.

But unlike the other men who'd taken my body and used it for themselves, I knew Jace would give as much as he took. More so, even.

When Jace didn't move, I dropped the shirt I'd been about to put on and then reached for my sweats. My hands shook as I slowly worked them down my body, my eyes never leaving his. I had no idea where my boldness was coming from, but I knew what it was that was keeping me from dissolving into a puddle of fear.

It was him.

I knew without a shadow of a doubt that he'd never hurt me. And I knew that if that fear made itself known, he'd be the one to stop things. If I hadn't had the events of this morning to rely on as proof, I'd have been terrified. But I wanted more of what he'd given me then and just now in the kitchen.

I just wanted him.

I left my underwear on as I pushed my sweats down. A flicker of self-doubt went through me as I bent over to work the pants off my legs. I'd never really given much thought to my looks before. I'd lost a lot of weight in the past couple of years and I'd already been kind of skinny before that. What if he liked guys who were more built, like him? I was technically experienced at sex, but I also kind of wasn't. Would Jace want me to just lie there and take whatever he did to me? Or would he want me to be an equal participant?

Because I didn't know how to do that.

Fuck, why was I doing this now? I finally had the chance to show him I was his equal and I was blowing it.

Because you're not his equal.

I shook my head at the thought and then lifted my eyes. Jace was still staring at me. Desire burned in the depths of his dark gaze, but there was something else too.

A certain softness that I couldn't put a name to.

But it was enough to have me stripping off my sweats the rest of the way. My plan had been to stand there, silently offering him my body, but I chickened out and quickly turned to rummage through the drawer for my jeans. Just as my fingers closed around the denim and I started to straighten, I felt Jace's heat at my back. I closed my eyes as I held there a moment, waiting for him to grab me.

Except he didn't. He just stood there, his thighs flush with the backs of mine, his groin brushing my ass. I straightened, fully expecting him to turn me around and kiss me. Maybe push me onto the bed.

Something.

Anything.

But his hands didn't reach for me. He didn't order me to my knees to suck him, he didn't demand I bend over the bed.

And all that actually relaxed me.

I ended up being the one to make the first move.

By leaning back against him, trusting him to support my body. His clothes felt rough against my skin, which was tingling all over. He felt solid against my back and I loved that.

I had no clue how long we stood there before he finally did something.

He nuzzled my neck.

Just nuzzled it.

It was such a simple thing, but it felt so incredibly intimate. He'd warned me that he was aggressive when it came to sex, but I'd yet to see proof of that. Yes, he'd been demanding this morning, but not in the way I would have expected.

I felt a soft kiss press against my pulse, then another a little lower. More kisses trailed down my throat and then skimmed over my shoulder. He took his time kissing me like that. Every once in a while, he'd let his tongue taste my skin, but he didn't demand anything. When I leaned more heavily against him, his hands came up to hold my waist. He kept up the butterfly kisses, even as his hands drifted down my hips. I expected him to pull my underwear down, but he didn't. His hands didn't stop their downward trajectory until they reached my thighs. He wrapped his hands around the outside of my legs so that his fingers were pressed along the insides of my thighs. I automatically widened my stance for him and pressed my ass against his groin. I could feel the hardness of his cock and an image of him bending me over right then and there flashed in my head.

I wanted it, but I couldn't deny it frightened me too.

"Not going to go that far," Jace murmured against my skin. "Just want to touch you, okay?"

I wasn't surprised he'd sensed my fear.

I'd been counting on that when I'd started all this.

I nodded and was rewarded with him sucking gently on the spot where my shoulder met my collarbone.

Jace used his hands to hold me in place as he began bumping his hips against mine. I let out a little moan at how good it felt. When I lifted my arm so I could reach behind me and clasp his head, Jace sought out my mouth and kissed me deeply. His fingers bit into my thighs, but not painfully.

"God, Jace," I whispered against his lips as my body lit up with heat. "I need…"

"What, baby?" Jace asked as he nibbled at my jawline. His hands came up to rest on my chest. He was still grinding his cock against my ass and I cursed the fact that there were so many layers of material between us.

"I don't know," I admitted honestly.

"Do you trust me, Caleb?"

I wanted to laugh at that. Did he really need me to answer that?

Was I even *capable* of answering it?

I twisted my fingers in his hair and held him in place as I kissed him. I plunged my tongue into his mouth. I liked how gentle he'd been with me up to that point, but I was ready for more.

"Say it," Jace growled right before he kissed me back.

I knew then that even though he already knew that I trusted him, he liked hearing it.

He *needed* to hear it.

And *I* needed to give him what he needed.

"I trust you, Jace. Always."

CHAPTER 13

JACE

I'd told myself this morning that I couldn't touch him again. That I'd pushed him too hard and too fast. I'd only meant to kiss him after he'd told me he wanted to leave, but I wasn't sure what insanity had been going through my head to make me think that one taste of him would be enough.

Sex was a means to an end for me. It was a way of feeling in control in those moments where the helplessness of my situation kicked in. It hadn't always been that way, but since my sister had disappeared and I'd been completely powerless to do anything to help her, I'd taken all those emotions and poured them into meaningless encounters with complete strangers. I was always careful about the men I selected. I was fortunate enough that I could read people pretty well, and I'd used that to my advantage when I'd searched out compatible partners. It often only took a few carefully planned words to confirm a guy would meet my needs. I was demanding and forceful, even when I propositioned them. Those who were into it ended up beneath me, their bodies becoming nothing more than tools for me to work out some of my issues. And I alleviated my guilt by making sure they got off, sometimes even more than once.

But things had been different with Caleb from the moment my lips had brushed over his. Hell, they'd been different from the moment I'd first laid eyes on him.

I hadn't actually asked Caleb if he'd ever had a consensual sexual relationship with someone else, but he'd pretty much confirmed that when I'd kissed him. He'd been completely clueless on how to kiss me back.

And fuck if I hadn't just loved that.

I'd wanted to be the first man who showed him that sex wasn't about someone just taking something from him that he didn't want to give, an irony not lost on me considering my own sexual history. But to have been the first man to show him the pleasures of kissing – that was something I couldn't have even dreamed up.

He'd been so responsive and trusting that I hadn't been able to stop with one kiss... or twenty. I'd kept telling myself to stop, that it was too much, too soon, but Caleb's innocent responses had driven me on. When he'd instinctively started fucking my hand, a need unlike any I'd ever known had gone through me. I'd had this image of Caleb sliding in and out of my ass, and once in my head, it had been impossible to shake. I'd never once bottomed for any man – hadn't even considered it. But the thought of Caleb's weight pushing me into the mattress as he fucked me from behind at first, then turned me over and held me in the snare of his beautiful eyes as he filled me, moved over me, in me... it was something I knew I needed to experience.

I sighed as Caleb repeated that he trusted me for what had to be the third time now. He always made sure to add my name when he said it – it was like he was making it clear that he knew who he was with... that I was the only one he'd give that gift to.

I kissed Caleb until he was so pliant that I was practically holding him up. I let my right hand slide down his chest and over his abdomen. I kept my moves slow as I played with the waistband of his underwear. When he was moaning and writhing against me, whispering my name, I did what he wanted and dipped my hand beneath the fabric. He cried out in relief when I closed my hand around his length. I could feel the moisture on his shaft, proof that he really did want this. I pumped my hand up and down his dick with enough pressure to tease him, but not drive him higher.

"Jace," he groaned, clearly growing frustrated.

"Turn around, baby, let me get a taste of you."

Caleb eagerly turned and wrapped his arms around my neck. His mouth crashed down on mine and I happily gave control over to him. I used the opportunity to push his underwear down enough so I could stroke my palms over his smooth ass. Caleb kissed me frantically as he began grinding against me. I gripped his ass, then lifted him like I had in the kitchen. He quickly kicked his underwear off and wrapped his legs around me. His fingers sifted through my hair and he gripped me hard as he plundered my mouth.

For someone who'd never been kissed before, he was an incredibly fast learner.

I turned him and walked him the few steps to the bed, then lowered him down onto it. He kept his legs locked around my waist as I took control of the kiss. I could feel his weeping dick pressed against my abdomen and my mouth filled with saliva in anticipation. I ripped my lips from his, then trailed them down his body. I gave each of his nipples some love, then toyed with his belly button for a bit. He kept trying to push my head lower, a move I knew was driven by pure instinct, but I solved the problem by grabbing his wrists and pressing his arms to the bed beside him. I held him there as I nuzzled the patch of rough blond hair at his groin. I bypassed his dick and pressed kisses against his inner thigh.

"Jace," he growled as he tried to lift his hips to force his dick closer to my mouth.

"Patience, Caleb," I murmured as I released his hands and worked my way down his legs.

"Fuck patience!" he groaned, then he levered up onto his elbows so he could watch what I was doing. I held his gaze as I lifted his foot to my mouth.

I'd never taken the time to explore past lovers like I was now, and while part of me was glad this was another new thing I was sharing only with Caleb, I had to wonder how that had made the men I'd been with feel.

As it was, Caleb's toes turned out to be of particular interest to me.

To him too, because he flopped back on the bed and groaned. He covered his face with his hands as I sucked each one into my mouth. After I was done, I braced his heel on the lip of the platform supporting the bed, then I went to town on his other foot. By the time I was done, he was splayed out before me, both feet braced on the platform. I had a nice view of his hole, but I ignored it because I knew he just wasn't ready for that.

This moment was all about him.

Well, mostly. My own dick was demanding attention, so I unzipped my pants and pushed them down enough so I could free my dick. But I didn't touch myself. Instead, I leaned forward and pressed a kiss to Caleb's balls, then licked my way up his shaft. Caleb let out a muffled curse. I wrapped my arms around his legs to keep him from moving too much, then sucked the crown of his dick into my mouth. I welcomed the sweetness of the pre-cum that flowed over my tongue, then began sucking gently on the crown.

Caleb bucked into my mouth, but I used my hold on his thighs to keep him from moving too much.

"God, Jace, please!" Caleb begged desperately.

More pre-cum slid over my tongue and down my throat and I knew it meant he wouldn't last. My own dick was leaking, so he wasn't the only one.

I wrapped my fingers around his base and took him farther into my mouth. Fingers dug into my scalp and the accompanying bite of pain did nothing but turn me on even more. I reached between my own legs and began jerking myself off. Since I no longer had a hold of Caleb's thighs, he began fucking my mouth. I managed to relax my gag reflex enough to take him all the way inside. Caleb pumped into me over and over, but when I gagged a little, he froze and then tried to pull out of my mouth.

"Jace, God, I'm sorry!"

I ignored the horror in his voice and released my own dick so I could wrap my arms around his hips. The move kept him from escaping me like he wanted. Since I knew he was only doing it because he thought he was hurting me, I held him still and sucked him to the back of my throat and began humming around his rigid flesh.

"Jace, yes, fuck, yes, please!"

More words spilled from his throat, but I couldn't understand most of them. He was back to fucking my mouth. Despite my hold on him, he suddenly lurched to a sitting position and dug his fingers into my hair. My own lust spiked as he took control and began to fuck me without any kind of hesitation. I shifted my body so I could look at him while he was doing it.

"Jace," he whispered in disbelief. His face was pulled into an expression that was a mix of near-pain and want and I reveled in knowing that I'd done that to him. That I'd sent him to a place where all he could do was respond to the needs of his body.

But I wanted to make sure he knew I wanted what he was doing to me just as badly. I had no doubt he'd freaked moments earlier when he'd heard me gag because he'd probably experienced that same thing before.

Never in a million years did I want him to equate what had been done to him to what he was doing to me.

With my hands once again free, I began jerking myself off frantically. It was all I could do to keep my throat relaxed enough to take Caleb's pummeling. Caleb saw me fucking my own hand and his mouth parted.

"Yes," he gasped. "Just like that."

I didn't know if he was talking about me fucking my hand or me deep-throating him, but I didn't really care. I was too lost in his glassy eyes to care.

"I'm going to come," Caleb said as he shook his head. "It's too much!" he cried out. Seconds later, he began spurting down my throat. I choked a bit, but then hollowed my cheeks to draw out the orgasm for him. He shouted in relief as he continued to pump into me. His climax set off mine and I was forced to pull off him to shout out my own pleasure. I felt cum hit my chin right before I looked down to watch my own release spew from the head of my flushed dick. My body was racked with spasms and I had to grab Caleb's thigh to steady myself.

The orgasm seemed to go on forever. When it finally eased, all I could hear was my own heavy pants as I tried to catch my breath. Caleb's fingers were linked with mine where they were pressed against his thigh. I looked up at him and saw him watching me with wonder. He didn't say anything, but he didn't need to.

His eyes were speaking for him loud and clear.

Caleb slid off the bed and dropped to his knees in front of me. His hands came up to clasp the sides of my face. I expected him to kiss me, but instead, he ran his tongue along my chin, collecting his own semen. Then he covered my mouth with his and I eagerly drank every drop of the salty, bitter fluid that he fed me. I reached down and covered his ass with my hands, then pulled him forward so he was straddling me. Our spent cocks brushed against one another as Caleb wrapped his arms around my neck.

"Thank you," he whispered against my mouth, then he tucked his face against my neck and just clung to me.

An unpleasant sensation went through me and it took me a moment to figure out what it was.

Fear.

But fear of what?

Losing Caleb?

Keeping him?

I wanted to laugh as the answer became obvious to me.

Both.

CHAPTER 14

CALEB

"We don't have to do this," I said as I followed Jace down the dimly lit sidewalk. "I'm sorry I blew up at you like that."

I felt my cheeks heat as I remembered the way I'd gone off on Jace that very morning. I'd called him an overbearing jackass after he'd refused to let me go ashore with him to the local convenience store that also had a small laundry attached. Between being confined to the boat for nearly two weeks and Jace's distant attitude, I'd been at my breaking point and I'd just needed some kind of change in my routine. When I'd insisted that no one would recognize me in the few minutes it took to toss our clothes into one of the half-dozen washing machines, Jace had calmly reminded me it wasn't safe.

An argument that had held little water with me, since there was still no evidence that I'd been linked to the shooting outside Richard Jennings' house.

Jace had insisted we still needed to be careful about anyone seeing me, but I hadn't been so sure that was the reason he'd been unwilling to even consider the idea of me going ashore with him. Maybe if he hadn't spent the better part of a week avoiding me even when we were in the same room together, I would have believed it was just his overprotective nature kicking in.

From the moment Jace had lifted me off the floor and settled me on the bed after the epic blowjob he'd given me, I'd sensed a subtle shift in him. He'd suggested I get cleaned up, even though he'd been the one covered in the remnants of our cum. Then he'd left the room without another word.

And my insecurities had kicked in big-time.

I'd obsessed over the fact that I'd been too rough with him, especially by the end when I'd fucked his mouth without any kind of consideration. I'd had that done to me more times than I wanted to admit, but when Jace had refused to let me pull out of his mouth, had even looked up at me with lust-filled eyes, I'd wanted to believe that he really was enjoying what was happening. I'd lost control after that. Jace had come too, but maybe it had just been his body's natural reaction to the stimulation.

My worry had continued to grow and grow as Jace had withdrawn from me both emotionally and physically over the subsequent hours, but when I'd tried to talk to him about it that night as we'd been getting ready for bed, he'd brushed off my query about whether he was okay or not with a comment about being tired.

He hadn't held me that night.

Or any that had followed.

And a part of me had died each time he'd said goodnight and then turned his back on me.

During the days, he'd spent most of the time moving the boat around the bay. We'd made several round trips over the same area, so even the scenery had started to feel stifling after a while. Jace had gone ashore a couple of times to get us groceries in the past week and each time he'd brought me back some Sno Balls.

Every time I saw them now, I just wanted to cry. It was almost like they'd become a consolation prize.

I didn't want the damn Sno Balls.

I wanted Jace.

"It's fine," Jace said. "It'll be dark and since it's a weeknight, there probably won't be many people around."

The answer stung. Not because of what he'd actually said, but because he hadn't responded to the hurt and confusion he must have been able to hear in my voice.

As bad as the last week had been, Jace had taken things to a whole new level of hurt. It wasn't something I'd even noticed until I'd been getting dinner ready almost a full forty-eight hours after our sexual encounter.

Jace had removed all the knives and forks from the kitchen and replaced them with plastic utensils.

It had been like a slap to the face, and I'd ended up going into the bathroom and crying into a towel so Jace wouldn't hear me above deck. Then I'd dug my fingers into my arm until there'd been several small bruises on my skin. It hadn't been enough damage for the bruises to last long or be noticeable, but my heart felt like it had been torn from my body.

I hadn't confronted Jace about the silverware.

I'd kept hoping something would change over the past week, but nothing did. To make matters worse, Jace was spending every evening above deck while I read or watched TV in the bedroom. On a few occasions, I'd heard him talking to someone on the phone. Since he'd told me himself that the only person he was in communication with was Dalton, I'd known it was the handsome former soldier he'd been choosing to spend his time with instead of me.

My anxiety continued to build as we walked. Another five minutes passed before we reached our destination.

It was a small movie theater and *Lord of the Rings* was spelled out in red plastic letters on the marquee. I'd known we were going to the movies, but he hadn't said which one.

"It's a marathon," Jace said. "I saw a sign in one of the stores that they were playing it all this week."

I stared at the letters for a long time until they started to merge together and I realized it was because I was crying.

He'd remembered that I'd said it was my favorite movie.

"Caleb?" Jace asked in concern when I stopped following him. "Are you okay?"

I let out a watery laugh, then shook my head. "God, Jace, you're such a fucking asshole," I whispered, then I turned on my heel. I wiped at my face as I began walking.

"Wait, what's wrong?" Jace asked as he caught up to me and grabbed my arm.

"Lord of the Rings?" I asked. "You gonna fuck me again now too, Jace?" I bit out.

"What—"

"Is this how it's going to be?" I practically spat as I began walking again. "You treat me like shit, then you do something nice and I'm supposed to forget that you can't even bring yourself to look at me? Maybe I blow you or let you fuck me and then it starts all over again?"

"Caleb—"

"Fuck you, Jace," I muttered, my voice breaking. "I get it. You don't do relationships, you don't fuck the same guy twice, you get off and you go. Shame on me to think I was the exception to the rule."

I quickened my pace. I knew Jace was still behind me, but he didn't say anything. It took only a few minutes to get back to the marina. Once on board the boat, I went to the bedroom and searched out the second burner phone Dalton had bought for Jace. We hadn't made use of it, but Jace had explained it was activated and that I should use it to call him or Dalton if there was any kind of emergency while Jace was on shore. Since I didn't have anything else that was truly mine on the boat, I turned to leave.

Not surprisingly, Jace was standing in the doorway.

Blocking it.

"You're not leaving," he said quietly.

Too quietly.

If he'd been any other man, I would have been scared. But he wasn't any man.

"What are you going to do to stop me, Jace?" I asked as I came to a halt not more than a foot from him. "You may not give a shit about hurting me here," – I pointed at my chest – "but we both know you won't lay a hand on me in anger."

His jaw ticked, but as expected, he didn't make a move toward me. But when I went to push past him, he grabbed my arm and propelled me back into the room. He slammed the door shut behind him.

"I never lied to you—"

"Yes, you did!" I snapped. "Every time you kissed me! Every time you shared some part of yourself with me, every time you—" – I hated that my voice cracked – "—every time you looked at me like I was the only person who existed for you!" I wiped at a stray tear that slipped unbidden from my eyes. "But you warned me, didn't you?" I whispered, my anger deflating as pain began to spiral throughout my chest. "You told me not to give you everything. So shame on me for that too," I murmured.

"It isn't like that, Caleb," Jace said in frustration as he thrust his hand into his hair. "I just… I just…"

When he didn't say anything, I pushed past him, saying, "Go tell it to Dalton" as I did so.

Jace grabbed my arm and dragged me back to him, then walked me backward until I hit the bed. His heavy weight pushed me onto the mattress and he instantly pinned my hands beside my head. "I don't fucking want Dalton!" he snapped. "Don't you get it, Caleb? It's you!" he practically snarled. "It's only ever been you! You're all I've ever wanted from the moment I met you."

Before I could even respond, his mouth closed over mine. The kiss was harsh, but my body welcomed it anyway. But it ended way too soon.

"You were seventeen fucking years old," Jace said, his voice quieter now. "You'd been brutalized in the worst way and I just wanted… I just wanted…"

"What?" I asked softly, some of my pain easing as I watched the helplessness flash in his eyes.

"I had to stay away," he said hoarsely. "Don't you understand?"

He didn't give me a chance to answer. Instead, he shook his head violently. "I couldn't go through that. Not again. Not with you."

"Go through what?" I asked. His body was shaking on top of mine.

"I couldn't love you and lose you like all the others. I just couldn't... I can't... I won't."

I held my breath. Had he just admitted he loved me? I knew the others he was talking about were the family members who'd all been stolen away from him.

I forced some oxygen into my lungs. "You wouldn't talk to me," I murmured. "We had that amazing moment when you... when we..." I cursed inwardly because tears began slipping down my face and with my hands pinned, I couldn't do anything about that.

Jace released one of my hands and skimmed his thumb over my right cheek, then my left. I let out a watery laugh because it was just like him to do something like that.

"When we had sex," Jace finished for me. "That's what it was, Caleb. And it was perfect."

"Then why didn't you speak to me afterwards? I thought I'd hurt you – that I'd treated you like my father and Rush had—"

Jace kissed me. "Don't," he breathed against my mouth. "Don't ever compare what happens between us to what those assholes did to you. I loved everything we did." He kissed me again and I couldn't help but kiss him back. "You want the simple answer?" he asked. "I freaked out. That may not seem like much of an explanation, but I was so fucking scared. And I had no clue what to do with that. There was no cutting it out... there was no fucking it away."

"You could have talked to me," I said softly.

"And say what? 'Caleb, if I lose you I think it might very well kill me.' 'Caleb, I'm so in love with you that it feels like I can't breathe with it sometimes.' 'Caleb, I'm so fucking clueless on what to say or do that will keep you with me forever.'"

I let out a harsh sob. "Yeah, for starters," I said. I reached up to stroke his face. "God, I love you so much, Jace."

He closed his eyes as if pained, then pressed his forehead against mine. "Caleb, if I lose you I think it might very well kill me," he whispered, his voice barely audible. "Caleb, I'm so in love with you that it feels like I can't breathe with it sometimes."

I smiled and settled my hand on the back of his head.

"Caleb, I'm so fucking clueless on what to say or do that will keep you with me forever."

I pressed a kiss against his cheek and then pulled his mouth down to mine. "I love you, Jace."

He sighed. "Love you, baby. So much," he whispered, then he kissed me deeply. "I'm sorry, I didn't mean to—"

I kissed him to shut him up.

I welcomed his weight as he settled completely on top of me and buried his hands in my hair. The kiss turned raw and needy fast, which I was completely on board with. Jace was the one who pulled back, and when I tried to follow, he accepted my kisses, but refused to deepen them.

"Caleb, wait," he insisted, then he was pulling me to a sitting position. "I need to move the boat out to open water. It's not safe to spend the night in the marina."

I sucked in a breath and nodded. I tried to get control of my raging lust while he went above deck to start the boat up. I busied myself with putting the burner phone away, but my mind was reeling too much to make it possible to sit still. I ended up going above deck. The cool air helped calm my libido, but I kept looking over my shoulder at Jace as he focused on getting us out of the inlet.

He loved me.

I couldn't believe it.

As much as I'd loved hearing the words, everything seemed even more insurmountable now. Knowing that my happiness and well-being would have such a strong impact on another person was overwhelming. I glanced down at my arm. I couldn't see the scars but I could feel them. They'd been so many things to me for so long.

My friend.

My confidant.

My escape.

I knew Jace would want me to stop hurting myself for good, and I wouldn't have expected anything different. But saying I'd give up the one thing that had kept me from losing myself completely, and actually doing it, were two very different things. Even now, the emotion I was feeling was overwhelming. Most of it was good, but the doubt and fear were there too.

What if Jace hadn't meant what he'd said? What if he decided I wasn't worth the effort when he realized I couldn't just fix myself and be everything he needed me to be? What if he got tired of being with someone who couldn't separate the monster from the father long enough to completely let go of the past?

Would I survive losing Jace?

I hadn't even noticed that the boat had come to a stop until Jace's arms wrapped around me from behind. He kissed my neck. "Don't overthink this," he murmured.

"How can I not?" I asked. "I have so much more to lose now than I ever did."

"You're not going to lose me."

"You can really do it, Jace?" I asked.

"Do what?"

"Love me even if I never find some of the pieces?"

He hugged me tighter. "I love you in this moment as much as I will ten years from now. Twenty, thirty, a hundred… doesn't matter. No matter how many times you fall and shatter into a million pieces, I'll spend every day of the rest of our lives helping you find any pieces that remain. The things I love about you can't ever truly be lost, Caleb."

I didn't know what to say to that, so I didn't say anything. Any words I might have spoken would have seemed inadequate to describe what he'd just done for me. With that one statement, he'd given me permission for so many things.

"Let's go to bed," Jace urged.

I held his words close to my heart as I turned to face him and said, "Jace, I've loved what we've done so far, but I don't think I'm ready for anything more. I know you said I could, um, take you, but I don't think I'm ready for that, either. The stuff I'm feeling, it's already too much and I don't know how to deal with it…"

As badly as I wanted to look at him, I couldn't. The embarrassment was just too great.

But of course, Jace wasn't satisfied, and he tipped my chin up. "We can do as much or as little as you want for as long as you want, Caleb. But I really need to hold you tonight. Five days without you in my arms has been pure hell."

I smiled and nodded, then accepted his kiss.

He took my hand and led me below deck. I tugged him to a stop when he started to walk past the kitchen. I reached into the fridge and pulled out two containers of strawberry milk and then snagged the last package of Sno Balls from the counter.

"I'll split them with you," I said as I nodded at the Sno Balls.

He eyed me and then took the package and ripped it open. He removed one of the cakes and handed it to me, then put the other back on the counter. As he reached for my hand again, he said, "Don't touch that one. I've got special plans for it."

"What plans?" I asked.

But he didn't answer me. It wasn't until we were in bed that he gave me a preview by sliding his finger through the pink frosting and then pushing my shirt up. He swiped the frosting over my nipple, then proceeded to lick it off. I was moaning by the time he covered my mouth with his.

"Any questions?" he asked.

I shook my head, because I was incapable of speech.

"Good," he said. He dropped a kiss on the tip of my nose. "Enjoy," he added as he motioned to the Sno Ball that I was still holding in my hand. He winked at me as he reached for his milk.

Yeah? Two can play that game, buddy.

"Oh, I will," I said as I made a big production of licking some of the frosting off the cake. I made sure to get some on my lip and then poked my tongue around my mouth to "find" it before I did the move all over again.

By the time I was finished, Jace was practically panting. "Did you enjoy that?" he asked.

"I kind of did," I said with a grin.

And a wink.

"Good," Jace said, then he brushed his mouth over mine. "Because come tomorrow, you're going to pay for that."

He kissed me deeply, then pulled me into his arms and all I could think was, *God, I hope so.*

CHAPTER 15

JACE

"You okay there, babe?" I asked casually as I watched Caleb squirm in his seat.

"Shut up," he responded. "Could they make that shower any damn smaller?" he asked. "It's impossible to reach all the important spots."

I chuckled because I knew exactly what spots Caleb had been trying to reach.

"Is that your way of telling me I wasn't very thorough this morning?"

He sent me a death glare. "You know you were, you cocky bastard."

I failed miserably at hiding my grin as I plucked a piece of bacon off my plate and took a healthy bite. I was rewarded with a forkful of scrambled eggs being flung at me.

"You did not just do that," I said, my eyes going wide.

Caleb was already dipping his fork into the eggs on his plate again when I lunged for him. He laughed and grabbed some of the eggs in his hand and tried to mash them in my face. I ducked and ended up with eggs in my hair. I managed to drag him from his seat and we crashed onto the floor. We were both laughing as we fought to control who ended up on top. I won, but once I closed my mouth over his, we were both winners. Caleb groaned into my mouth.

"You want me to double-check some of those spots you missed in the shower?"

Color suffused Caleb's cheeks and I knew he was very tempted to have a repeat of the events of the morning.

I'd ended up following through on my threat from the night before with the Sno Ball, but I'd made sure Caleb was asleep when I'd started. He'd slept without a shirt so it had been easy to get some of the frosting on him without waking him up. I'd had the pleasure of watching his body become aware of my touch long before his gorgeous eyes had actually opened. By the time they had, they'd been bright with need and the first word out of his mouth had been my name.

I'd tortured his front for a while, but when I'd turned him over onto his belly, he'd tensed just the slightest bit. I hadn't asked him to trust me, because I already knew he did. But I had leaned over his back and kissed him until he'd relaxed. I'd put some of the frosting on his back and had slowly licked it off until he'd once again gone completely pliant beneath my touch. He'd chuckled when I'd spread some of the frosting on his ass cheeks, but his laugh had died a quick death when I'd split him open and swiped a generous amount of frosting on his crease. I hadn't given him time to think about what I was doing. He'd jerked as soon as I'd run my tongue up his crack, but I hadn't given him the opportunity to question what was happening. I'd merely closed my mouth over his gorgeous hole and kissed it like I'd so often kissed his mouth.

He'd moaned as he'd buried his face in the pillow. After that, I'd taken my time, since any resistance he'd shown to the taboo act had fallen by the wayside. I'd eased his dick underneath him so I could reach it while I played with his ass. I'd used what was left of the frosting to toy with him. When I'd finally allowed Caleb to come, it had been with my tongue in his ass and my hand stroking his dick. I'd been so turned on that I hadn't managed to hold back and I'd ended up coming all over Caleb's ass myself. Between the frosting and my cum, it didn't surprise me in the least that he might have a sticky spot or two left in some sensitive places.

"Maybe," he admitted shyly.

I chuckled and kissed him, then helped him to his feet. We were both covered in food, and I regretted for the umpteenth time that Dalton's boat didn't have a bigger shower.

Caleb and I began cleaning up the mess. As we worked, I brought up an issue that I knew we needed to deal with sooner rather than later.

"Caleb, I need to call Ronan to tell him about Jennings."

Caleb stiffened. He was in the process of scraping some food from his plate into the garbage can. "Why?" he asked. "Jennings won't help me."

I hated that he even thought that there'd been a chance Jennings would have helped him. The man was a predator, just like Caleb's father.

"He needs to be held accountable for what he did to you," I began. Before Caleb could object, I said, "But going to the cops is too risky. If Jennings feels cornered, he might tell them it was you the morning of the shooting."

"It's over, Jace. It doesn't matter anymore. Sending him to prison won't undo what he did."

I was tempted to bring up the fact that it was very likely that Caleb wasn't the only kid Jennings had hurt, but that would only add to Caleb's guilt and shame.

"We need to tell Ronan so we can try to figure out if Jennings is the one who put that hit out on you."

Caleb set the plate in the sink. "You don't think it was my dad?" he asked. He almost looked hopeful.

"Honestly, it could be both of them. We won't know unless we do some digging. But I need Ronan's help with that. He's got resources that I don't."

"What will you do if you find out it's one or both of them?" Caleb asked.

I dropped my eyes. "We'll deal with that when we know for sure," I said.

Caleb appeared in front of me and gently grabbed my face and forced me to look at him. "What will you do?"

I held his gaze. "We'll make sure they can't hurt you or anyone else ever again."

Caleb settled on one of the benches that were on either side of the small table. "He's my father, Jace," he whispered.

I knelt in front of him and cupped his cheek. "Your safety, Eli's... that will always come first. You understand that, right? That man isn't your father anymore, Caleb. He stopped being that the moment he touched you and your brother."

Caleb managed a nod. "Does that mean we're going back to Seattle?"

"I think we have to. You're due back there next week for the pre-trial hearing."

He shook his head. "I didn't tell the prosecutor about the letter. He's going to be so mad."

"No, he won't. He'll understand, Caleb. We all do. And people will believe you. Your father is desperate to keep you from talking. He'll say anything at this point."

And do anything.

But I kept that part to myself.

"Promise me things won't change, Jace. Promise me that everything you said last night—"

"I promise, Caleb. I meant every word. I'm not going anywhere."

He pushed into my arms. I stood, taking him with me. "I need to make the call," I said.

"Okay."

"Everything will be okay, Caleb. I know I said those words to you before—"

"I believe you."

I relaxed and kissed him. I released him and went to my room to get my regular phone, since I wasn't worried about hiding our location anymore. I returned to the kitchen and sat down. I watched Caleb moving around the kitchen as I waited for the phone to power on and find a signal. I couldn't help but think how nice it was just to have him there, puttering around. I had no clue what was going to happen next in terms of our relationship, but I wasn't having even a single doubt. I loved him more than I feared losing him. I'd just have to figure out how to keep him safe. I'd do better by him than I had Maggie.

My phone beeped in my hand, a surefire sign it had found a signal. Message after message began appearing on the screen. Most, not surprisingly, were from Mav. I sighed because I knew I had a lot of bridges to repair, starting with him. He wasn't going to like that Caleb and I were together. He hadn't said as much, but I knew he didn't think I was good enough for the young man he considered a brother.

I skimmed the messages just to make sure there was nothing of importance. That was when I noticed a message from a number I didn't recognize.

A foreign number.

I stilled for all of two seconds, then frantically opened it.

Treptower Park. Friday, 3pm.

"What the hell?" I whispered. My heart began racing as I dialed the number.

"Jace?" Caleb said. "Everything okay?"

I didn't answer him because someone picked up at that precise moment. My German wasn't great, but I was able to get enough information from the woman speaking on the other end to determine that she did in fact live in Berlin and that her phone had been stolen two days earlier. I ignored her question about who I was and hung up.

"What is it?" Caleb asked, his voice filled with concern.

"Someone texted me from Germany," I said. "They used a stolen phone to do it. They put down the name of a park and Friday, three p.m. in the message."

"This Friday?" Caleb asked. "That's the day after tomorrow."

I nodded. My fingers were shaking as I looked up the name of the park. It, too, was in Berlin.

"It has to be Maggie," I said. "It has to be. She's the only one over there who would know my cell phone number."

So why hadn't she called? Or left a better message?

Fear consumed me as I jumped to my feet. "I need to go. I need to go!"

"Jace, calm down," Caleb said as he grabbed my arms. "Take a breath and just talk to me. Tell me what needs to happen."

"Have to get back to Dalton's. Find a flight…"

"Okay, how do I come with you? I don't have a passport."

"Caleb…"

"Jace, just answer the damn question. And don't tell me no, because I *need* to come with you. I know Mav can do shit like make up fake passports because I've seen it, so you must know someone!"

He was almost frantic as he hung onto me. I knew it wasn't smart because the trip could prove to be dangerous, but part of me needed him there.

My gut was telling me so.

"I do," I said with a nod. "I'll call him. But Caleb, if I can't pull it all together in time…"

"I know," Caleb said. "I know." He hugged me, then released me and motioned to the phone. "Do what you need to do. I'll get us back to Dalton's."

"Do you know the way?"

"I do. Trust me."

I did. I absolutely did. And I told him so. He smiled and kissed me hard, then hurried above deck. By the time I started dialing Dalton's number to tell him what was going on, the boat was already moving, and I sent Maggie a silent message.

Hang on, Maggie, I'm coming.

CHAPTER 16

CALEB

I had no clue how Jace had managed it, but I didn't care. I was where I needed to be.

By his side.

I reached down to close my hand around Jace's and he automatically linked our fingers. We were sitting in the back of a taxi that was taking us to a hotel near the park that had been mentioned in the text. We had almost a full twenty-four hours to kill before the three-p.m. deadline. Jace had already mentioned going to the park the following morning to scope it out, but until then, we were left to helplessly wonder what was going on.

Jace hadn't said anything, but I knew he was terrified. The fact that the text had been sent to a number which only Maggie would have known, but hadn't included any kind of personal message from her, had him worried. It had *me* worried. If Maggie was okay, why *hadn't* she called? In the time it took to send a text, she could have made the call. If she'd been in danger, a call would have made more sense.

That was the problem, though. Nothing about any of this made sense.

And I knew that made it harder for Jace to deal with.

When he'd admitted that he loved me, but that he was terrified of losing me, I knew it was because he'd lost so many people in his life. His parents had died young, many of the men he'd served with had lost their lives in battle, and his younger sister, who he'd sacrificed his own physical well-being to protect when they'd been kids, had been stolen from him.

So to be faced with the prospect that his sister could very well be gone too was tearing him apart. I didn't need him to tell me that to know it.

After I'd gotten the boat back to Dalton's place, Jace and I had driven to New York to both meet up with the man who had the skills needed to create a passport, and catch our flight to Berlin from the JFK airport. We'd stopped only long enough to get my picture taken for the passport and for Jace to withdraw a large sum of money from his bank. He hadn't let me come into the apartment building with him to get the passport, but when he'd come back out, I'd been relieved to see the small manila envelope in his hand.

We hadn't told anyone besides Dalton what was happening. Jace had received multiple calls and messages throughout the day on his cell phone, but he'd ignored them, so I'd had to assume they were from Mav or Ronan. I'd been a nervous wreck when we'd gone through security at JFK. I'd been certain they'd be able to tell the passport was a fake. But there'd been no issue and we hadn't been stopped at customs in Berlin, either.

It only took about twenty minutes to reach the hotel. Once we were in the room, Jace busied himself with his phone while I put our toiletry items in the bathroom. Neither of us had slept on the plane and I doubted we'd get any sleep tonight, either.

"Jace," I said softly. He was pacing back and forth in front of the sliding doors that led out to a small balcony. He didn't even look up from what he was doing. I'd never seen him so agitated; it reminded me of how I'd get when things just became too overwhelming to deal with.

I went to him and stepped in front of him to stop his pacing. He was aware of me enough not to bowl me over. "What?" he asked impatiently.

"Come lie down with me for a bit," I said softly as I eased the phone from his fingers.

"No, I need to study this map."

He was talking about the map of the park. On the plane, he'd used the onboard Wi-Fi to pull up different versions of maps of the park and surrounding area and he'd spent hours going through them. I hadn't been sure what he was looking for, but I'd left him to it.

"You need to rest," I said. "Please," I added. "I want you to be at your sharpest tomorrow so you can keep us both safe."

He looked at me for a long time, then nodded. He took my hand and followed me to the bed. I worked his jacket and shoes off. My intent had been to leave it at that and urge him into bed, but when he captured my mouth in a bone-melting kiss, all thoughts of rest went out the window.

He kissed me over and over as his fingers began tearing at my clothes. I knew exactly what he was doing and I felt my insides drop out. He needed me, but it was the one thing I just couldn't give him. No matter how badly I wanted to, I just wasn't ready yet.

"Jace—"

"I know," Jace said with a nod. "You're not ready. I need… I need you to fuck me, Caleb. If you're not ready for that either—"

I kissed him to silence him. I wasn't ready for him to be inside of me, but I was more than ready to know him in that way. And to be able to give him something besides just pleasure, to give him the escape he needed, meant everything to me.

"I need to feel good," Jace continued, his voice cracking. "I need to not think about what's coming."

His voice broke and I clasped his face. "I'll take care of you, Jace. Now, tomorrow, always. You'll never be alone again, do you hear me?"

He choked back a sob and nodded. "Love you."

"Love you," I whispered back, then I kissed him and began tugging at his clothes and mine.

He ended up on top of me on the bed, but I welcomed his weight. It was the first time we'd both been naked at the same time and feeling his hot skin against mine was like nothing I'd ever experienced before.

I let my hands roam over his back and ass as he kissed me. We began grinding against one another and I could feel one, or both, of us leaking. It was a sure sign that if we weren't careful, we'd end up coming before we'd even gotten a real taste of one another.

I managed to roll Jace onto his back. I took his hands and placed them above his head. I kissed him deeply, then said, "Leave them there."

Jace pulled in a breath and nodded.

"Just feel, Jace."

He sighed, then closed his eyes. I took my time exploring his body, but bypassed his dick. My confidence grew as Jace began to respond to my every touch. By the time I finally did close my hand around Jace's cock, he was fisting the bedsheets and a fine sheen of sweat had broken out all over his body. His dick was thick and hard in my hand. A shimmer of anxiety went through me as the past threatened to intrude on the moment, but when I looked up at Jace, I saw that his eyes were on me.

"Caleb, you don't have to," he said softly.

Pure, unadulterated love for this man poured from every part of my soul. Despite him being the one who needed comfort, he was still so very aware of me. It changed how I viewed what I was about to do.

It was no longer about me performing an act that was a means to an end. It was about bringing the man who saw me – who knew me better than I knew myself – a little bit of what he'd given me. It was a sex act, but it wasn't about sex.

It would be like that when he made love to me for the first time, too. I wouldn't forget that when the time came.

I held his gaze for a moment, then shimmied down his body as I gave his dick a few more tugs. He never stopped looking at me.

Not as I nuzzled his cock.

Licked it.

Sucked on the head.

There were times that I would draw my eyes away from him long enough to pay attention to what I was doing, but every time I looked at him, he was watching me.

With hunger.

Need.

Awe.

Love.

But as much as I loved seeing all those emotions, I really wanted him to experience the freedom that came with not having to do anything *but* feel. So I took Jace to the back of my throat and sucked hard. He let out a hoarse shout and then I felt his fingers in my hair. But he didn't try to hold me on his dick and he didn't punch his hips up so he could fuck my mouth.

Something I was grateful for, since I really wanted to be the one to control his pleasure.

I sucked him until he was calling my name, then popped off his cock and made my way up his body. I covered his mouth with mine. He groaned and kissed me back and I knew he could taste himself on my tongue.

"Tell me what to do," I said. I hated that I had to ask him the question, but the reality was that I didn't know what came next. My own initiation into anal sex hadn't been gentle and there was no way I wanted to hurt him the way I'd been hurt. I understood things in theory, but I needed him to guide me.

"You need to prep me," he said. "There's a condom and lube in my wallet."

I climbed off him and searched out his wallet, then found what I needed.

I put the condom on the bed and then began fumbling with the packet of lube. My nerves got the better of me. "Fuck," I muttered as I felt my cheeks heat.

Jace sat up and leaned against my side. "Breathe, baby. It's going to be perfect."

I sighed. "I'm supposed to be the one telling you that," I groused. He took the lube from me and opened it.

"I don't need to hear the words to know it," he responded. He handed me the lube, then reached for the condom. As he opened the package, he said, "One finger at first, then two."

My response got caught in my throat as Jace's fingers wrapped around my dick so he could roll the condom down my length. When he was done, I managed to ask, "Um, like this or, um, from behind?"

He kissed my shoulder. "Do you want to know what I was envisioning when I first told you this was what I wanted?"

I loved how relaxed he sounded. It eased some of my own fears.

I nodded in response to his question.

"I want both. I want to feel your weight on my back as you're moving inside of me. But when you come, I want to see you."

I practically swallowed my tongue at that. He'd really given this some thought.

"Okay," I said, my voice hoarse.

He smiled and turned over. His back was just as beautiful as his front and I couldn't help but run my fingers down the length of his spine. But it was his ass that I couldn't take my eyes off of. I slid my palm over his warm, smooth skin, then trailed my finger down the crease. On the one hand, what I was about to do seemed so forbidden, but on the other, I needed it as badly as he did. My dick was hurting like a son of a bitch, but I ignored my own lust and shifted so I was straddling his lower legs. I used my hands to split him open and took in the sight of his fluttering hole.

Oh God, there was no way I was going to fit without hurting him.

I blanched as the memories of the many times I'd been hurt in this very way went through me.

"Caleb," I heard Jace call and I looked up at him.

"It's not the same," he murmured. "Remember that."

His ability to read me was just uncanny. I nodded because he was right. What we were doing was nothing like what I'd known in my previous life. I needed to stop comparing the two acts. Everything Jace and I did was about showing one another love. What had been done to me before had been about power and cruelty. It had no place in this room with us.

I sighed and cast out the memories, then focused on Jace's perfect body. I tentatively touched his entrance with the pad of my finger. I rubbed him gently and used the sounds he was making to gauge if he liked what I was doing.

No doubt that he most definitely did.

I was about to reach for the lube when I remembered what he'd done to me the previous day.

Did I dare?

Did I even want to?

The sight of Jace's opening flexing just a little under my perusal answered that question for me.

With a big fat *yes*.

Before I could overthink it, I leaned down and pressed a kiss to Jace's entrance.

"Jesus fucking Christ!" he shouted.

His bellow startled me, but before I could even issue an apology he said, "Oh God, please do that again."

So I did.

And smiled when he reacted accordingly. His incoherent pleas emboldened me and I began licking him. His musky flavor was strange, but I found it weirdly addicting. Not to mention the way his hole would relax under my tongue, then contract as soon as I removed my mouth. Jace's whole body was shaking and he had his face buried in a pillow. As much as I was enjoying what I was doing, my own lust had spiked exponentially, so I searched out the lube and got some on my finger. My nerves came back as I pushed against his opening. He let out a groan when my digit breached him.

He was so hot and tight, I was sure I'd die right there on the spot. I instinctively went slowly, giving his body time to adjust to my finger. I worked the lube in and out of him. Before I added the second finger, I said, "Jace?"

"I'm good, baby," he said as he turned his head so he could look at me. "I'm so fucking good, Caleb," he said with a smile.

I put some more lube on my fingers, then carefully pushed two inside of him. He closed his eyes and whimpered, but he didn't ask me to stop. I knew there was probably at least a little bit of pain, but I wasn't sensing it was anything bad.

I fucked him with my fingers a few times, then put the last bit of lube on my sheathed cock.

"I'm... I'm ready," I said awkwardly.

Jace lifted to his hands and knees, then looked at me over his shoulder. "Make me yours, beautiful," he said with a lopsided grin. The lightness made me less nervous. I got into position behind him and put my dick against his hole. I settled my free hand on his back and then began to push forward.

"Fuck," Jace muttered as he began to push back on me and his body enveloped the head of my dick. I knew this would be the worst part and I fought every instinct that told me to shove into him so I could feel his heat and tightness around my entire cock. I put my hands on his hips to steady us both. Jace was the one who ended up moving first. He pushed back onto me, slowly sucking my dick into his body inch by inch.

"Oh God, it feels so good," I whispered. "Jace, does it..."

"*So* good, baby," Jace responded. "Need more. Need it all."

I took that as permission to slide deeper into him. We both cried out when my balls pressed against his ass.

My body's natural instincts took over at that point. I was still in tune to everything Jace was saying and doing, but I no longer felt completely clueless. I thrust into him slowly at first, but once he started meeting my thrusts, I increased the pace. It was at that point that I applied pressure to his back. I followed him down as he lay flat on his stomach. I curled my arms around his shoulders and buried my lips against the crook of his neck. "So beautiful, Jace. You're just so fucking beautiful," I whispered into his ear as I began sliding in and out of him.

Jace seemed incapable of speech, because all he could do was grunt and moan as I fucked into him. My orgasm was threatening to consume me when I remembered what he wanted. It took everything in me to slow, then stop. I eased my dick out of him and lifted my weight off him.

"Turn over," I urged.

His moves were languid and heavy as he did what I said. I felt a gut-punch when his warm eyes settled on me. I'd never seen him look so at ease.

Like he was right where he was supposed to be.

Somehow my dick found its way back inside of him without me having to take my eyes off him. I kissed him over and over as our bodies began a natural rhythm of give and take. Jace's legs were wrapped around me, but something in my brain told me we both needed just a little more – that last little bit to take us to the edge.

I shifted my arms so that I was bracing his legs. The move had his ass canting higher, which let me slide even deeper inside of him. Jace shouted my name and then wrapped his arms around my neck. I maneuvered my body so that I was lying flat on top of him. I managed to get my arms around him while still holding his legs. It meant his body was folded in on itself, but with the way he was clinging to me, I knew it wasn't bothering him.

"Harder, Caleb. Fuck me harder," Jace demanded. His mouth latched onto my neck and sucked hard.

I began slamming into him. His dick was mashed between our bodies, but I had no hope of reaching it. I was at a point where I could no longer release him, not even long enough to make sure he got off. It was like my body had taken over and it began pummeling Jace for all it was worth.

"Jace," I cried out desperately. I was so close, but I didn't want to leave him behind. But he was just so damn tight and hot that I couldn't stop fucking him for even a second. The need inside of me kept building on itself with every stroke.

"Harder, Caleb, I'm so close." I felt his fingers rake down my back and then his hands were on my ass, urging me on. "Yes, just like that," he cried.

I felt his inner muscles tighten on me even more. It felt like he was pulsing around me.

My body ached with the need to come and I felt like my head was going to explode. I couldn't breathe or think.

All I could do was fuck.

I wanted to tell Jace I was right *there*, but I didn't have enough oxygen in my lungs to form actual words. I was making sounds that didn't even seem human. I pressed my cheek against Jace's in the hope he'd somehow feel how much I loved him.

Jace suddenly shouted in my ear and then his ass clamped down on my dick. At the same time, I felt his teeth close over the skin of my collarbone. The idea that he was marking me in his own way set off my own orgasm and I lost all awareness as white-hot pleasure tore through me. A brutal sob tore from my throat as the pressure in my balls exploded and I began filling the condom. The need to be even deeper inside of Jace had me crushing him to me. My body jerked as it emptied itself inside of Jace's hot body.

I felt Jace grab my face and then he was pushing me back enough so he could do what he'd wanted to all along.

Watch me as I came.

I had no idea what I looked like as the pleasure consumed me, and I didn't care. I had no control of any of that, anyway. I was just going along for the ride.

The orgasm seemed to go on forever. When it finally began to ease and I started to come back to myself, I found myself lying on Jace's chest. I was still buried deep inside of him. My body was rocked by the occasional aftershock as Jace's rough palms ran up and down the length of my back. At some point, I'd released his legs because I could feel them resting on mine. I could feel something warm and sticky against my stomach. There was no question as to what it was.

We lay there in silence for several minutes as we waited for our breathing to slow. I crossed my arms on his chest and rested my chin on my hands and looked at him. He was watching me with an almost dreamy expression on his face. One hand came up so he could tuck my hair behind my ear.

There were a million things I wanted to say to him, and I had no doubt he felt the same, but we were both content to just stare at one another as our bodies made the slow descent to earth.

There'd be plenty of time to talk later.

The rest of our lives, in fact.

CHAPTER 17

JACE

I was tempted to reach for Caleb's hand just so I could assure myself he was still there, but I didn't want to draw attention to ourselves. The last thing I needed was some homophobe verbally berating us in the middle of the park. Something like that could scare off whoever it was we were there to meet.

"This is fucked," I muttered. "We don't even know where we're supposed to be."

Caleb patted my back, but kept the contact brief.

We hadn't spoken much this morning. Neither of us had been able to eat anything and we'd ended up spending most of the day wandering around the park.

For what reason, I had no idea.

Just to be closer to Maggie, I supposed.

Even though my gut was telling me I wouldn't be seeing her, despite the dreams I'd had of hearing her calling my name from across the park and then running toward me. In the dream, she never made it to me. She just disappeared into thin air moments before she reached me. But not before I got a look at the desperation in her eyes.

Or heard the agonized way she screamed my name.

All the fear and helplessness Caleb had helped me escape for a while had come crashing back with a vengeance this morning when I'd woken up. Caleb had already been awake, but he'd instinctively known I hadn't wanted to talk about what the day might bring.

To say my first time bottoming had been a pleasurable experience was an understatement like no other.

It had been goddamn life-altering.

I doubted it was so much the fact that Caleb had taken me – it was more that he and I had finally gotten to taste that intense level of intimacy. We'd literally been as close as any two people could be. It had been incredible. I'd actually felt like I was a part of him. There'd been no need for words afterwards, because I'd known exactly what he was feeling and thinking.

It had been a bittersweet moment, because even though it had been one of the best nights of my life, my gut was telling me it would always be marred by the outcome of whatever happened today.

I glanced at my watch, then my phone to make sure I'd set my watch ahead enough hours. It was five minutes after three.

"Fuck," I whispered.

Caleb pressed into me a little more. Enough that I'd feel it but not enough that anyone would really notice. We were sitting on a park bench by a river that had numerous little boats traveling up and down it. Tourists went about their business while I tried to remember the last time I'd seen Maggie.

I'd been seeing her and her boyfriend off at the airport. I'd spent a good five minutes rattling off warnings about staying safe when she'd wrapped her arms around me and said, "I'll see you soon."

I could feel tears stinging my eyes, but I managed to stem them. I did end up closing my fingers over Caleb's, though, homophobes be damned. I needed his touch to keep me from completely losing it.

Caleb pulled my hand up to his lips and pressed a gentle kiss to my knuckles.

When another ten minutes went by, I turned to Caleb. "Maybe we're not in the right spot."

Caleb was about to respond when his eyes shifted away from me. "Jace," he said softly. He nodded at something behind me. I turned to see someone standing about a dozen feet from us. I couldn't tell if it was a man or a woman because the jacket they were wearing had a hoodie that hid their hair. The weather wasn't quite cold enough for the heavier jacket, but I suspected that wasn't the reason the person was wearing it anyway.

I stood, pulling Caleb to his feet, and automatically stepped in front of him.

The figure remained in the same spot for a moment, then slowly began walking toward a cluster of trees just behind us. I followed, pulling Caleb along behind me.

The figure stopped by the trees. He or she didn't remove the hood, so I still couldn't see their face.

"What did your sister give you for your twenty-seventh birthday and what color was it?"

I couldn't be sure from the voice alone, but if I'd been forced to guess, I would have said the person before us was a man. The mention of my sister had my heart in my throat.

"Where is she?" I asked.

He didn't answer me and when he turned to leave, I quickly said, "A butterfly. She gave me a butterfly." When the man didn't respond, I pulled the collar of my shirt down to reveal part of my tattoo. "It looked like this."

There were several beats of silence before he said, "Come with me."

"No, tell me where she is!" I said sharply.

But he ignored me and turned away. I fought the instinct to grab him because there were too many people around. If he managed to get away from me, I'd never see him again. I knew we could quite possibly be walking into a trap, but there really was no choice. I didn't have time to try and convince Caleb to stay behind in the park, and I knew he wouldn't have, anyway. I kept his hand in mine as I followed the figure across the street. We walked for a good twenty minutes, the neighborhood becoming a little more run-down and seedy looking with every block that went by. The figure remained a few feet ahead of us and refused to engage with me when I asked questions. Warning bells were going off in my head that this could all be a trap, but I was too desperate to call the whole thing off.

"Caleb—"

"Don't," Caleb said softly. "I'm not going anywhere," he said as he clutched my fingers tighter.

I ground my teeth together. It'd been wishful thinking. And for all I knew, we were being watched and the second Caleb and I separated, someone could grab him. At least I was armed. It was something.

I had no clue what part of the city we were in. The figure kept scanning our surroundings, and when we reached a brick building that looked like it could come down at any moment, he ducked into the alley next to it. I forced myself to remain calm as we followed. About halfway down the alley was a chain-link fence that had been cut open. We followed the guy through the fence, then to the back of the building and through a back door. The building was dark and smelled bad. I could hear blaring televisions and people fighting as we walked past the doors on the first floor. The man led us to a set of stairs, which we took to the fourth floor of the six-story building.

He stopped outside a door near the top of the stairs and knocked once, then used a key to open the door. An older woman stood just inside the door and I stiffened when I watched the man give her some money. The women ducked her head as she hurried past us and went up the stairs, rather than down them.

"Hurry," the guy said as he waved us inside. He locked the door and engaged the deadbolt too. It was only at that point that he pushed his hood back.

He could have passed for a woman if he'd wanted to. His thick, straight brown hair hung to just past his shoulders. His stunning face was a unique mix of feminine and masculine features, but it was his eyes that stood out.

They were an eerie shade of blue that was so clear that they almost looked silver. I wondered if he was wearing contact lenses.

I estimated him to be in his mid to late teens at the most.

The apartment was small and shabby with just a few pieces of stained furniture.

SLOANE KENNEDY

"Where's Maggie?" I asked.

When the man's eyes fell, I felt it like a punch to the gut.

"No," I said, shaking my head. "No!" I practically yelled. "Where is she?"

"Jace," Caleb began, but I tore free of his hold and grabbed the young man. "Where is my sister?"

"I'm sorry," was all he said.

"No!" I snapped. I started to shake him, but Caleb stepped between us and forced me to release him.

"Jace, baby, look at me," he said firmly.

"He's lying!" I declared. "He has to be," I added, my voice breaking.

Caleb's warm hands closed around my neck. "We need to hear him out."

I shook my head because I didn't care. I wouldn't believe a word this man said to me.

I *couldn't*.

"No," I whispered again.

Caleb turned to the guy. "What's your name?"

"Silver," he responded.

I wanted to laugh at that.

A fucking kid with silver eyes named *Silver* was the one to tell me my sister was gone?

No fucking way.

"Where is Maggie?" I ground out.

"She's gone," Silver said quietly.

I reached for him again, but Caleb stopped me. "Tell us what happened," Caleb said. "Why did you bring Jace all the way here if you knew his sister was dead?" Caleb sounded calm, but I didn't miss the anger in his voice.

Silver studied us both for a minute, then turned and disappeared through a door that presumably led to the bedroom. I automatically reached for my gun. Maybe it really was a trap – an elaborate trap. Maybe he and someone else were holding Maggie hostage...

My mind spun with different possibilities, all of which had my sister alive and well.

"It's a trap," I said to Caleb. My instincts were screaming at me to get Caleb out of there. I grabbed his hand. "We should go."

Caleb didn't hesitate to follow me to the door, but we both stopped short when we heard a soft gurgling sound. We turned just in time to see Silver returning to the room.

But not alone.

"Oh God," Caleb whispered at the sight of the baby in Silver's arms. I couldn't move as he approached us. He was talking to the baby, who was watching him with bright eyes. The baby's little fingers were hanging onto Silver's hair.

Silver came to a stop directly in front of me.

"Your sister named her Willa. After your grandmother."

"No," I whispered as I covered my eyes with my hand. "No, it can't be true," I said as I shook my head. But I knew it was.

My sister was dead.

My beautiful, fun-loving, kindhearted, perfect baby sister was dead.

I felt Caleb tug me against him and then his arms were around me. "I'm sorry, Jace."

I pressed my face against his shoulder and nodded. As badly as I wanted to let go of my emotions, I knew I couldn't. I forced myself to straighten and wiped at my face. I settled my eyes on my sister's child.

Her daughter.

I knew Silver could be lying about the baby, but I couldn't even come up with one reason why he would. And to have known my grandmother's name? Maggie would have had to have told him that.

"What happened to Maggie?" I asked as I tried to process that the little bundle in Silver's arms was my last link to my sister.

I had a niece.

I was an uncle.

"I met Maggie about a year ago. She was brought to the house I was living at."

"Living at?" I asked. "Were you like her? Were you taken?"

"Not exactly," Silver hedged. "I was sold... by my parents."

"Sold to who?" I asked.

"His name is Ivan Petrov. He's a well-known businessman over here. Has ties to the Kremlin. But his business is just a front."

"For human trafficking?" Caleb asked.

Silver nodded. "He has an estate in Brandenburg. It's near a lake called Trebelsee. He keeps some girls there... for private parties."

I felt bile rise into the back of my throat.

"How did you and Maggie meet?"

"I had more free rein than most," Silver murmured. "It meant I could move around the house more freely than the others. Ivan trusted me with the girls and would have me take care of them when one of the customers got too rough with them."

I was grateful when Silver didn't bring up details about whatever circumstances had led to him meeting Maggie.

"After a couple of months, Maggie confided in me that she was pregnant. She knew what happened to the girls who ended up in that condition." Silver dropped his eyes and said, "Most of the girls welcomed the forced abortions, but Maggie was different. She wanted the baby. But she knew it was impossible."

"What happened?" Caleb asked.

"She hid the pregnancy as long as she could. When it was finally discovered, she was almost five months along. Ivan told his men to get rid of it, but the guy who was in charge of the day-to-day stuff told Ivan that a white newborn of American descent would fetch a hefty price tag. He agreed to let Maggie carry it to term."

Caleb's fingers dug into my hand, but I welcomed the distraction. It kept me from collapsing into a ball on the floor.

"They let Maggie keep the baby with her while they found a buyer. Maggie begged me to help her escape. I knew it was impossible, but she pleaded with me to help her. She didn't want her baby to end up with people that could do to it what was done to her... to me."

Silver bounced Willa in his arms as she began to fuss a bit. "It ended up taking almost six weeks for Ivan to find a buyer and make the arrangements. When I found out he'd located someone, I managed to steal the key for the fence surrounding the estate from the guard assigned to watch me. I was able to knock him out, and Maggie and I made a run for it that night. But when we were climbing out the window from the second-floor room she was in, she hurt her ankle. I tried to help her, but she couldn't run. The alarm was sounded when she was discovered missing. We were nowhere near the fence and Maggie knew she'd never make it. She told me to take Willa and run."

Silver's eyes met mine. "She told me to get the baby to you, no matter what. She made me memorize your number. I didn't want to leave her, but I knew there was no way I could get her and Willa out of there. I'm so sorry," he whispered. Tears coasted down his face and he quickly wiped them away.

"How do you know she's dead?" Caleb asked.

"I saw them kill her," Silver murmured. "I managed to reach the woods beyond the fence. None of the guards had seen me make a run for it, so they didn't chase me. I hid in the woods. She was surrounded by guards on the patio and then Ivan came outside and demanded to know who'd helped her and where the baby was. She wouldn't tell him. I… I saw him shoot her."

The baby seemed to sense Silver's distress because her little face scrunched up and she started to cry. The young man immediately set out to soothe the baby by rocking her back and forth in his arms.

"How long ago was all this?" I asked. I felt numb inside.

Maggie really is dead.

"Six days ago," Silver said.

The baby was still fussing, so he looked at me and said, "Can you hold her a second while I get her bottle ready?"

I was frozen in place and couldn't force myself to reach for her. Thankfully, Caleb stepped in and took her from Silver. I couldn't even bear to look at the baby, so I began moving around the small apartment. Caleb followed Silver to the kitchen and spoke softly to the baby as Silver got the bottle ready.

I was dimly aware of the two young men talking, but I tuned them out. My limbs felt heavy and my head hurt. It felt like my body was shutting down.

Maggie's dead.

I lost all sense of everything until Caleb asked, "Jace, do you want to hold her?" I hadn't even noticed him appear at my side. I shook my head, even as shame curled through me. The last thing I wanted to do was hold her. It was wrong, but I couldn't stop thinking that maybe Maggie would have been alive if the baby had never existed.

"Here," Silver said as he came out of the bedroom. There was a bag slung over his shoulder and he had a small stuffed panda in his hand. "This one's her favorite."

Understanding dawned.

We were taking the baby with us.

Because that was what Maggie had wanted.

Maggie is dead.

God, why the fuck couldn't I think clearly?

Before I could say anything, there was the faint screech of tires outside. Silver froze in place for a split second as his gaze swung to the window. Then he was pushing past us. I followed him and saw several black SUVs sitting in the middle of the street. I felt my gut clench as more than a half-dozen men got out of the vehicles. They were dressed in dark clothes and immediately began looking around. They weren't holding weapons, but I saw the outline of more than one gun underneath their suit jackets.

"You have to go," Silver said as he shoved the diaper bag and toy into my hands.

"Who are they?" I said, though I was pretty sure I already knew.

"Ivan's men."

I automatically reached for my gun at my back, but as soon as Silver saw it, he frantically shook his head. "No! You have to go! You have to get Willa out of here!"

I'd dropped the diaper bag, so Silver snatched it up and then handed it to Caleb. He kissed the now sleeping baby's forehead and carefully tucked the toy into the folds of her blanket.

"Stay here until they're gone," Silver said.

My brain finally seemed to kick in and I caught up to him just as he reached the door. "Wait, no," I said. "Stay here, I'll go."

"No!" I heard Caleb call, then he was at my side.

"No," Silver said. "There's too many of them. I don't care how good you are with that thing" – he motioned to the gun – "you won't be able to stop them. And if they find Willa, your sister will have died for nothing."

"You can't go out there!" I bit out. "They'll kill you!"

"No, they won't," he declared. "Ivan will never let that happen."

"Why not?" I asked, but Silver ignored me.

"Take care of her," he said to Caleb. He grabbed the door handle, but I slammed my hand against it to stop him from opening it.

"I can't let you go out there," I ground out.

"I know you don't feel it yet, Jace," Silver said softly as he turned to face me. "But you will." His eyes shifted to Willa. "You'll love her because your sister loved her and she's proof of how strong your sister was. There will be a day you won't see her as the reason your sister is dead and you'll be glad you let this happen. Take her home, Jace. Take Willa home where she belongs."

The fact that he'd known exactly what I was thinking had me stepping back.

"I'll be okay," Silver repeated. "Promise."

I knew he was lying. I could see it in his pretty eyes. But when I shifted my gaze to the baby in Caleb's arms, I knew it wasn't a choice. I dropped my hand from the door and Silver took off out of it like a shot. I hurried to the window, making sure to stay out of view. I had no idea what the young man's plan was, but my question was answered about a minute later when Silver rounded the corner from the alley. His hands were in his pockets and he began casually walking along the sidewalk away from the men, like he hadn't even noticed them.

I heard one of the men call out to him in German and Silver looked over his shoulder. He pretended to be surprised, then he took off running. I expected some of the men to stay behind and search the building, but to my surprise, they all jumped into their cars and took off after Silver. I could only assume that by him using the alley to get to the street, instead of the front door, the men hadn't realized he'd been in this particular building.

Either way, I didn't care.

The coast was clear.

"Let's go," I said as I grabbed Caleb's arm.

I took the diaper bag from him and led him from the building. I took us out the very door we'd used to enter the building, but led Caleb toward the opposite street. It took just minutes to find a taxi, but I didn't breathe a sigh of relief until we were a good mile from the area.

I looked over at Caleb, who looked pale. His eyes met mine and I could see the same question in them that kept repeating on a loop in my head.

Now what?

CHAPTER 18

CALEB

I found him standing over the baby's crib. I'd left one of the smaller lamps in the living room on, since I hadn't been sure if the baby would be okay with sleeping in total darkness, so I could see the outline of Jace's body as I approached him.

His back was to me. I could tell he had his arms crossed, and his stance looked rigid.

It was well past midnight. I was surprised I'd even managed to fall asleep, but between the lack of sleep while flying to Germany and the events of the day, I'd reached my breaking point. I had no doubt Jace had, too.

After getting into the taxi, Jace had spoken to the driver, but I hadn't understood what he'd said. He'd revealed to me that he'd asked the driver to take us to one of the nicer hotels in the city. I hadn't understood why he'd made the request until we'd reached the hotel. They'd spoken English so I'd heard all the requests Jace had made.

A suite with either two bedrooms or a living room.

A crib.

And someone to pick up some diapers and formula and bring them to the room.

We'd gotten all those things within twenty minutes of the bellman showing us to the room. Willa had woken up by the time we'd gotten to the room, so I'd spent a few minutes changing her diaper – a task I'd probably mangled since I'd never done it before – and feeding her again, since she'd seemed fussy. Jace had disappeared into the bedroom and I'd left him alone, because there'd been no doubt in my mind that he'd needed a few minutes to try and understand what the hell had happened.

He'd clearly been in shock from the moment Silver had confirmed Maggie was dead.

And there'd been nothing I could do for him.

It had been hard for him to look at the baby and know that his sister had died protecting the infant. I couldn't blame him for the very thing Silver had brought to light – that he held some level of resentment toward the baby for being the reason his sister was dead. If Willa had been aborted or even sold, Maggie would still be alive. I knew the fact that Jace was even thinking those thoughts probably made him hurt almost nearly as badly as the fact that he'd lost his sister.

But I also knew him well enough to know that once he got past the shock, he'd fall in love with the baby as surely as I already had.

I'd never held a baby before, but from the moment Silver had handed her to me, I'd felt a sense of rightness go through me. I'd never known that feeling before, except maybe when Jace held me. The way Willa looked up at me with such trust...

Was that what Jace had felt when I'd given my trust so freely to him?

It wasn't exactly the same thing, but maybe some of those emotions were the same.

When Willa had fallen asleep, I'd put her in the crib. I'd used Jace's phone to search the internet for what position she was supposed to sleep in, and then I'd tried to figure out what kind of feeding schedule she was supposed to be on and how much she was supposed to eat and when. From what Silver had told us, the baby had to be around seven weeks old, so I'd used that as a guide for determining what I needed to give her and when. Once I'd made sure the little girl was out, I'd gone to the bedroom and had found Jace lying on the bed. He hadn't spoken to me as I'd gotten into bed with him. Since he'd been facing the wall, I'd had no choice but to wrap my arm around him from behind. I'd been able to tell he hadn't been sleeping, but I hadn't pressed him to talk because I'd known it was just too soon.

I'd spent the rest of the afternoon feeding, changing and playing with Willa. Jace had ordered us some room service, but neither of us had eaten.

He'd also completely ignored the baby.

I had to hope he'd come around sooner rather than later, because I was clueless as to what to do next.

The fact that he was now standing over her crib, watching her sleep, could be both a good thing or a bad thing.

I had the answer to my question when I moved around him so I could see his face.

It was both.

Because tears were streaming down his face.

Reality had finally set in and while it was terrible to see his world implode around him, I knew it was the only way for him to eventually find his way back to the surface.

"I really thought I'd find her," he said softly.

"I know," I acknowledged.

"I promised I'd always look out for her."

I pressed against Jace's side and settled my hand on his chest as I looked at a still-sleeping Willa. "Come back to bed, Jace," I murmured. I slid my hand into his and pulled him behind me. He meekly followed.

I let him lie down first, and not surprisingly, he turned so his back was away from me. But instead of just holding him, I braced my head on my arm and used my free hand to move his hair off his face. I didn't speak, because there were no words I could say that would take the pain away.

He lay frozen like that for several long beats, then a harsh sob tore from his throat and he covered his eyes with his hand.

"Oh God, Maggie, I'm so sorry."

I wrapped my arm around him and held him as tight as I could as I dropped my mouth to his ear. Every time he tried to stifle his sobs, I told him it was okay to let go.

So that's what he did.

Completely.

Terribly.

And I felt every moment of it deep in my soul.

He eventually quieted, then fell asleep.

But I knew it wasn't over.

It would be something he'd have to endure over and over again, especially in those moments where he momentarily forgot his new reality. I didn't even know if there would be a time where it wouldn't hurt like hell, because even two years after losing my brother, the pain was as raw now as it had been back then.

It wasn't until Jace turned in his sleep and burrowed against my body that I finally felt my own tension ease a bit. I fell asleep, but woke up a short time later when Willa started crying. Thankfully, Jace slept on and that proved to be the case the second time Willa woke up a few hours before dawn. Not surprisingly, when my head hit the pillow, I was out within seconds, and when I woke up again, it was light outside.

And the bed was empty.

I sat up and looked toward the bathroom, expecting to see Jace in there, but it was empty. I finally noticed that the French doors that closed off the bedroom from the living room were shut.

I'd left them open the night before so I could hear Willa.

I climbed out of bed and hurried to the doors. I eased them open and froze at the sight that greeted me.

Jace was standing in front of the large window that overlooked the city. He was wearing just a pair of sweatpants and had Willa pressed up against his chest. I could see the baby's face – she was out cold, but her cheek was resting on the butterfly tattoo her mother had designed. Jace was gently patting her on the back and shifting his weight back and forth on his feet.

I'd never seen a more beautiful sight.

I felt tears sting my eyes when I realized Jace was talking to Willa. I couldn't hear what he was saying, but the fact that he was being so gentle with her...

"Hey," Jace said softly, and I looked up to see him watching me.

"Morning," I said, my voice cracking a bit. "Everything okay?" I asked.

His eyes held mine and I felt my heart lurch because I finally saw Jace in them... *my* Jace.

Jace sent me a warm smile and nodded.

And I knew in that moment that everything would be okay.

"I was just explaining to my niece here that this waking up before the sun even rises isn't going to work for us."

Us.

I breathed a sigh of relief. We were still an *us*.

"What did she say?" I asked.

"We're still in the negotiation process," Jace explained, keeping his voice low. "But I think she'll see my side of things soon."

"I have no doubt," I said. "Did you feed her?" I asked.

He nodded and pulled his phone from his pocket. "Thank God for the internet."

"No shit," I said. "Um, poop, I mean. No poop."

Jace chuckled. "I think you have time to practice the substitute swear words."

I crossed my arms. "Does that mean you're keeping her?" I asked. I'd meant to save the conversation for a better time, but I was desperate to know what role the baby would play in his life.

And I wanted to know that I would play a role in both their lives.

Jace held out his hand to me. I walked toward him and took it. He tipped my head up and kissed me. "I'm keeping both of you," he said. "Willa's not the only one who needs a family."

I leaned into his side and stared out the window.

"Do you want that, Caleb?" Jace asked.

Did I want to spend the rest of my days with the man I'd been searching my entire life for and the baby who'd manage to steal my heart with one look from her innocent blue eyes?

Hell yeah, I did.

"You bet your ascot I do," I said.

Jace chuckled. "That was a good one," he said.

We held there for a moment before I asked, "What are we going to do, Jace?"

I knew Jace wouldn't be satisfied until he both recovered his sister's body and punished the man who'd taken her from him, and like me, I knew he was probably worried about Silver. But spending even another second in the dangerous city scared the hell out of me. Whoever this Ivan guy was, he seemed to have far-reaching power and I wasn't sure to what lengths he'd go to get Willa back. In theory, Jace could send me and Willa back to the States and stay behind to deal with Ivan, but that terrified me even more.

"We're going to go home," Jace murmured.

I breathed a sigh of relief and pressed my forehead against his chest. I felt him kiss the top of my head.

"I just don't know how we're going to do it," Jace said softly. "I think I'll need a passport to get Willa out of the country, but I don't have any contacts here."

I sighed and looked up at him. "Can I have your phone?" I asked.

He handed it to me.

"Do you trust me, Jace?" I asked.

"Always," he responded without hesitation.

I smiled, then turned my attention to the phone. Once I dialed the number I wanted, I leaned into Jace's side as he put his arm around me. When the voice on the other end picked up, I said, "Mav, it's Caleb. Jace and I are okay, but we need some help—"

That was all I got out before Mav interrupted me to ask where we were and that he was coming to get us.

I closed my eyes and smiled.

Thank God for family.

CHAPTER 19

JACE

We'd been here before.

Driving in Ronan's SUV from the private airport where we'd landed mere minutes earlier in his personal jet.

A few things were different, though.

Mav and Eli weren't with us.

But we were plus one infant.

And the Caleb who was pressed against my side was no longer the vulnerable teenager I'd saved two years earlier.

Sure, he was technically still a teen, but he'd acted with more maturity and responsibility than many adults I'd met.

Myself included.

While I'd been practically paralyzed with grief, Caleb had taken on the task of caring for a newborn with next to no experience. As if he hadn't already had enough on his plate, he'd somehow still managed to be there for me, too.

I'd been drowning.

Pure and simple.

The second we'd gotten to the hotel room and we'd been safe from the reach of the man who'd murdered my sister, I'd given in to the numbness my body had been craving. I'd spent hours in a place in my mind where my sister was still alive and I was back on that boat with Caleb, contemplating what our future would look like.

Now I had to contemplate a different future.

One in which I was now a father.

I didn't even know what to do with that.

But I'd known that was what I was as soon as I'd picked Willa up this morning. She'd been crying pretty loudly when I'd woken up. The fact that Caleb had slept through it had been proof of how exhausted he must have been. Strangely enough, having Willa wake me up kept me from having to go through the stages of grief all over again. Acknowledging that my sister really was gone had taken a back seat to trying to figure out what Willa needed from me at that moment.

Silver had been right.

The second I'd picked her up and she'd looked at me with her big, watery eyes, I'd felt it. And the resentment I'd felt had slipped away as if it'd never been. There'd been no question that Willa was my future.

It was what Maggie had wanted.

It was what I wanted.

I hadn't been one hundred percent sure about Caleb, but I'd had my answer the moment I'd turned to see him watching me and Willa. The look of contentment in his eyes had been enough to assure me that whatever I was facing, he'd be at my side.

What I hadn't been expecting was all the help that Caleb brought with him. It was utter insanity that my first thought when I'd been trying to figure out how to get Willa out of Germany *hadn't* been to reach out to Ronan and Mav. I'd been trying to determine if Dalton would be able to work with my contact in New York to get me what I needed. The fact that Caleb was the one who'd had to remind me that Dalton wasn't the only one in my corner had been an eye-opener. Despite my behavior toward Ronan, Mav, and Memphis, there was no chance in hell they would have left me to my own devices, even if Caleb hadn't been with me.

Asking for help wasn't something I knew how to do, and I'd need to work on that.

For Caleb's sake.

And Willa's.

While Mav had been the one Caleb had talked to, it'd been Ronan who'd flown to Germany to pick us up, passport and a mess of baby stuff in tow. There'd been no issue with getting Willa out of the country, and Caleb and I had practically passed out on the plane, leaving Ronan to take care of Willa.

Caleb's fingers tapped against mine as he held my hand. We were getting closer to the house that Ronan and Seth owned on Whidbey Island. Ronan had informed us that Mav and Eli had gone to the house to escape the crush of reporters that had descended after Jack's acquittal. Fortunately, Eli had managed to get through his finals for his second year of medical school before all hell had broken loose with the trial, so he at least had some time to recover from the ordeal without the added stress of school. Ronan had determined that it made sense for Caleb and me to stay at the house as well, since it already had top of the line security. Caleb still hadn't been implicated in the shooting at the Jennings' house, but I also had no clue what kind of progress, if any, Ronan, Mav, and Memphis had made in determining who'd put the hit out on Caleb. Until we had some answers, he'd be under twenty-four-hour guard.

I knew Caleb was nervous about seeing his brother again. With the way he'd left and his refusal to return home with Mav more than two weeks earlier, Caleb was carrying a heavy dose of guilt. Not to mention everything he'd put Mav and Eli through over the past couple of years as they'd tried to help him recover from his ordeal. And, of course, now there was the added complication of my and Caleb's relationship.

As we got closer and closer to the Whidbey Island house, Caleb's tension continued to edge up. I saw him reach for his forearm a few times, then catch himself. He hadn't cut himself since that day when we'd first boarded the boat, but I knew that didn't mean he was cured. I'd used some of the time while we'd been waiting for Ronan to arrive in Germany to research Caleb's condition. I'd learned that it was very much like any kind of addiction. With therapy and hard work, he'd get to a point where he learned to use different methods of coping, but the urge to cut would likely always be there.

Caleb and I hadn't talked about the self-injuring with all that was going on, but I knew it was something we needed to address in the near future. For my part, I was trying to learn how to deal with the fear and helplessness that came with knowing I couldn't just make him stop. I knew I'd hurt him deeply when I'd hidden the silverware and knives on the boat – it had been a knee-jerk reaction and I wasn't proud of it. I'd selfishly wanted to avoid having to interact with him because of the feelings I'd been dealing with, but the fear that he'd hurt himself without me knowing had been at the back of my mind, so I'd replaced the silverware with the plastic cutlery. I'd learned during my research that trying to remove sharp objects from Caleb's immediate vicinity wouldn't solve anything – he'd just find other ways to hurt himself. I'd apologized to Caleb the morning I'd found the text about Maggie, and we'd talked about the issue enough that he'd agreed to try and reach out to me first whenever he was feeling the stress that drove him to hurt himself.

The same stress he was feeling now.

I leaned in to kiss his temple and said, "Breathe, baby."

He drew in a breath, but didn't look at me. His eyes were on Willa, who was asleep in her car seat. The back seat in Ronan's SUV was the bench kind and Caleb and I had been able to squeeze onto it, along with the car seat. The irony wasn't lost on me that despite the rough start that had come with learning of Willa's existence, neither Caleb nor I could take our eyes off her for very long.

"He'll hate me," Caleb whispered. "They both will."

"You know that's not true," I said softly.

"Does Mariana know I'm back?" Caleb asked Ronan.

"She does. She thought you and Eli could use some time to talk, so she'll be coming out to the house tomorrow. At least, I think that's what she said – she couldn't stop crying when I told her I was going to pick you guys up," Ronan said.

As we reached the house and began the short trek up the driveway, Caleb looked at me. "You won't leave, right?"

"Martha Stewart couldn't drag me away, baby."

He laughed and leaned against me. When the car pulled into the circular part of the driveway, Eli's Rottweiler, Baby, was already waiting at the bottom of the steps. I could see that the front door was open, but didn't see Eli or Mav.

Once we were out of the car, Caleb went to greet Baby while I got Willa's car seat. I turned in time to see Caleb standing stock-still with Baby eagerly nuzzling his fingers. But Caleb's attention wasn't on the dog anymore.

It was on Eli, who was standing in the doorway.

Also frozen.

Eli moved first.

In fact, he was the only one who moved. Caleb seemed stuck in place.

Eli moved slowly down the stairs, his eyes never leaving his brother. He looked terrible. It was clear he'd lost some weight and his expression was almost haggard.

Caleb didn't move, didn't react as Eli neared him. But when Eli was within a couple of feet of him, his expression unreadable, Caleb suddenly let out a harsh sob. "I'm sorry," he blurted, then he covered his face with his hands.

Eli didn't even slow his step. The second he reached Caleb, he enfolded him in his arms. Caleb kept repeating he was sorry as he sobbed in Eli's arms and Eli just held onto him. I could hear him saying something to Caleb, but I wasn't sure what it was. It had Caleb nodding, though, so that was encouraging. I glanced up to see Mav standing at the top of the steps, his eyes on the brothers. He gave them a moment, then descended the stairs. When he reached the pair, Eli relinquished his hold on Caleb and Mav immediately wrapped his arms around him. There were more muffled words spoken between them and then Mav kissed Caleb's temple. He released Caleb, who wiped at his eyes. Caleb and Eli started speaking as Mav made his way to me.

I tensed, because the last time I'd seen Mav, I hadn't exactly been welcoming. Not to mention I'd pretty much kidnapped the young man he considered a little brother.

When he reached me, he extended his hand.

But not to shake mine.

No, he wanted Willa's car seat.

I didn't know what to make of the silent request, but since I knew he wouldn't hurt her, I handed her over. He immediately gave the car seat to Ronan.

And I prepared myself for the worst.

But I wasn't about to apologize for what I'd done. Yes, I was sorry I'd worried him and Eli, but taking Caleb had been the smartest thing I'd ever done in my entire life. If that earned me a punch or two, so be it.

Only there was no punch. There were just Mav's arms sliding around me. "Thank you for keeping him safe," Mav murmured. He slapped me on the back. "Welcome home, brother."

I let out a harsh breath.

Because fuck if I hadn't needed that.

I nodded, but didn't manage to say anything. Mav released me and then turned his attention on Willa, who was being gently nuzzled by Baby. The infant had woken up at some point and was just staring at all the new faces.

"What do you say, baby girl?" Mav said. "Wanna go see what your Uncle Mav and Uncle Eli have for you?"

I smiled at the sing-song voice he used as he took the car seat. Willa looked completely entranced as Mav continued to talk to her as he began walking toward the house. Eli automatically fell in step next to him and began cooing at the baby. Ronan followed and then Caleb was at my side. I wiped at the remnants of his tears. "What do you say we go introduce Willa to her uncles?" I asked.

He slid his hand into mine and nodded. "I think I just found another piece, Jace," he murmured softly. I smiled and kissed him, but refrained from telling him I had a feeling it was the first of many.

Because I knew he'd have to see it to believe it.

CHAPTER 20

CALEB

"I'm not exactly an expert at this," I said as I rolled up the dirty diaper and secured it with the Velcro tabs and then grabbed a baby wipe. "I mean, did you know there was a right way to wipe the baby if it's a girl... how do parents know this stuff?"

I knew I was babbling, but I couldn't seem to make myself stop.

"I saw this thing on the internet about cloth diapers being better, but can you imagine the mess?"

"Caleb," Eli said softly, and I forced myself to look at him. We were in one of the guestrooms that I figured had probably once belonged to Seth as a child. There was a full-size bed in it, but also a crib and a changing table, which I suspected were new, since Seth and Ronan's youngest child was too old for those things.

"You're doing great," my brother said. He shook his head and smiled wide. "You're incredible with her," he added.

I breathed in a sigh of relief, because I'd needed to hear that. Jace had said the same to me already, but hearing it from Eli was nearly as important to me. Maybe because I felt like I had something to prove to him.

That I wasn't the same young, reckless kid who'd run away when things had gotten too hard.

I got the new diaper on Willa and picked her up. I reached for the bottle Jace had made, but when I saw the way Eli was looking at the baby, an almost hungry expression on his face, I asked, "Do you want to feed her?"

His eyes lifted to mine. "Really?"

I nodded. It was no secret how much my brother loved kids. He was planning to practice pediatric oncology when he finished school.

Eli was sitting cross-legged on the bed, so I reached across it and handed Willa to him, then gave him the bottle. Unlike me, he knew right away what to do and I had no doubt it was because he'd handled many of the babies in the extended family at the weekly family dinner celebrations.

Celebrations I'd often avoided.

I climbed up onto the bed and sat so that I was facing him. He looked so at peace holding the baby.

"You need this in your life, huh?" I asked.

Eli looked at me, then glanced at Willa again. "Mav and I have talked about it, but it makes more sense to wait until I'm finished with school," he explained, though there was a certain hollowness in his voice as he spoke. "A lot of things made more sense before…"

He didn't need to finish the statement for me to know what he'd been about to say.

Before the trial.

The trial against my father had consumed so much of all our lives, but none more so than Eli and Mav, who'd even ended up putting their wedding plans on hold until after my father was convicted. I'd heard Mav and Eli tell my stepmother that they wanted to start their life together on a positive note, but I had to wonder what would happen now that everything had changed so dramatically. Would they wait until my father's second trial was over? Or until after the one he was likely to face in Virginia for Nick's death?

Silence descended between us until the only sounds in the room were of Willa eagerly sucking on her bottle. When she finished, Eli handed the bottle to me, then put her against his shoulder and burped her. I was about to offer to take her to put her in the crib, but something in Eli's gaze stopped me.

I'd seen him in the hours after the acquittal and he'd been an absolute mess. And physically, he still looked completely worn out. But the way he was smiling down at the baby made me think that he needed this moment of peace.

Just like I'd needed the peace I'd known I would only find in Jace's arms.

"I'm sorry, Eli," I said. "I shouldn't have just left like that."

Willa had grabbed onto Eli's finger, so he let her hold it as her eyes drifted shut. His eyes shifted to me. "Why did you?" he asked.

I dropped my eyes and shook my head. "Desperation, I guess," I said softly.

"To get away from us?" he asked.

"What?" I said in surprise, lifting my gaze. "No... no, not at all. I just..." I snapped my mouth shut and turned to look out the window. I stared at the view of the water for a minute before I said, "Someone played me a recording of your testimony. I could hear it in your voice."

I chanced a glance at Eli. He was the one staring out the window now.

"It was like it was happening all over again, wasn't it?" I asked.

Eli nodded and I saw a tear slip from his eye. He used his shoulder to brush it away. "I thought I'd prepared myself for anything, but between the questions and Jack staring at me the whole time, I was right back there, you know?"

I nodded and dropped my eyes. "It was still just me up until that moment that I heard you talking about it on that tape," I admitted. "I'd never let myself think about what it was like for you. That's why I never wanted to talk to you about it. It made it all more real. Does that make sense?"

"It does," Eli acknowledged. "But if I've learned anything, it's that not talking about it won't make it go away. It'll just destroy you from the inside out."

I managed a nod. "Did Mav tell you? About what I've been doing to deal with it?"

"Yes," Eli said softly. "I'm so sorry, Caleb. If I'd known…"

"If you'd known, I would have run even sooner," I admitted. "It was the only thing making it possible for me to put one foot in front of the other every day." I began toying with my fingers so that I wouldn't be tempted to reach for my arm to make sure the scars were still there. "I have some things I want to tell you, Eli, but I don't know if I'm ready yet."

"Caleb…"

He waited until I looked up at him to say, "I'm not going anywhere."

I felt tears threatening, but I managed to stem them. "Promise?" I whispered.

Eli's hand covered one of mine. "Promise."

I wasn't sure what to say next, but Eli took care of that by saying, "So tell me about Jace."

I couldn't stop the smile that spread across my mouth at just the mention of the man's name.

Eli chuckled. "So that's how it is, huh? Mav owes me fifty bucks."

"For what?" I asked with a laugh.

"We had a bet going on how long it would take before Jace got his head out of his ass and realized you were it for him. I said it would be by the next time we saw you. Mav thought Jace was going to run again and he'd have to hunt him down and drag him back here and knock some sense into him."

"Really?" I asked as more tears threatened. Would Mav really have gone that far… for me? "You don't think I'm too young for him? For anyone?" I asked.

Eli shook his head before I even finished the question. "You're not a kid, Caleb. I wish to hell you were a regular nineteen-year-old whose only concern was getting his ass out of bed every morning to make it to class on time and deciding which frat party to go to on Friday night. I wish you'd had the chance to experience your first kiss, your first time falling in love, fumbling through sex for the first time.

But those things were taken from you. You've had to deal with things no adult should ever have to, let alone a little kid. I have no doubt you were always meant to be with Jace, but I would have given anything to have you guys find each other in some benign way like bumping into each other at a coffee shop." Eli eyed me for a moment and added, "Or in your case, in the snack food section of the local grocery store."

I laughed and wiped at my eyes as some of the heaviness in my chest eased.

"He brings me Sno Balls," I said with a grin.

Eli smiled. "See, it's true love."

We fell silent for a moment before I said, "Eli, he gave me some of those things – the first kiss, the falling in love for the first time... other stuff I probably shouldn't mention."

Eli chuckled and softly said, "A lifetime of firsts." He looked at the engagement ring on his left hand. He must have seen my confusion because he removed the ring and handed it to me. "Turn it over," he said.

I did and saw that the phrase *A Lifetime of Firsts* was inscribed in the ring. "Wow," I said. I handed it back to him and watched him slide it on. What would it be like if I wore a ring that Jace gave me? Was that something he even wanted? He'd talked about us being a family, but there hadn't been time to get into any details of what the future held. Hell, I didn't even know if he was okay with me telling Eli that he and I were together. What would happen once the threat to me was gone? Hell, what would happen tonight? Was he even going to stay here at the house? There was plenty of protection now – I'd seen the men walking the perimeter myself. There was no reason for Jace to stay.

I admonished myself for the bout of insecurity that went through me. Jace had said he wasn't leaving. I had to believe he wasn't only staying because he wanted to make sure I was safe.

"Hey," Eli said gently as he touched my hand. I looked up at him and saw him pointedly look at my arm.

The arm I was currently digging my nails into.

God, what the hell was wrong with me?

"Why won't it stop?" I whispered.

"What?" Eli asked softly.

"This voice in my head that's telling me that none of it is real. That Jace is going to leave me when he realizes I'm not worth it. That you're going to hate me when you realize some of the shit that's going through my head about you, about Dad." I looked at my arm. "Why is *this* the only thing that makes sense to me?"

Eli got up and quickly put Willa in the crib, then came around to my side of the bed and forced me to shift so I was sitting on the edge of the bed. He did the same and faced me so he could take my hands. "That stuff in your head, Caleb… it's your mind's way of trying to protect yourself from more pain. If you believe Jace will leave you, it might hurt less when he actually does. If you prepare yourself for me to hate you, then it won't matter as much if that's what happens. *That's the shit that's not real*," he said.

"It's been two years and I'm still figuring out how to ignore that voice in my head that says I deserved what Jack did to me. I watched the video. I *saw* him rape me. But I couldn't stop making excuses that it was somehow my fault. It's Jack's lies that speak the loudest. It's the lies of the men who used me when I was a kid that try their damndest to still be heard. I wish I could tell you it will all just stop when Jack goes to jail or you and Jace embark on the next chapter of your lives or" – he looked pointedly at Willa – "you become a parent yourself." He shook his head. "But I'm not going to add to the lies. It's work, Caleb. It's such fucking hard work. But that voice will get quieter and, God willing, when it goes silent for the final time, you won't even realize it at first."

I nodded and then he was easing me into his arms. "You hear that voice, you come ask me if I'm going to turn my back on you. You go find Jace and you look at the truth in his eyes when he tells you he's exactly where he wants to be. You pick up that little girl and then ask yourself if she'd really be better off without you. I'll bet you all the fucking Sno Balls in the world that you won't ever hear the answer that voice in your head is trying to convince you that you will."

I sighed and leaned into him, then wrapped my arms around him.

He held me for a long time. When I pulled back, I wiped at my face for what had to be the hundredth time. "Eli," I said as I held his gaze, "I need to go ask Jace a question."

He smiled and nodded. "Go, I'll make sure Willa is settled."

I got up and started to leave the room, but then turned to look at him. "Eli, don't put your life on hold for him, okay?" I said softly. "Not even for another minute. He's not worth it."

He knew who I was talking about, of course. "Yeah," he said, his voice sounding strangled. He dashed at his face and said, "Can you send Mav up here? There's something I need to ask him." He sent me a wobbly grin.

I nodded and left the room to go find my man.

CHAPTER 21

JACE

"How's Memphis?" I asked as Mav slid the cup of coffee in front of me.

"He's fine," Ronan said. "He'll need to wear a sling for a couple more weeks, but he won't need any kind of physical therapy or anything."

I nodded.

"Jace, there's something we need to talk to you about. Mav heard from Daisy just as the plane was landing. I didn't want to say anything in the car with Caleb there."

I stiffened. "Okay, what is it?"

"Jennings is dead," Mav said, keeping his voice down.

"What?" I asked in surprise. "How?"

"It appears to be a suicide. His wife found him hanging in the basement of their house. His home office was down there. There was no evidence of foul play, but also no suicide note. Daisy was scanning the local dispatch feeds when she saw the address come through. It'll hit the local papers in a matter of hours, if it hasn't already."

"Fuck," I muttered. As badly as I'd wanted the fucker dead for what he'd done to Caleb, it would be Caleb who suffered when he learned what had happened. He'd blame himself for somehow driving

Jennings to it after the confrontation more than two weeks earlier. I ran my fingers through my hair. Why the fuck couldn't Caleb just get a damn break already?

"Caleb's given me permission to talk to you about this," I said to Ronan. "You too," I added to Mav. Even though Caleb and I hadn't actually talked about Mav learning the truth about what Jennings and Rush had done to Caleb, I had no doubt that Caleb had known it was inevitable that his brother's fiancé would need to be clued in. "Jennings and a guy named Rush raped Caleb when he was fifteen. It happened on a camping trip with Caleb's father. The fucker handed Caleb to them on a silver platter. He may have taped both rapes on his phone to use against the men."

Mav lurched out of his chair and went to the back door that overlooked the back yard. He gently pounded his closed fist on the glass. I suspected if it'd been an actual wall, he would have unleashed the anger I could see cascading throughout his entire body. Ronan looked just as pissed, but he remained seated. "If he stored them on his computer…" he murmured.

He didn't need to finish the sentence. If they'd only been stored on the one computer that Nick had copied the other videos from, then there'd be no proof. The pedophile had been smart enough to install software on his computer that would wipe the hard drive after a certain amount of time if he didn't log into it. By the time Daisy had hacked into the computer the day after Jack had been arrested, the files had already been gone. The only evidence of Jack's depravity had been the flash drive. There'd been no videos on his phone or his cloud account.

"Caleb said he thought Rush worked with his father, but that Rush wasn't his real name."

Mav returned to the table and sat. His expression was drawn tight with anger. "We can search the DoD records for someone with a last name or known nickname that's a variation of Rush, but it's a long shot."

"Maybe go back further," Ronan suggested. "College, high school even."

"Caleb said Jennings was friends with his father when they were both in high school. Start there," I said. "The timing with this Jennings thing is too convenient," I added. "Caleb had a gun on him and still the guy refused to confess to what he'd done. Assholes like that don't feel guilt. He strung Caleb along for years with promises that he'd help him, but he didn't do shit. He was only trying to keep Caleb quiet long enough to keep him from telling anyone what happened."

"You think Jack put a hit out on Jennings like he did Caleb?" Mav asked.

"He's got the resources," I said. "The guys who hit us out in the woods were pros."

Mav nodded in agreement and said, "Talent like that could've made Jennings' death look like a suicide."

I looked at Ronan. "Any chance the coroner will be able to tell?" I asked.

Ronan shook his head and put out his hands. "All depends on the coroner. Some are more experienced than others. If he doesn't see any signs of a struggle, he's not likely to order the specific drug tests that will show if he ingested anything that would have knocked him out. Something like GHB would've made it easy for someone to string him up without any kind of struggle."

"We can't risk tipping the cops off to look at it as something more," I said.

"*We* can't," Ronan agreed. "But Declan probably can. He's the one who arrested Cortano. If he can find anything that shows Cortano and Jennings were still in contact in the past couple of years, he can feed that to the cops in Bethesda."

I knew who Ronan was talking about. Declan Barretti was a captain in the Seattle Police Department. He was also the brother-in-law of Dom Barretti, Eli's adopted father. Declan and Dom had both been present when Eli had admitted that Jack had raped him repeatedly as a teenager.

"Are you sure he won't figure out Caleb was the one who was at the Jennings' house that day?" I asked.

"I have no doubt he *will* figure it out," Ronan said. "But Caleb's family, and if we've learned anything about the Barrettis, even the ones who are a Barretti by law and not blood, you don't fuck with their family."

Mav nodded in agreement.

"I'll talk to him," Ronan said.

"I'll have Daisy see if she can find a link between Jennings and Jack that's more recent. If Jennings panicked after Caleb showed up and reached out to Jack, it would explain how he knew Caleb was no longer in Seattle. It would have been the perfect time for him to silence him." Mav looked at me and said, "We found a tracker on the rental car we used in West Virginia. I was the one who rented it. Jack probably knew I'd be one of the people going after Caleb and had someone scanning all the rental car agencies for my information. We had the car delivered to the airfield we landed at – the tracker was probably already on it. I'm sorry, Jace. It never even occurred to us to check it."

I shook my head. "It wouldn't have occurred to me either," I said. "I shouldn't have insisted on radio silence," I added. "I panicked." I shook my head. "I can't stop seeing that laser sight on his chest. If I'd moved just a fraction of a second slower…"

Ronan put his hand over mine. "You didn't. Nothing else matters. You got him back here and he's safe now. Jack isn't getting another shot at him."

I nodded. "I need to ask you guys a favor. I need to go back to Germany for a few days. Can Caleb and Willa stay here?"

I realized after the question that I hadn't even pointed out that Caleb and I were together now and that he would be staying with me going forward. Hell, Caleb and I hadn't even had a chance to talk about what would happen once things settled down. I hadn't even given thought to where we'd end up. Though after everything that had happened, I was pretty sure that the *where* was the easy part. Caleb's family was here.

And, as it turned out, so was mine.

I just hadn't realized it.

"You can't go after him, Jace," Ronan said.

I sighed. Leave it to Ronan to know what I'd been referring to. "He killed my sister, Ronan."

"And he'll pay for that, but you won't be anywhere near him when it happens. You're one of the first people the cops will point the finger at."

"They won't make the connection," I insisted.

"Yes, they will," Mav said softly. "We have a source who works for Interpol. He's confirmed that Petrov is already on their radar and that an arrest is imminent. He's also confirmed that a body was discovered in one of Petrov's known dumping grounds – the body matches Maggie's description."

I felt my heart sink. Even though I'd believed what Silver had told me about seeing Maggie die, a tiny part of me had wanted to believe he'd somehow gotten it wrong.

"You supplied DNA to the Berlin police, so they should have confirmation that it's Maggie within a couple of days. If the time comes, I'll go with you to claim the body," Ronan said gently.

I managed a nod. "Petrov's got ties to the Kremlin. We all know he won't serve a day behind bars."

Mav and Ronan exchanged glances. "We'll be taking care of that. But the police will connect Maggie's death to Petrov. You'll be their first suspect if something happens. The plan is to use them as your alibi."

"Who, the Berlin police?" I asked.

"You'll be at police headquarters in Berlin answering questions about your sister when Petrov is terminated. We've already got someone in place. He's just waiting for the order," Mav explained.

"It's the surest way to keep you with your family, Jace. Nothing, not even revenge, is worth risking losing Caleb and Willa, is it?" Ronan asked.

I automatically shook my head. He was absolutely right.

Which meant I had to rely on these men to take care of everything. To give my sister justice, to help me bring her home, to keep my new family safe, to make sure I came back to them… it was a hefty ask, but I already knew what my answer was.

"Tell me what you need me to do," I said.

"We'll keep you in the loop on everything, Jace," Ronan vowed.

"The kid who saved Willa," I began. "We need to get him out of there if he's still alive. His name is Silver. He said Petrov wouldn't kill him for helping Maggie, but I'm not sure if that's true or not. But if there's even a chance he's alive—"

"We'll look into it," Ronan said. "The man who's going to take Petrov out should be able to give us that information."

I didn't ask how they were going to manage any of that, because I didn't care. I just wanted to find the young man and do for him what he'd done for me and my sister.

The sound of Baby's nails clicking on the linoleum had me looking over my shoulder. The big dog had spotted Caleb as he was making his way toward us. That ridiculous flip-flopping sensation in my belly that always seemed to happen around him had me climbing to my feet. He walked right into my arms and I didn't give a shit that Mav was watching as I leaned in to kiss him.

"Everything okay?" I asked, because I could feel the tension in him.

He nodded. "Willa's asleep. Eli's with her." To Mav he said, "Eli wants to talk to you."

Mav instantly stood and hurried from the room. He patted Caleb on the shoulder as he walked past.

"I need to talk to you," Caleb said nervously. "Ask you something, really," he murmured.

"I'll just go call Daisy," Ronan said as he smoothly excused himself.

"Can we go for a walk?" Caleb asked as he motioned to the back yard.

"Sure." I took his hand in mine and led him from the house. Baby came with us. I noticed him take off toward the woods. Moments before the big dog reached the tree line, a man stepped out and knelt down to greet the dog. I smiled because I had no doubt the friendly animal had gotten in the habit of checking out all of Ronan's men who were guarding the perimeter of the property.

I led Caleb down to the beach where I knew we'd have a little bit of privacy. Ronan's men would still see us, but they wouldn't be privy to our conversation.

There was a huge bleached-out log sitting about a hundred feet up from the water, so I led Caleb to it and sat down. When he didn't automatically sit down next to me, I assumed he was feeling stressed enough that he didn't want to talk face to face, so I was about to offer that we sit on the sand so he could sit in front of me, but he surprised me when he stepped over my legs and settled his weight on my thighs. I automatically put my arms around him to support him.

"What is it, baby?" I asked when he remained quiet.

"I'm not fixed, Jace. I wish I was, but I'm not. No matter how many times you tell me you aren't leaving me, my mind refuses to believe it."

"Then your mind and I are going to need to have a serious talk, because I'm not going anywhere."

He stared into my eyes for a long time. "I want to get some help," he finally said. "I want to be worthy of you."

When I went to respond, he covered my mouth with his hand. "I know I am, here," he said as he removed his hand from my mouth and placed it over his own heart. "But I'm not so sure up here." He pointed to his head. "I know you're right... that the things people love about me can't be lost, but I want more than that. I want there to come a day where I don't have to ask you the question that I'm going to ask you today and probably every day for the foreseeable future. Not because I think you'll get tired of answering, but because I shouldn't have to ask it. I need my own voice to be the one I listen to first. Does that make sense?"

I nodded, since I was struggling to find my own voice. I finally managed to say, "Ask me the question, baby."

"Promise me you're not leaving me, Jace," he whispered.

"I promise, Caleb. Martha Stewart couldn't drag—"

He let out a watery laugh and kissed me before I could finish. "I love you, Jace."

I tucked him against my neck and settled my lips against his ear so that there was no doubt he'd hear me. "I love you, Caleb. I'm so fucking proud to call you mine. Promise me you'll never leave me."

"Never," he croaked, his words almost getting lost on a warm breeze. "And if Martha Stewart ever makes a play for you, she better watch her back because I'll kick her ass."

I let out a bark of laughter and then wrapped my arms even tighter around him. "Everything will be okay, Caleb," I murmured. "Do you believe me?"

He nodded against my neck. "I believe you, Jace."

CHAPTER 22

CALEB

"Finally!" I jerked at the sound of Jace's voice at the same time that a blast of cool air went through the shower as the door was pulled open. I was about to protest the interruption when my eyes fell on Jace's body.

Jace's naked body.

Jace's gorgeous, naked, ripped body.

He stepped into the shower and pulled the door shut, then pressed up against me, stealing some of the water from the spray.

"Finally, what?" I asked. "Did you have trouble getting her down?"

"No, she was out before I even put her in the crib." He nuzzled the back of my neck. "*Finally*, we get a shower that's bigger than a phone booth."

"A phone booth? What's that?" I joked.

Jace's teeth closed over the lobe of my ear. "You'll pay for that, whippersnapper."

"Promise? Because I don't see any Sno Balls in here, and I'm not sure you can top what you did with those."

Jace's hands slid up and down my sides. "Challenge accepted," he murmured, then he turned my head and sealed his mouth over mine. I moaned into the kiss, then turned around in his arms and practically attacked him.

We'd been back in the U.S. for only three days and things had gone into overdrive. The pre-trial hearing I'd been scheduled to testify at had been pushed back by a week so that the lawyers could do yet more legal wrangling. I'd already been stressed about the whole thing, but also eager to get it over with so the actual trial could get scheduled and the entire ordeal would finally have an end in sight. So I hadn't exactly taken the news of the delay well. Especially when I'd learned the very same day that Jace was returning to Germany to claim his sister's body.

We'd ended up having our first real fight as a couple when I'd insisted on going with him and he'd refused to budge on the matter. We'd gone to bed angry, but when I'd had a chance to get past the irrational fear of losing him, I'd recognized how selfish I was being. I'd apologized to Jace and we'd spent several hours talking about his sister and family. It'd been a way to grieve her loss and still celebrate her life. The next morning, I'd helped Jace plan the funeral, which would happen when he returned. He'd decided to bury Maggie in Vermont with the rest of his family, so the plan was for me to fly out there and meet him for the service. Ronan was going with Jace to Germany, and Memphis and a couple of Ronan's other men were going to accompany me to Vermont. We'd decided to leave Willa with Mav and Eli so that Jace could focus on saying his goodbyes to his family.

That conversation had eased the way for others about our future. I'd been worried Jace would want to return to D.C. – something I would have done if he'd asked me to, despite the relationship I was finally starting to build with Eli – but Jace had been the one to suggest that we make our home in the Seattle area. We'd already started the process of looking for a house near Mav and Eli's, something I'd fully expected my brother and his fiancé to oppose with arguments about Jace and I not knowing each other well enough to make that kind of commitment. But they'd surprised me by being on board with the idea and letting us stay with them until we found a place. Of course, everything was contingent on the danger to me being eliminated.

Which wouldn't happen until my father was convicted.

I didn't even know what would happen if he wasn't.

Jace returned my desperate kiss as he maneuvered me back against the wall. The tiles were cold against my back, but it actually felt good because my entire body felt like it would go up in flames.

Since returning from Germany, Jace and I had fooled around some more, but we hadn't had sex again, mostly because I was weirded out at the prospect of getting off with my brother and his lover only a couple of doors down. I wasn't exactly quiet when it came to the things Jace did to me.

"We should have thought of this sooner," I said against Jace's mouth as his hand wrapped around my dick.

"Thought about what?"

"Bathroom," I muttered right before I let out a loud moan. Jace's talented fingers were massaging my balls in the most sinful way.

"Still gotta be quiet, babe," Jace reminded me. "You're a bit of a screamer."

No argument there.

"Then I guess you'll be doubly challenged tonight," I responded. I gasped when his hand returned to my dick. I pressed my head back against the wall and between breaths managed to say, "Top the Sno Ball thing *and* try to make me scream."

"Mmmm," Jace said as he grazed his teeth over my neck. "Let me see what I can do about that."

He gave my cock a few more strokes, then his hands slid to my ass and pulled me forward so our dicks were flush with one another. He began grinding against me, sliding our shafts along one another until I was certain that was how he was going to get us both off. But he surprised me by lifting me up.

"Put your legs around my waist," he urged.

I did.

He stepped forward until my back was once again against the wall. He used his body to pin me against the smooth tile, then reached between us. I thought he was going for my dick, but he went for his instead. Using his left hand, he slid his dick between my legs and canted my hips until his cock was riding the edge of the crack of my ass. Only he didn't leave it at that.

No, he tucked his dick *between* my crack and splayed his hand over my backside to keep his shaft lodged between my globes.

"Hold on to me," Jace ordered. I already had my arms around his neck, but when he used his other hand to grab my dick, I tightened both my arms and legs to keep from falling to the ground.

Jace began rocking against me and I groaned at the sensation of his dick sliding along my crack. Besides rimming me the one time, he hadn't messed with my entrance at all in the times we'd been together, so to feel his thick cock there now was a new sensation.

And a welcome one.

I knew he wasn't going to penetrate me with his dick – that wasn't something he'd ever do until he had my express permission – so I was able to relax enough to enjoy the pleasurable sensation of riding his cock. Not to mention that his other hand was slowly jerking me off, the drags on my flesh matching his thrusts against my ass.

Jace's mouth searched out mine. He kissed me gently and said, "Ready, baby?"

I nodded. I was ready for anything he gave me.

Jace shifted slightly to change the angle of how he was holding me and on his next thrust, the head of his cock brushed my hole. I gasped at how good it felt and ordered him to do it again.

He did.

Over and over he fucked my ass without actually fucking it. The sensation of his crown pressing against my entrance, but not actually penetrating it, became the ultimate tease and I found myself trying to move my body so that I could get him inside me.

Anything to deal with the sudden emptiness I was feeling.

"Oh God, Jace, fuck me, please."

I wasn't sure if I meant literally or not, but I knew Jace would take care of me. He'd ease the ache inside of me.

He continued to torment me with a dozen or more strokes that left me writhing against him. I demanded more and he gave it to me. I was sure he'd make me come that way, but I was suddenly afraid I'd still have the strange, bereft feeling when I finally did come.

"Jace—" I whispered, though I didn't really know what I was asking.

But Jace knew.

He suddenly released my dick and settled me on my feet, then dropped to his knees in front of me. His mouth closed over my cock and I immediately fisted my hands in his hair and began fucking the hot cavern. His right hand slid between my legs and up my ass, disappearing into my crease. When the pad of his finger massaged me, I groaned my approval. But when it began to press inside me, I lost the first part of our unofficial bet and screamed, "Yes, please!"

It should have hurt, but my body was eager for the intrusion after all the teasing. Not to mention that Jace was sucking my dick like he was my own personal Hoover. By the time his finger sank all the way inside me, I was slamming my dick into his mouth over and over, and fucking myself on his thick digit. It was heaven and hell. Too much and not enough.

My orgasm came rushing to the surface and I let out a wail of satisfaction when it finally crashed over me. Jace somehow managed to cover my mouth with his free hand, even as he kept up the powerful suction and smooth thrusts of his finger inside my body. I was certain the pleasure couldn't become any more intense until Jace did something with his finger inside of me that had an almost blinding light piercing my closed eyelids. Wave after wave of white-hot pleasure consumed my body and I literally could not control anything anymore. I emptied myself down Jace's throat as I screamed over and over into his palm. I was practically riding the arm he had between my legs, because that was all that was keeping me upright. I heard Jace let out a muffled shout around my cock and then he was pulling his mouth free and pressing his cheek against my thigh. My own climax was starting to ease, so I managed to look down just in time to see cum shooting from the head of Jace's dick.

The dick that he wasn't currently touching.

How the fuck was that even possible?

Like me, it took several minutes for Jace to recover from his release. He carefully pulled his finger free of my body and let me slide down the wall. We ended up in a tangle of limbs beneath the spray of hot water. There was no kissing or touching, just clinging.

And the only words I could manage to muster in my exhaustion were, "You win."

CHAPTER 23

JACE

Some of the pain in my chest eased as soon as I felt Caleb wrap his arms around me from behind. The funeral had ended nearly an hour earlier, but I'd stayed behind to watch the men work to put my sister's casket in the ground. I'd insisted that Caleb go with the others to the lodge for the wake, saying I'd be along shortly.

But it had ended up being harder to leave than I'd thought.

So it didn't surprise me in the least that Caleb had returned for me.

It had been Caleb's idea to ask the owners of the lodge my family had once owned to allow us to hold the wake there. They'd been very accommodating and Caleb had been the one to work with them to make all the arrangements.

The trip to Germany had gone off without a hitch. I'd still been sitting with a representative from the police department working out the arrangements for my sister's body when there'd been a flurry of excitement around us. The baffled-looking police captain had come striding into the room the representative and I had been in. He'd studied me for a long time, like he couldn't believe I was there, then he'd announced that Ivan Petrov had been shot in the head by an unknown assailant while in the parking garage of his office building. All four of Petrov's bodyguards had been taken out as well.

While he'd spoken to me in English, he'd conversed with the representative in German. I'd been able to follow along enough to understand what he was asking.

How long had I been with her and had I left at any time or made any phone calls? When the man had asked to see my phone, I'd readily handed it over.

Although suspicious, he'd left us alone after that. I'd played dumb, of course, by asking all the right questions about who Ivan Petrov was. But the officer had said he'd have to get back to me once the investigation had been concluded. He'd called me the following day as I'd been watching my sister's casket being loaded onto Ronan's plane. I'd only half-listened as he'd explained that Ivan Petrov was the primary suspect in my sister's murder. I'd faked my surprise and subsequent confusion about the man's death and then had thanked the officer for all he and his department had done to find my sister.

I hadn't meant a single word of any of it.

It was while at the airport waiting for the plane to go through its final preparations before takeoff that a black SUV had rolled onto the tarmac and Ronan and another man had gotten out of the front seats. I hadn't recognized the man, though I'd had a good idea of who he was, and I'd gone to shake his hand.

It'd been the least I could do to thank him for getting justice for my sister.

While I'd been thanking him, Ronan had opened the back door. If it hadn't been for the eerie silver eyes, I wouldn't have recognized the young man covered in bruises. Silver had clearly been right that Petrov wouldn't kill him for his betrayal, but I had no doubt he'd suffered every second of every day after having been returned to the man. Once we'd gotten Silver settled on the plane and he'd fallen asleep, Ronan had told me that the young man had refused Ronan's offer to examine him. The plan had been to get Silver on U.S. soil and take him to a hospital, but when we'd told him as much after landing, he'd lost it and tried to get off the plane while it was still taxiing. It was only after I'd promised him on Willa's life that we wouldn't take him to the hospital that he'd settled somewhat.

I'd tried to talk to Silver a few times about what he'd endured after being returned to Petrov, but he'd barely spoken to me. It was only when I'd shown him pictures of Willa on my phone that he'd shown any kind of emotion. I'd explained that the plan was to stop in Vermont for the funeral and then continue on to Seattle in a couple of days, but Silver hadn't acknowledged the information in any kind of meaningful way.

We'd gotten him a room at the lodge, but hadn't seen much of him. He had shown up for the funeral, but he'd remained on the outskirts of the small crowd. My hope was that he'd gotten a ride back to the lodge with someone, because I'd been too preoccupied to make sure.

"Did you see Silver at the lodge?" I asked Caleb.

"Yes," he said softly. He came around to stand at my side. "But he went to his room right away. I tried to talk to him, but he asked me to leave him alone. Do you think he'll be all right?"

I shook my head because I just didn't know. The young man had clearly been traumatized and I had no clue how to help him.

"It was a beautiful service, Jace. She was well-loved."

I nodded. Many of Maggie's friends had attended the funeral and said really nice things about her.

I stared at the row of five headstones.

"I need to make sure she's always a part of Willa's life," I said. "Will you help me do that?" I asked.

Caleb nodded. "She'll always be with us, Jace. We'll make sure of it. And when Willa's ready, we'll bring her back here and show her where she comes from. The lodge, the gift shop, the dreaded bunny hill…"

I smiled and tightened my arm around him.

"Let's go back to the lodge," Caleb suggested.

I nodded and dropped my hand to search out his. He linked our fingers and led me to the waiting car. I was glad to see he had two of Ronan's men with him.

Once back at the lodge, we ran into Dalton, who was making his way through the lobby, his bag in hand. He was moving slowly, which meant he was probably in a good deal of pain.

"Are you heading out?" I asked.

He nodded. "It's a long drive."

I wanted to tell him he shouldn't have come, since I knew how hard traveling was on his body, but my argument would have fallen on deaf ears. "I could find someone to take you home," I offered, though I knew what his answer would be.

He shook his head.

Yep, it was exactly the answer I'd expected.

Dalton was a man of few words.

"Thank you for coming. Will you let me know when you make it home?" I asked.

Dalton nodded. I didn't try to embrace him, because he wasn't a big fan of physical contact. I shook his hand.

"You two take care," he said, then pushed past us.

"He hates me," Caleb murmured.

"He hates just about everyone," I said. I knew Caleb thought Dalton had feelings for me, but I wasn't so sure. I'd known Dalton long enough to suspect what the issue was. Just like he'd been my only friend, I'd been his only link to the outside world. He'd known just from the way I'd talked about Caleb two years earlier what it would mean when the day came that Caleb came back into my life.

And he'd been absolutely right.

I'd been able to spend a few minutes with Dalton the night before and had told him that I was making the move to Seattle a permanent thing. He'd already suspected as much, but when I'd asked him to consider moving himself, he'd almost instantly shot me down.

"He doesn't do change well," I said to Caleb. "It took him a long time to get to where he is and he won't give that up for anyone – not even if it means he's going to spend the rest of his life alone."

Caleb sighed. "We'll keep working on him," he said, his voice ringing with determination. I looked at him and he smiled. "He's your family, Jace. That makes him my family, and he should be with his family."

I brushed my mouth over his. "You're an amazing man, Caleb Cortano."

"Let's go collect some more stories about your sister to share with Willa," he suggested.

I sighed and followed him to the room where the wake was being held. The hour that followed was bittersweet. I got to hear a lot about my sister that I hadn't known, but the ache in my chest that came along with knowing she wasn't going to walk through the door at any moment and announce it had all been a mistake was profound. By the time the wake ended and Caleb and I were back in the room, I was completely worn out.

But just as Caleb and I were getting ready to lie down, Ronan came to our room to tell us that Silver was nowhere to be found. Ronan had gone to check on him and when there hadn't been a response, he'd grown worried that the young man had passed out because of his injuries. He'd gotten the manager to open the door for him, but there'd been no sign of Silver, and the few belongings we'd gotten for him, including some toiletries and a couple of changes of clothes, were still in the room.

"Let's search the lodge," Ronan suggested. "I'll have my guys head toward town to see if he went there for some reason."

My phone rang before Ronan even finished. Seeing that it was Dalton, I answered. "Hey, you okay?" I asked.

"Yeah," Dalton said. "Listen, about that kid you guys had with you… the one with the weird eyes?"

"Have you seen him?" I asked as I snapped my fingers at Ronan to keep him from leaving the room. I put the phone on speaker.

"Yeah, he's with me."

"What?" I asked in surprise.

"I picked him up when I saw him walking along the highway leading to the interstate."

"Thank God," I muttered as I sat down on the bed. "Where are you? We'll come to you."

"Um, yeah, well…"

"What?" I asked at Dalton's hedging.

"He only agreed to get in my car if I promised not to take him back to the lodge. I tried to find out why, but he won't talk to me. Just told me to take him to the nearest bus station. I asked him if he even had money for a bus ticket."

"What did he say?" I asked. I knew Silver likely didn't have any money.

"Said it wasn't a problem. Said he'd be able to earn some."

I swallowed hard because I knew exactly how the young man was planning to earn it.

"Don't take him there, Dalton. We'll come get him. We'll talk to him."

Dalton was silent for a moment. "I got him to agree to come with me, Jace. Back to Elkton. He fell asleep a few minutes ago, so I wanted to call you to give you a heads-up."

"You're taking him home with you?" I asked.

"Well, I wasn't going to let him fucking do whatever it was he was gonna do to get money for a bus ticket," Dalton snapped.

Dalton's agitation surprised me. He rarely showed any kind of anger – he was more of a slow burn type who was likely to shut down before blowing up. "What are you planning to do with him, Dalton?" I asked.

"No fucking clue," the man muttered. Dalton lowered his voice. "But the kid is messed up. Only way I could get him to agree to come with me was to promise I'd give him the money he would have earned at the bus station."

"I don't understand," I said.

"He thinks I'm buying him for the night, Jace," Dalton said in a harsh whisper.

"Dalton—"

"Don't, Jace," Dalton snapped. "You know I wouldn't—"

"I know that. That wasn't what I was going to say."

I took the phone off speaker to give Dalton privacy for what I wanted to say next. "Dalton, I know you're hurting right now… more than usual. Silver isn't your responsibility. Let me come get him."

"Silver? That's his name?" Dalton asked softly. He went silent and I could practically see him looking at the young man in his passenger seat. "He wouldn't say how he knew you guys."

"He saved Willa. We owe him everything."

The man was silent for a moment, then said, "I'll call you when we get to my house, Jace."

With that, he hung up. I shook my head and looked at Ronan. "Let's see what things look like in the morning."

Ronan nodded. "We can fly down there and get him if your friend can convince him to come with us. But we can't force him."

I nodded. Caleb sat down next to me and put his hand on my knee. Ronan said his goodbyes and left the room. To Caleb, I said, "He'll be okay. Dalton will take care of him."

Caleb sent me a small smile, then reached up to tuck a stray lock of hair behind my ear. "Let's get some rest, Jace. Things will look brighter tomorrow."

I wasn't as certain, but I nodded anyway and didn't argue when Caleb took my phone and set it on the nightstand, then did what he did best.

He took care of me.

~

Things didn't look brighter the next day or any in the week that followed. We hadn't had much time to dwell on the fact that no amount of convincing could get Silver to come to Seattle. Fortunately, he was still with Dalton, but I wasn't sure how long that would last. The idea of the young man disappearing all together terrified me. With no money or family, he literally had nothing, and there were only two places he could end up if he left Dalton's place.

Either on his knees in an alley somewhere servicing a random stranger for a few bucks.

Or dead.

As much as I would have liked to go to Maryland myself to try and talk to Silver, Caleb had to be my first priority.

Because for all the progress he'd made in the past few weeks, it had become more and more difficult for him to hold it together as we'd neared the date of the pre-trial hearing. I'd managed to get him to share his feelings, rather than him bottling them up, but he was still a wreck about the whole thing.

"It'll be okay," I said softly as I squeezed my fingers tighter around Caleb's hand. We were standing outside the judge's chambers waiting for the prosecutor.

Caleb nodded, but didn't say anything. He was holding onto my hand so tight that if he'd been a stronger man, he likely would have caused me some serious pain.

"There he is," Eli said. He was leaning against Mav, who had his arm around him. I followed Eli's nod and saw a tall man in his early thirties walking toward us.

"Eli," he said as he shook Eli's hand, then said his hellos to Mav.

"Caleb, good to see you again," he said.

"Mr. Morrison," Caleb said with a nod. "Um, this is Jace, my boyfriend."

I forced myself to nod politely as the man introduced himself to me. Caleb had been worried the man would rail at him for the letter Caleb had sent his father in prison, but he'd assured Caleb that he'd seen the letter and it could easily be explained away in court - a fact that had eased some of Caleb's attention.

Morrison turned his attention went back to Caleb. "Are you ready? I got a text from the defense that they're already in there," he said as he motioned to the doors.

Caleb sucked in a breath and said, "I'm ready."

But the second the four of us fell into step behind the prosecutor, the man turned to us and said, "Oh, I'm sorry, it's a closed hearing. You won't be able to join us. It's just me, Caleb, the defense attorney, his client, and the judge."

"What?" Caleb croaked. "His... his client?"

Caleb's startled eyes swung to me, then Eli. "Dad... Dad will be in there?"

"Baby," I said, desperate to get his attention, but he jerked his hand free of mine.

"No, no, you never said he'd be in there," Caleb said to the prosecutor. Then he turned to me. "Jace, I can't," he cried. "Please, you have to come with me!"

"Caleb—" the prosecutor began, but Caleb cut him off with a wave. He grabbed my wrists.

"Jace, please, I can't go in there. I can't see him. I'm not ready!"

"It's okay," I said as calmly as I could, even though I wanted to punch the prosecutor in the face. To him I said, "There must be something you can do. Talk to the judge—"

"No, I'm sorry, that's not possible." To Caleb he said, "Caleb, I'm sorry, but it needs to be this way."

Caleb shook his head frantically. He'd gone so pale that he was scaring me.

"Can you delay the hearing?" Eli asked.

The prosecutor shook his head. "No, we've already delayed once. Without a legitimate reason..."

The man let his words hang.

Caleb stepped back. He was struggling to pull in oxygen. "Caleb," I began, but he cut me off.

"I'm... I'm okay. I just... I need a minute." Despite his words, he didn't look okay. His gaze fell on the prosecutor. "Can I go to the bathroom?"

"That's fine," he said. "I'll just head in and let the judge know. The bailiff will escort you in when you're ready." He nodded at the stern-looking court officer standing a few feet away.

Caleb was already hurrying away before the prosecutor even finished talking. I only half-listened as the man apologized to me, Eli, and Mav for the confusion. I kept sight of Caleb as he made his way down the hall to the bathroom.

Not liking how calm Caleb had suddenly gotten, I said, "I'm going to go check on him." I didn't care that I'd cut the prosecutor off mid-sentence.

It took a good thirty seconds to work my way through the small crowd that had emerged from one of the courtrooms near the bathroom and my anxiety crept up with every single one of those seconds.

The first thing I noticed when I walked into the bathroom was that it was empty, except for one closed stall at the end. The second thing I noticed was that a small corner of the large mirror was broken and that several pieces of glass were on the floor.

My heart was pounding in my chest as I rushed to the last stall. "Caleb!" I shouted.

"I'm sorry, Jace," I heard him softly say.

I was about to break the door down when the latch flipped. I yanked it open and felt my heart sink at the sight of Caleb leaning back against the side of the stall, his jacket removed and his sleeve rolled up.

And there they were.

Three perfect cuts on the inside of his lower arm.

I felt my throat close up with tears as my eyes lifted to meet Caleb's gaze. He looked both heartbroken and relieved at the same time. "I'm sorry," he whispered. A couple of tears slipped down his face.

"Caleb?" I heard Eli call behind me.

Caleb let out a choked sob and I quickly pulled him into my arms, not caring about the blood on his arm. "It's okay," I whispered softly into his ear. Caleb began to cry.

"I had to," he croaked.

"I know, baby," I assured him.

I heard a gasp behind us, but didn't need to see who it was.

"I'll stand guard outside," I heard Mav say.

"Caleb," Eli cried out, and as I released Caleb, I saw Eli turning to get some paper towels from the dispenser.

"I'm sorry," Caleb told his brother.

"It's okay," Eli said, his voice shaky as he gently pressed the paper towels to the wounds.

Caleb let out a rough sob and then he was pushing into Eli's arms. I took over holding the paper towels against Caleb's arm as his brother held him and just let him cry. When Caleb had calmed, Eli released him and gently pulled him from the stall. We got him to the sink and Eli held onto Caleb as I quickly cleaned the cuts. Fortunately, they weren't deep.

"I'll go tell the prosecutor we're not doing this today," Eli said as he wiped at his brother's face.

"No," Caleb said, grabbing Eli's arm before he could leave. "Please, I need to do this now. I'll... I'll be okay." His eyes fell to his own arm, then he was looking at me. "Jace, please, I have to do this."

"We can talk to the judge... try to explain."

Caleb shook his head. "If he finds out about this," – he motioned to his arm – "he might say I'm crazy or something. He'll believe my father's story that I made all of it up."

Part of me knew he was right, but the other part of me just wanted to get him home where I could keep him safe. I traded glances with Eli and could tell he was just as reluctant as me to let this continue. But Caleb *did* seem calmer and while I hated how he'd gone about it, I couldn't take this from him – he'd never be able to move on with his life if his father walked.

I finally nodded, and when Caleb looked at Eli, he said, "If you have to stop at any time while you're in there, you just tell the prosecutor and that's it. No arguments," he said firmly.

"Okay," Caleb said solemnly. "Promise."

As he and Eli talked, I covered the still-bleeding cuts with some more paper towels and used my hair tie to secure the makeshift bandage to his arm, much like he had the day he'd hurt himself when we'd boarded Dalton's boat. Luckily, there wasn't any blood on his shirt. Eli helped him get his jacket back on and then I took his hand in mine and led him from the bathroom. When we reached the judge's chambers, I held him for a long time and whispered in his ear that I'd be there the moment he was done and that I loved him. He nodded against me, but didn't speak.

My gut was screaming at me that I was making a terrible mistake by letting him do this, but I forced myself to let Caleb go.

For once, I hated that my instincts were usually spot-on.

Because less than thirty minutes later, a very pale and deathly silent Caleb emerged from the room.

And I completely lost it.

Because I'd only seen him like this one other time - that first night in the cabin when I'd discovered the scars on his arm and he'd told me that he was too far gone to fix.

"Caleb, baby, talk to me," I said, gathering him in my arms as soon as he exited the doorway. But it was like he wasn't even hearing... or feeling me.

My eyes fell on Jack Cortano as he left the room in cuffs, sandwiched between two guards. He threw us a smug smile over his shoulder, which had me releasing Caleb and striding after him. But Mav got in my way.

"Don't!" he bit out when I tried to push past him. "Caleb needs you now," he said firmly.

I turned to see that Caleb was in Eli's arms, but he wasn't reacting to his brother either.

He was just... gone.

"What the fuck happened?" I snapped at the prosecutor as I returned to Caleb's side.

The man looked stricken. "His father said something to him."

"What?" I asked. "What did he say?"

"He was smart – waited until the hearing was over and the judge had left," the man muttered.

"What did he say?" I asked impatiently.

The prosecutor opened his mouth, then seemed to think better of it. He grabbed my arm and pulled me aside so Caleb wouldn't hear us.

"He said, 'Caleb, I love you, my sweet boy. We'll be together again soon.' The second he said it, Caleb just froze. It was like... like this switch got flipped inside of him," the man said softly, his gaze going to Caleb.

A chill went through me because I had no doubt that that was exactly what had happened.

Mav was the one to say our goodbyes to the prosecutor because Eli and I were still trying to get any kind of response out of Caleb.

By the time we got Caleb back to the Whidbey Island house, he was barely functional. He hadn't spoken or cried. Even seeing Willa didn't have any kind of effect on him. I got him settled in our bed and crawled in with him, hoping like hell I'd get some kind of reaction out of him.

But there was nothing. Just like there was nothing three days later.

He stayed in the same position in bed, no matter how much I begged and pleaded with him to come back to me. He roused from bed only long enough to drink something or go to the bathroom, and nothing more.

It was like I wasn't even there.

"Caleb," I whispered as I settled my lips on the back of his neck. We were in the same place we'd been from day one. Lying in the middle of the bed with my arms wrapped around him from behind. Baby had become Caleb's shadow from the moment we'd gotten back to the house, and I had no doubt the big animal could sense something was very wrong with the young man. He was currently lying along Caleb's front and while Caleb wasn't interacting with him, the dog only left his side when Eli took him outside.

I rubbed Caleb's arm. "I'm here, baby. I'm not going anywhere. So you take as long as you need to, but I *will* be here when you're ready to come back to me." I leaned over him as I spoke and while the sight of the single tear sliding down his cheek hurt like hell, it also brought a certain measure of relief.

Because it was *something*.

And right now, I'd literally take any proof that he could still hear me.

Wherever he was.

CHAPTER 24

CALEB

You're Daddy's sweet boy, aren't you, Caleb?
Yes, Dad.
Daddy... say it.
Yes, Daddy.
No one will ever love you like I do, you know that, right?
Yes, Daddy.... but it hurts, Daddy.
It'll only hurt this first time... Do you believe me, my sweet boy?"
"Yes, Daddy."

I squeezed my eyes closed even tighter as bile crawled up the back of my throat. I waited for the nausea to pass and tried to take in my surroundings.

I was really warm, almost hot, even. There was a body at my back... and front. The body at my back was long and warm and fit me perfectly. The one at my front was shorter, stocky, smelled a bit and was very, very hairy.

And unlike the body at my back, the one at my front was awake... and could tell I was too because a wet tongue lapped over my face a couple of times before a cold nose pressed against my neck. I stifled a chuckle and ran my hand over Baby's head.

"Someone's been feeding you hot dogs," I said softly. They were the dog's favorite.

"He wouldn't eat," I heard someone say. I lifted my eyes to see Eli sitting in an armchair near the bed. "Neither of them would."

I knew who he was talking about. I put my hand behind me so I could feel Jace's body. He stirred a bit and tightened his hold on my waist, but didn't wake up.

"What day is it?" I asked. Eli looked like shit, so I had no doubt it wasn't just Jace and Baby who hadn't left my side for however long I'd been lost in my own little world.

"Saturday."

Four days.

I'd gone silent for four days.

And I'd hurt myself again.

In front of Jace.

And Eli.

All because I hadn't had the strength to deal with the idea of spending even a single second in the same room as my father or the thirty minutes that followed in which my father had pretended to watch me lovingly from his seat not ten feet from me. But he'd really sealed the deal by calling me *sweet boy*.

He hadn't called me that in a long time, but the second he'd uttered the two words, it was like my body had been once again lying beneath his as I'd sought to escape into the darkness of my mind where there was no pain, no sense of betrayal.

"Where's Willa?" I asked.

"She's with Seth and Ronan. They were going to take her to Magnus and Dante's house today. It's Leo's birthday, so Dante and Magnus are going to watch her while Ronan and Seth take their kids to the party."

"Will you take me to see her?" I asked.

Eli nodded. He didn't ask why I was making the request.

I figured it was because he probably already knew why.

"I'll give you two a second," Eli said. He got up and urged Baby to follow him. I gave the big dog a pat as he got off the bed, then carefully rolled over so I was facing Jace. He looked as exhausted as I felt. I ran my fingers over his face and through the curls of his hair. I smiled as I remembered how often I'd imagined being able to do this very thing. Now he was mine and I could do it to my heart's content.

And probably would.

He came awake slowly, but the second his eyes landed on mine, he closed them and let out this huge sigh of relief. "Thank you," he whispered, though I wasn't sure who he was thanking. He opened his eyes again and then tugged me closer to him.

"I'm sorr—"

That was all I got out before he kissed me. It was a sweet, searching kiss that I felt in the very marrow of my bones and it chased away the little bit of the remaining chill that my father's words had left behind.

"Missed you," Jace said softly.

"Missed you too," I responded. "I heard you, Jace. Every word. I felt every touch. It made it easier to come back to you."

He nodded and caressed my face. "Not going anywhere, Caleb," he reminded me.

I knew we'd have to talk about what I'd done at the courthouse to deal with my stress, but I instinctively knew Jace would let me talk to him about when *I* was ready.

"Eli's going to take me to see Willa."

"I'll come with you," Jace said, but when he started to move, I grabbed his wrist.

"Stay here and sleep, Jace. I know you haven't," I said as I ran my thumb along one of the dark circles beneath his eyes. "Mav and Eli will be with me, and I'm sure we'll take at least one other of Ronan's guys with us. Knowing Mav, it'll probably be ten."

Jace didn't smile. I could tell he didn't want to heed my request.

"I need this, Jace."

I was glad when he didn't ask me to explain. It wasn't something I really understood myself. While I loved being able to lean on Jace, I wanted there to be a day where I didn't *have* to. But I needed to start with baby steps.

"Okay, call me when you get there," he said with resignation.

"I'll text you so I don't wake you," I amended.

He nodded and I kissed him. I could tell it was hard for him to let me go, but he did.

I took a few minutes to get cleaned up in the bathroom and changed my clothes. Eli and Mav were waiting for me downstairs. Eli had a bottle of water for me and what had to be the biggest sandwich I'd ever seen. He thrust it at me and said, "Eat every bite or no kid."

I smiled and wrapped my arms around him. He looked like death warmed over, but he was still taking care of me. I released him and said to Mav, "When we get home, he doesn't leave your bed for at least a week, do you hear me? I don't care what you have to do to keep him there."

"I'm sure I can think of something to keep him occupied," Mav said with a wink. Color flushed my brother's cheeks.

To me he said, "Eat your sandwich." To Mav it was, "Get in the car before I take you up on that offer right now."

I followed them out to the car, forcing myself to eat the sandwich. I wasn't particularly hungry, but I knew I needed to get something in my system.

The drive to Magnus and Dante's house took a couple of hours, since we had to take the ferry to the mainland. It gave my addled mind time to clear and by the time we reached the house, a thought had started to take form in my mind. I set it aside as Magnus ushered us inside. I knew the party was taking place across the street at Leo's house, because I'd seen several balloons in the shape of Avenger characters attached to the mailbox, and I could hear kids shouting from the back yard.

"How are you feeling?" Magnus asked.

"Better," I said.

"Well, she's back here," Magnus said as he led me down a hallway. Mav and Eli stayed in the living room, presumably to give me privacy with Willa.

Magnus opened a door for me. I'd assumed it would be either his and Dante's room, or the room I knew they kept for Magnus's grandson, Matty, for when he spent the night with them, but I was wrong on both counts.

It was Aleks's room.

I could tell from the simple furnishings and lack of superhero paraphernalia. Not to mention that Aleks himself was in the room. He was lying on the floor next to Willa, who was lying on her back on a blanket. Aleks was holding the small stuffed panda that Silver had given us in Germany – the one he'd said was Willa's favorite.

He'd been right.

The toy never failed to soothe the baby when she was particularly fussy.

"Aleks," Magnus called. Despite how quietly he'd said Aleks's name, the young man still jumped. His wide eyes went from Magnus to me and it took him a second to relax.

"Oh, sorry," he said as he sat up. He carefully picked Willa up and cradled her against his chest.

Magnus put his hand on my back and sent me a nod before leaving me and Aleks alone. As I entered the room, Aleks said, "I just gave her a bottle and burped her. I hope that's okay."

I nodded. "Of course, thank you."

Aleks shifted nervously. "She's a really good baby," he offered.

"She is," I agreed. I couldn't help but think he almost seemed reluctant to give her up. I couldn't say I blamed him.

"You didn't want to go to the birthday party?" I asked, more to give Aleks a few more minutes with Willa than anything else.

"Crowds aren't really my thing," he murmured. "I know I need to push myself a bit more, but a party for twelve seven-year-olds?" He smiled and shook his head.

I wasn't sure what he'd meant by pushing himself more, but I suspected it had to do with his past. Knowing he'd gone through what Maggie had, but for even longer, broke my heart. But I knew he probably didn't want my pity.

"I didn't like those parties when I *was* seven," I said. "So I hear ya."

Aleks relaxed a bit more, then stepped forward and handed Willa to me. He looked a lot like his older brother, though he had short hair while Dante's was long like Jace's. I knew both brothers were of Brazilian descent, but that was all I really knew. I guessed Aleks to be a little older than me.

Willa gurgled and sent me a lopsided smile as I took her from Aleks. The tightness I'd been feeling in my chest eased.

"It's incredible, isn't it?" I whispered. "Those eyes…"

I shifted my gaze to Aleks and he nodded. "Makes everything else go away for a bit."

"Yeah," I said. "That's it exactly."

A look of sadness passed over Aleks's features, but he masked it by dropping his eyes. "Well, I'll leave you two alone."

"Or you could stay," I suggested. "I don't know the first thing about kids and everyone's always talking about how you have a way with them."

Aleks seemed reluctant, but there was also something in his eyes that looked a lot like longing. He finally nodded. "If you're sure," he said.

I nodded. There was a minute or two of awkward silence as we got settled on the floor. I held Willa while Aleks pretended to attack her with the panda, which had Willa making all sorts of cooing noises. Our conversation was stilted at first, but by making Willa the focus of it, it got easier and easier, and as she fell asleep in my arms, we started talking about other things.

Simple things.

And as we talked, things began to fall in place and my mind felt less and less jumbled.

It was a good hour before Eli came to check on us. Aleks helped me to my feet. I surprised him when I handed Willa back to him. "Do you think you can watch her for a while longer?"

"Yeah, sure," he said, slightly confused.

I turned to Eli who seemed equally confused. "Don't you want to take her home?" he asked.

"I need to do something first." I pushed past him and went to the living room. As expected, I found Mav there. He got to his feet when he saw me.

"Everything okay?" he asked.

"No," I said. "But it will be. I need you to take me to see my father."

～

They were putting me in the same room with him.

I hadn't been expecting that.

I'd assumed there'd be a pane of plexiglass separating us and we'd have to talk through phones.

Clearly, I'd watched way too much television.

The guard who'd explained the rules to me wasn't the same one who was going to bring my father into the room, but both he and the guard with my father would stay to monitor us.

A fact I was supremely grateful for.

Because even though I was determined to do this, I was still scared shitless.

The guard had explained that because my father needed to be kept separate from the other inmates for his own protection, it would just be us in the room, despite there being several tables and chairs available so multiple visits could happen at once. I hadn't asked why my father was being kept separate, though I had a pretty good idea. I had a feeling the crime shows I'd seen had gotten the part about suspected child molesters not doing well in prison right.

I hadn't been allowed to take my phone into the room with me, so I had to use the clock on the wall to check what time it was. By now Jace probably knew where I was, since I'd asked Mav only to wait to call him when he was sure Jace wouldn't be able to get to the prison before us to stop me. I'd have a lot of explaining to do to Jace, but I was prepared for it.

I might not have been as strong as he would have liked me to have been before doing this, but I needed it to be now. I'd told Eli not to let my father have so much power over him, but I'd been a hypocrite. The proof had been in my behavior before and after the hearing.

I'd had a lot of time to think as we'd made the trip to Magnus and Dante's house, and interacting with Aleks and Willa had cemented the deal for me. I didn't need to know Aleks's entire story to know how he must have suffered. And yet he battled on every day to build a life for himself. He'd spent more years being brutalized than not, and he was still here. And Willa... Willa just changed the game entirely. I'd spent the last four days not being there for her because of my father and his manipulations.

That just wasn't acceptable to me on any level. It was like some of his ugliness was reaching through me and down to her.

No, it had to be today, now.

I forced myself to sit still and not reach for my right arm like I wanted as I waited. When the door on the opposite side of the room opened, I felt my mouth go dry and a bitter chill ran through my body, then I suddenly went hot all over. The need to run was great, but instead, I looked over at the guard. I wasn't sure, but I thought he sent me a little nod, like he wanted to make sure I knew he wasn't going anywhere.

But I was probably overthinking.

I forced my eyes back to my father. Amazingly, he looked very different from when I'd seen him at the hearing. I knew it wasn't possible for him to have suddenly aged dramatically overnight, so I had to assume I'd been seeing him through a child's eyes at the hearing.

Now all I saw was an old, frail man. He'd clearly lost a considerable amount of weight and his skin was pale. He wasn't wearing any cuffs on his wrists or feet, but he still moved slow for someone his age. It was hard to see any of the man who'd so often held me down as he'd brutalized me.

But the cruelty was still there in his eyes, which latched on to me the moment he entered the room and held on for the slow walk to me.

For once, though, I didn't feel the urge to look away.

He settled in the chair across from me and I was supremely glad the table was wide enough that he couldn't inadvertently touch my legs beneath it. He'd have to actually extend his leg to make contact with me and with the guards watching, I doubted he'd be that brazen.

My father's face softened as he took me in, but it wasn't real. His eyes were dark and cold.

"My sweet—"

"Shut up," I bit out.

I was satisfied to see his eyes go wide for a moment. When he made a move to touch my hand where it was resting on the table, I said, "You sure you want to do that?"

At the same time, the guard called out, "No contact!"

My father's brittle eyes held mine for a moment before he looked at the guard who'd escorted me into the room. "Sorry, Officer Phelps. I've just really missed my boy, here."

Despite the silky smoothness of my father's words, Officer Phelps didn't relax his stance even a little. When the big man's eyes met mine, I saw that thing again.

That silent message that gave me this weird boost.

Like the man knew what I was trying to do.

I turned my attention back to my father.

"Caleb," he began, but I cut him off.

"They gave me fifteen minutes with you, but I only need two... if even that."

My father's mouth tightened a bit, but he remained silent.

"I keep asking myself how my father could do the things he did to me and still claim to love me."

"Caleb, son, I didn't do anything—"

"But earlier today when I was holding the little girl who will someday call me her father, I realized that you stopped being that to me the moment you laid eyes on me and no longer saw your son. Because fathers don't do that shit to their kids. Period. Monsters do, not fathers. So I don't know the exact moment you stopped being my father and became that monster, but I know the exact moment I stopped being your son. It was thirty seconds ago when you walked through that door and I felt absolutely nothing for you. Not fear, not love, not regret, not even hatred. I came here for some kind of closure, but looking at you now, I understand that to need closure gives you too much credit. It means you still have some kind of hold on me."

I shook my head. "So do your worst, old man. Because nothing is going to stop me from showing up in that courtroom and telling the world what you did to me, to Eli, to Nick. And they'll believe me," I said confidently. "Because you said it yourself. I was your sweet, perfect boy. No skeletons in my closet. But there are plenty in yours and I'm going to make sure the world knows about all of them."

I pushed my chair back, ignoring the fury in the eyes of the man across from me. The man I refused to even mentally refer to as being my sire.

"By the way, Eli is getting married in two weeks. *Before* the trial. Because he's done trying to find closure too. He's done putting his life on hold for you. It won't be a small wedding, either. He and Mav are going to let the world know how much they love each other... they aren't going to slink off and hide because a handful of people believed your lies. They're even looking into having a baby. They're going to live their lives. We all are." I stood up and leaned down, hands pressed to the table. There was barely a foot separating us and I repeated the words that I'd believed for so very long.

"No one will ever love you like I do, my sweet boy." I held his gaze and said, "You're right, they won't. They're going to do it so much better."

With that, I turned to go.

"Caleb!"

I ignored his hoarse shout.

And the next one.

And every one that followed me out the door. I ignored the pounding on the door behind me and the shouts and muffled orders of the guard that was still in the room. The guard next to me didn't say anything until we reached the waiting area.

"Good luck to you, Mr. Cortano," he said.

"It's Galvez-Christenson," I said, figuring Eli and Jace wouldn't mind me borrowing their names going forward. Caleb Cortano didn't exist anymore.

As I made my way toward the parking lot where I knew Mav would be waiting for me, I smiled at how everything around me seemed different. Brighter, louder. It would definitely take some getting used to.

As I reached the final locked gate that guards had to let me through to get to the parking lot, I felt my mouth pull into a smile at the sight of the man waiting for me on the other side. He looked like he could spit nails, but the second I stepped through the gate and walked into his arms, he closed them around me and took in a deep breath.

"You okay?" Jace asked.

"You have no idea," I said as I tipped my head back to look at him.

"Found another piece, huh?"

I shook my head. "More like got rid of one."

He kissed me again. I knew there was a lot he probably wanted to say to me, and I sure as hell had a lot I wanted to tell him, but when I said, "Jace, let's go get our daughter and go home," he simply nodded and took my hand in his and led me to the car.

CHAPTER 25

JACE

It was the most overwhelming wedding I'd ever been to.

Not that I'd been to many, but still, I could categorically say I was completely lost.

Mostly because I had no hope in hell of remembering any of the names of the people I was introduced to, let alone their relationship to one another. By the time Mav had explained that Eli's younger brother, Tristan, was in a relationship with Brennan and Memphis, and that even though Brennan and Tristan had been raised as if they were cousins, they really weren't, I'd stopped trying to make any sense of it. Mav must have seen me zoning out, because he'd handed me off to the care of Matty Hawkins, the son of one of my teammates. Matty had taken over the introductions, which had actually been easier to follow than Mav's, but he'd gotten sidetracked by a conversation about Captain America, Thor, and Hawkeye. There'd also been mention of Spiderman, but when his two little friends had arrived, one wearing Spiderman pajamas and the other carrying a Spiderman doll, I'd given up again. Matty had mentioned something about flashcards and the next family dinner, then he'd ditched me for his buddies.

I'd lost Caleb to his best man duties. He and Brennan, who I *did* remember from the shooting at Eli's apartment two years earlier, were both standing for Eli, while Ronan and a man named Mace were standing as best men for Mav. I'd managed to hang on to Willa until Caleb's stepmother had arrived, at which point she'd promptly stolen away the little girl she'd started referring to as her granddaughter on the very first day she'd met the infant, and I'd been left on my own again. I'd gotten glimpses of Willa being passed around now and then, but I'd resigned myself to the fact that I wouldn't be getting her back any time soon and I'd found myself a seat.

The wedding was being held in a church on the outskirts of downtown Seattle in a surprisingly run-down neighborhood. I'd heard that the church was actually run by a pastor who was friends with one of my other teammates, Phoenix, and his husband Levi. The chapel was small, but everyone squeezed in, and those who couldn't find seats stood along the sides. There were flowers everywhere, courtesy of Aleks, who apparently worked for a florist. The young man was in attendance, but I'd gotten the impression that the large crowd made him nervous, so he'd spent most of his time in the back rooms, which had become a staging area of sorts. I'd seen Caleb disappear into the room several times, and it warmed my heart to know he was checking on his new friend.

The weeks before the wedding had brought about some profound changes in all our lives, the biggest being what had happened to Jack Cortano just two days after Caleb had visited him.

There was no explanation for it, but somehow there'd been a mix-up at the prison and Jack had been put into the general population. He'd been dead within a matter of hours. His body had been discovered in the showers. He'd been stabbed repeatedly with several homemade shivs. The prison had launched an investigation, but they'd yet to determine which inmates had killed him or how the mix-up had happened in the first place.

I'd been certain Ronan had somehow had a hand in the whole thing, but he'd assured me that he hadn't. We hadn't gotten any answers until a few days later when a guard from the prison had shown up at Mav and Eli's house on the mainland. Since Jack's death had meant the danger to Caleb was gone, we'd returned to Mav and Eli's home so it would be easier to finalize the plans for the wedding. The guard, a man named Phelps, had brought Caleb his phone back, which he'd left behind when he'd visited his father.

Caleb hadn't been home, but I'd used the opportunity to ask Phelps about the murder. He'd merely shrugged his shoulders and made an offhand remark about mistakes happening and inmates sometimes ending up in the wrong place at the wrong time. He'd then asked me to wish Mr. Galvez-Christenson well and he'd walked away. I'd mentioned the visit to Caleb, but I hadn't voiced my suspicions that the guard had somehow been involved in the "mistake" that had led to Jack's death. Caleb hadn't reacted much to the news of his father's murder. I'd been worried that he hadn't really processed it at first, but as the days had passed and he'd continued to act as relaxed as he'd been since the day he'd gone to the prison, I'd started to accept that Caleb had accomplished what he'd set out to do.

He'd said goodbye to that piece of his life and he didn't want or need it back.

Despite an exhaustive search, we were no closer to determining Rush's true identity. What we *had* discovered was a single call between the Jennings' house and the office of Jack's lawyer. It wasn't definitive proof that Jack had hired the men to kill Caleb, but the fact that Jennings had called Jack the morning Caleb had held him at gunpoint was pretty telling. And since the coroner investigating Jennings' suicide had ruled the man's death as such, we were at a dead end. Declan had planted the seed with the Bethesda police to investigate the death as a possible homicide, but they hadn't found any definitive proof of foul play.

To be safe, Caleb was still being accompanied by myself or one of Ronan's men at all times, but I'd finally agreed this morning to end the twenty-four-hour protection because Caleb needed a sense of normalcy that he hadn't ever really had.

Cutting ties with his father hadn't been some miracle cure for Caleb, a fact he'd acknowledged himself. The urge to cut still hit him when he got stressed, though he hadn't acted on it. And he still needed

Eli's and my reassurance on a daily basis that we weren't going anywhere. He'd started seeing a therapist, though he'd asked Eli if it would be okay if he saw someone different from the woman Eli saw. Caleb knew there would be a day where he'd want to tell Eli the truth about the level of Jack's obsession with him and the subsequent jealousy Caleb had felt as a result, but he wanted his relationship with Eli to be stronger before he tackled that particular issue. Seeing a different therapist gave Caleb a sense of being able to open up about everything without having to worry that the therapist would judge him out of deference to Eli.

Caleb's relationship with his stepmother had greatly improved and he often took Willa over there for visits. Mariana had given us both a crash course on the basics of caring for an infant and whenever we did have a burning question about something, we called her or any of the half-dozen people in our immediate circle of friends who knew their way around the ins and outs of babies. Caleb and I were still searching for a place of our own, but we weren't in any real rush. The proximity to Mav and Eli meant we had help with Willa and it gave Eli and Caleb a chance to reconnect.

Caleb had also started making some decisions about his life beyond therapy. He'd already begun the process of getting his GED with the hopes that he could go back to college to study computers. He was particularly interested in web design. It wasn't something he'd ever given a lot of thought to as a career, but one afternoon when he'd been visiting Aleks at the flower shop with Willa, he'd helped the woman who owned the shop fix a problem with her webpage. She'd gone on to ask him if he could redesign it, and while he considered the changes he'd done mediocre – a sentiment not shared by the grateful shop owner or Aleks – it had stirred an interest in him to learn more about the business of designing websites. It fed both his creative side and his intellectual side.

As Eli's brother Tristan began playing a small piano, the wedding guests got settled into the pews as the minister took his place at the front of the aisle. Dozens and dozens of strings of white lights strung across the ceiling lit up the dim interior of the church. When Tristan switched to the typical wedding march song, everyone shifted in their seats to watch the procession.

I felt my heart expand at the sight of Caleb walking next to Brennan. My man looked amazing in his tuxedo, but I also couldn't wait to get him out of it tonight when we got home. Caleb flashed me a smile as he passed, then he put his fingers out. I was sitting along the aisle, so I lifted my fingers to trail along his and I felt the familiar jolt of electricity that went through my arm and straight to my balls. But along with it came the rightness of it all. I knew this would be us someday – we'd have a big wedding like this one so that all the people who'd accepted us so willingly into their family could celebrate with us. But the honeymoon? I already knew what we'd do for that. I'd just have to see if Dalton would lend me his boat again.

Up next down the aisle were several little girls in dresses throwing flowers all over the place. After that came Eli. He was flanked by his father, Dom, and his mother. I automatically scanned the crowd to see where Willa was and was pleased to see that Aleks had her. He was standing near the doorway leading to the back rooms. He was pointing Caleb out to Willa and Caleb sent the little girl a discreet wave. I had no doubt our daughter recognized him.

Warmth spread through my chest and I instantly thought of Maggie. Moments like these were always bittersweet for me – I knew in my heart that it was best for Willa to see me and Caleb as her parents and that it was what Maggie would have wanted, but I would've gladly played the role of doting uncle for the rest of my life if I'd had any kind of say in it.

Mav came next down the aisle. His best men accompanied him. Following closely behind the men were the ring bearers.

To say they stole the show was an understatement.

Jamie, the youngest of the three boys, was holding one of Matty's hands. In his other hand was the Spiderman doll. In Matty's free hand was a pillow with one of the rings tied to it. Right behind Matty was his best friend, Leo. Even if I hadn't remembered him as Matty's bestie, he was hard to forget because he was still wearing the Spiderman pajamas. I had no clue what the significance of the outfit was, but I couldn't help but notice how relieved little Leo's fathers, who were sitting on the opposite side of the aisle from me, looked as they watched their boy make his way down the aisle, pillow with the second ring on it in one hand, Baby's leash in the other.

Once the boys reached the front, they handed the pillows to the best men closest to them, then went and found their seats in the front row. Mav and Eli couldn't take their eyes off one another throughout the entire ceremony and both cried at different points as they spoke their vows to one another. I felt myself choking up by the end, and when the two men were pronounced as husbands and kissed, I joined the rest of the guests as they got to their feet and cheered. It took a good thirty minutes for the church to empty as the guests made their way to the hotel ballroom Dom and his husband, Logan, had rented for the occasion. I was feeling pretty restless by the time Caleb made his way to me, but when I saw that he had Willa with him, I was able to relax.

It should have been frightening to think that being away from them both even for a couple of hours had been as stressful as it was, but I wasn't going to make excuses for it. Willa and Caleb had literally become my entire world in a matter of weeks, and nothing and no one was going to change that.

"Hey," Caleb said as he leaned in to kiss me. "Look what I found," he said as he gave Willa a little tickle. The baby made the familiar gurgling sound she always made when she was happy. One of Eli's female relatives had surprised us with a beautiful white dress she'd made for the baby – something we'd both been grateful for, since we hadn't even considered that the little girl should be dressed up for the occasion.

"They took her from me as soon as I walked in and wouldn't give her back," I whined. Caleb laughed and handed her to me. "Here you go, Papa," he said.

I held Willa in one arm and wrapped the other around Caleb as we headed toward our car.

"It was a beautiful ceremony, wasn't it?" he asked.

"It was," I agreed. "Got me thinking about some stuff," I admitted.

"Oh yeah?" Caleb asked, his eyes twinkling. "I might have been thinking about some stuff too."

"Hmm, interesting."

"What do you say we compare notes tonight?" Caleb suggested.

"I say H-E-double-hockey-sticks yeah," I responded.

Caleb laughed. "What do you say we do it in a suite at the hotel?"

I stopped and looked at him. He seemed suddenly nervous. "I, um, asked Mariana if she might want to babysit Willa tonight at Mav and Eli's house, since they're staying at the hotel tonight too. She said yes."

Before I could respond, he rushed on. "I, um, think I'm ready to, um, you know..."

I did know.

And it was something I really wanted, but was more than willing to wait for. Caleb and I had experimented some more with me using my finger on him, but that had been the extent of it. Even whenever he begged me to fuck him in the throes of passion, I held back because I wasn't about to take our first time together for granted. And when Caleb was ready, he would need to tell me. I'd told him as much.

And now he was telling *me* as much.

"What do you think?" Caleb asked.

"I think we need to google what the minimum amount of time is that you have to attend a wedding reception for before you can sneak away."

Caleb smiled wide and said, "You drive, I'll google."

~

Turned out that it was harder for a best man to sneak out of a wedding reception than the average guest. So I'd had to settle for dragging Caleb into alcoves and even the coat closet at one point to get things started and to remind him to hurry his ass up. It was on our second trip to the coat closet that we found the opportunity we needed to get permission to check out early.

But only because the coat closet was already taken.

By the very men we'd been about to plead our case to.

There'd been no need to tell Mav and Eli that I had a headache after the men had literally tumbled out of the closet when I'd pulled the door open. With Eli's pants undone and Mav's long hair pulled free of his hair tie and his bowtie askew, it had been a simple matter of Caleb and I agreeing to stall Dom, who was searching the ballroom for his son so he could start the speeches, for ten minutes. By buying the horny grooms those minutes, we'd been rewarded with permission to ditch the festivities early. We'd said our goodbyes to both men once they'd returned to the ballroom looking flushed and very, very satisfied, then we'd headed for the elevator. We'd also said our goodbyes to Mariana and told her we'd check in with her later in the evening. Aleks had offered to take Willa home to Magnus and Dante's house until Mariana picked her up. I suspected it was as much to escape the party as it was to help us and Mariana out.

I couldn't keep my hands off Caleb once the elevator doors closed us off from prying eyes. Fortunately, the elevator didn't make any stops, but we ended up giving some people waiting on our floor a bit of a show before we realized the elevator had stopped. Luckily, the older couple seemed more amused than anything else.

By the time we reached our room, Caleb was already working my jacket off my shoulders. As badly as I wanted to fuck him right there up against the door, I managed to get control of my raging need. I pinned him to the door and held him in place long enough to ease him back from his desire a few notches. When we next separated, we were both breathing hard, but my libido was back in check.

"Are you sure, baby?" I asked as I threaded my fingers through his hair.

"Yes," he said. "I've always trusted you, Jace. That was never the problem. I finally trust *me*. Even if I have a moment where the past tries to take this from us, I trust myself to get us past it. And if I can't do it, I trust myself to tell you, instead of trying to deny what I'm feeling."

I kissed him gently. "So proud of you, Caleb. I knew you'd see what I and everyone else see."

"I'm starting to," he said softly.

I took his hand and kissed it, then led him to the bedroom. The suite was extravagant, but in truth, I would have been just as happy to be back on Dalton's boat in the too-small bed. I stopped by the huge bed, but didn't lower Caleb on it. Instead, I began kissing him again. I took my time worshipping his body, careful not to take him too close to the edge. I knew there was probably a part of him that wanted to get the whole thing over with, just to prove to himself he could, but to me, he was a virgin, and I was going to make sure that his first time taking a man inside him was as memorable as he'd made the experience for me.

By the time I urged Caleb to lie down on the bed, he was shaking, but I knew it wasn't with fear. I urged him on his stomach and then lavished attention on his back. There wasn't a single part of him that I left unexplored. He was whimpering and grunting with nearly every caress of my tongue, but it wasn't until my tongue found his hole that he began calling out my name.

It would hopefully be the first of many times he did that as I finally made him mine in every way.

CHAPTER 26

CALEB

By the time Jace rolled me onto my back and covered my body with his, I was begging him – literally begging him – for relief. He'd been torturing me for the better part of an hour. He'd rimmed me, he'd buried his fingers inside of me, he'd wrapped his gorgeous lips around my cock – he'd done all three in different combinations – but he hadn't once sent me over the edge. He'd known just when to back off and when to start the blissful torment all over again. I could barely see for the sweat that was pouring down my brow, the words coming out of my mouth made little sense anymore, and my dick was so hard that it had become almost painful to have the expensive sheets scraping against the sensitive skin. Jace's mouth seemed to be the only thing my dick wanted anywhere near it.

"Baby, open your eyes," Jace murmured against my mouth. I could feel him hot and hard against my leg and I automatically tried to open my own legs so I could get his cock against mine. Maybe then he'd finally get us both off.

"Open your eyes, Caleb," Jace repeated. I did as he said and immediately got lost in the burn in his gaze.

"Do you still want this?" he asked.

I managed a nod. When that didn't seem to satisfy him, I quickly said, "Yes. I'm good, Jace. So very good."

And it was true.

With all the sensual torture Jace had inflicted upon me, there hadn't even been the possibility of comparing any of what he'd done to me to what I'd experienced in the past. Yes, I was still nervous about him actually being completely inside of me, but I knew that as long as I focused on him, everything would be okay.

Jace reached for a small bottle of lube sitting on the nightstand. I hadn't even noticed it there before, but I realized he must have come up to the room during the reception at some point to get things ready so it would be one less thing to worry about. We'd stopped using condoms about a week ago after Jace had gotten tested. I'd been tested two years earlier as part of the case against my father, and since I hadn't been with anyone since, it wasn't something Jace had asked of me.

Jace kept his eyes on me even as he began working some of the lube into my body. I was pretty loose from his tongue and his fingers being inside of me several times already, so there was next to no pain – just a slight burning sensation that felt more good than bad. When Jace settled more of his weight on top of me, he said, "Keep your eyes on me."

I nodded and closed my hands over his upper arms. He used his hand to guide himself to my opening. The second he began to push into me, I tensed up. Jace stilled and I shook my head. "No, keep going. I'm okay, Jace. I swear. It just feels... weird." It wasn't exactly the sexiest word to use, but it was what it was. Jace didn't seem to mind, because he dropped his mouth onto mine and kissed me gently.

"I wish we were back in our little bed, don't you, Caleb? The one on Dalton's boat."

I was surprised by the shift in topic, but when he continued a moment later, I knew what he was doing.

"The bed was small, but that's not why you pressed up against me, was it, baby?"

I shook my head. I automatically thought of all the times Jace had held me, never once demanding anything from me. My body relaxed, allowing Jace to ease inside of me a bit more.

"That's what I was thinking about during the wedding. The bed, the boat... it was our own little haven, wasn't it?"

"It was perfect," I said, right before I let out a harsh gasp as Jace sank deeper inside of me.

He punctuated his next words with a few kisses. "I want our first night together once we're married to be on that boat."

I closed my eyes at that and nodded. I knew he wasn't proposing to me, because it was way too soon for that. But he was making me a promise that I could hang onto. I could add it to the mental list I kept in my head that I sought out whenever the doubts would threaten to creep in. Jace and Willa took up much of that list. Eli was there too.

"Do you want that, baby?"

"More than anything," I admitted.

"Open your eyes, Caleb."

I did as he asked. He pressed deeper inside of me, stretching me full as his balls bumped up against my ass.

It was done.

He was inside of me and I was still me. Jace was still Jace. And another piece slipped into place. One that started to finally show the hint of a picture in my mind's eye.

A perfect picture that I couldn't have dreamed up even if I'd tried.

"I love you, Jace," I said.

"I love you, too, Caleb. More than you'll ever know."

I doubted that, because I couldn't conceive that it could be any greater than how much I loved him.

Jace began to move and the need for words drifted away. He spoke with his body and I answered with mine. There was no frantic rush to the finish line as he moved in and out of me. I was so lost in all the sensations exploding through my body that he could have been fucking me for minutes or hours and I wouldn't have been able to tell the difference. By the time the end was in sight, we were clinging to each other and Jace had started whispering in my ear.

That he loved me.

That he wasn't leaving.

That he was going to marry me.

It went on and on like that and I swore it was his words that drove me higher and higher. When I was flung over the edge, he was right there with me, but there was no crashing down to earth. It was just him and me floating as his release burned my insides, proving that he was now a part of me forever.

My most important piece.

~

It hurt to watch Aleks suffering. Even though he'd been the one to ask me to go with him to the waterfront, I felt completely helpless as I watched my friend try to deal with his fear.

In the two weeks since the wedding, I'd gone to visit Aleks several times at the flower shop he worked at and a few times at Magnus and Dante's house. While the young man did okay in scenarios where it was just me and him or his family members, he got tense whenever he had to deal with more than a stranger or two at a time. The flower shop was the one place where being around a few more people than he was used to wasn't as hard for him, because he had a tendency to get lost in the flowers themselves. He'd even gotten comfortable enough in the past year that he'd started working there by himself.

It was striking how many things Aleks and I had in common. Like me, he'd had to get his GED, since he'd never had the opportunity to go to school. He'd only recently earned the equivalency degree, but wanted to someday go to college. He was still living with Magnus and Dante, but outings like the one we were currently on were meant to get him to a point where he could get his own place. And like me, he'd avoided therapy to deal with the trauma of his past. It was something I was trying to encourage him to reconsider, but I wasn't going to push it, since I knew it was a decision he needed to make for himself. The few times I'd gone to therapy when I'd been seventeen, I hadn't really wanted it and had done it only to please the people around me. I doubted I would have made anywhere near the progress I was making now.

"Do you want to go?" I asked as I watched Aleks check our surroundings for what had to be the hundredth time. We were sitting on a small grassy area near Pike Place Market. It was a weekday and still relatively early in the morning, but it wasn't quiet by any means.

Aleks shook his head. He was plucking at a leather bracelet he wore on his left wrist. He forced in a deep breath, then turned his attention to Willa. I'd already offered to let him hold her, but he'd declined, saying he would in a minute.

That'd been ten minutes ago.

I suspected he was worried he'd somehow upset the baby with his anxiety.

"I'll be okay," Aleks said softly. "Just keep talking, okay?"

So I did. Mostly about nothing at all.

Life with Jace had fallen into this blissful state that I couldn't put a name to. To outsiders, it would have seemed routine, mundane even, but to me, it was perfection. With Eli and Mav still on their honeymoon, Jace and I had the house to ourselves, and while that brought about a certain amount of freedom, sexually speaking, the presence of a baby definitely kept things interesting. Like this very morning when I'd had Jace's cock down my throat and he'd been on the verge of coming when Willa had made her displeasure about the state of her diaper known. Even though it had been the fastest diaper change and bottle feeding in the history of the world, Jace's passion had cooled by the time I'd gotten back to our room.

Of course, that had presented a new opportunity in itself, and neither of us had been complaining when he'd come deep inside of me as I'd ridden him to completion.

Another fifteen minutes passed before Aleks seemed to relax a bit more. He was still fingering the bracelet, though. "Can I ask what the words mean?" I asked. Aleks looked at me and I pointed at the small oblong piece of metal that had some words I didn't recognize stamped into it. The rest of the bracelet was made of thin, braided leather.

"Oh, um, meu melhor... it means 'my best.' It's this saying my brother and I have."

"It's beautiful," I said. "Did Dante give it to you?"

Aleks nodded. "I, um... I'm not used to carrying a phone yet. I know I should be after two years, but I was never allowed to own anything, so carrying something around with me is sometimes hard to remember. I often forget my phone at home. Sometimes my wallet and keys too. I've had to start keeping cash in all my pants pockets just in case."

I felt a shard of pity go through me at his words. He hadn't told me about his past, but I didn't need the details to know it had been horrific.

Hell, that word probably didn't even adequately describe it.

"Anyway, I still have this fear that... that someone is going to take me like when I was a kid. It's stupid, I know—"

"It's not," I cut in. "It's absolutely not."

Aleks held my gaze for a moment, then nodded. "I keep thinking someone will take me and if I don't have my phone or they take it from me, Dante won't be able to find me again and they'll take me away... so Dante had this bracelet made for me so I could always wear it. He says it has something in it that makes it so he can always find me, but no one will be able to tell by looking at it."

I nodded in understanding. He was talking about a tracking device. It was what Jace had used to find me at Mr. Jennings' house.

"Hopefully someday I won't need it," Aleks said with a shrug of his shoulders.

"There's no shame in it even if you do," I said. I'd told Aleks about my cutting when he'd asked about the scars on my arm. Like the others in my family who knew, he hadn't judged. And while my therapist had given me some alternative ways to cope with stress, I still found myself sometimes wishing I could have the security back that came with making myself bleed. My therapist had said the urge would fade, but probably never fully go away. There was always the potential that the strangest thing could trigger the behavior, so I understood where Aleks was coming from.

I gladly agreed to the topic change when Aleks asked about Mav and Eli and how their honeymoon was going. My brother and his husband had elected to spend a month on Mav's Harley. They hadn't had any particular destination in mind. They'd just gotten on the bike and started driving. As of that morning, they were somewhere in New Mexico.

While I was talking, I felt a prickle of unease go through me. I tried to pass it off as a momentary thing, but when the hair on the back of my neck stood up, I began searching our surroundings. Nothing stood out at first as I scanned the dozens and dozens of faces. But as soon as I widened my search, I felt my stomach drop out.

Because one face *did* stand out in the crowd.

Fear gripped my insides as I watched the man talk to another man that was with him. When they both looked in my direction, I fought the urge to scream. Terror for Willa took over and I quickly handed her to Aleks. "Here, take her," I said.

"Wha... what? Why? What's wrong?" Aleks asked, picking up on my frantic tone.

"Aleks, take her." I kept my eyes on him even as I tried to keep the other two men in my periphery. God, what if it wasn't just the two of them? They were standing about three hundred feet away, near the entrance to the marketplace.

Aleks took Willa from me. "I'll lead them away," I said. "You go to the nearest store and tell them to call the cops. Don't leave until the cops come, do you hear me?"

"Caleb—"

"It's Rush, Aleks. Tell Jace it's Rush. He'll know what that means."

I quickly climbed to my feet. Aleks did the same, but when I made a move to leave, he grabbed me. "Caleb, wait—"

I pushed Aleks's hand away where he was holding onto the waistband of my pants to keep me from leaving. "They can't get her, Aleks," I bit out. "Get her to safety."

With that, I hurried away from Aleks and Willa and climbed up the small rise. I pretended not to have noticed Rush and the other guy. But I kept them in my line of sight as I neared the road leading into the marketplace. But instead of turning toward the marketplace, I went the opposite direction. I managed a discreet glance over my shoulder and saw that Aleks was moving toward a small gift shop near where we'd been sitting. When he disappeared inside, I chanced a glance over my shoulder.

Rush and the other guy were following me.

And they'd gained a lot of ground.

I was about to duck into a store myself, when I slammed into someone in front of me.

"Whoa there," the guy said. "You seem like you're in a hurry or something."

I tried to push past him, but he refused to release me. Before I could say anything, a gun was pressed against my belly. The man's body was so close to mine that I knew there was no way anyone was going to see it.

A few seconds later, I heard a familiar voice at my back – the one that had haunted the worst of my nightmares.

"Make a sound and Steve here will go into that little shop and kill everyone in it, including your friend and your kid."

I held perfectly still. When Rush's fingers bit into my arm and began propelling me forward, I didn't fight him. I had no idea which guy Steve was, but since the other two guys stayed with us, I had to hope it meant that no one was going to pursue Aleks into the store.

As we walked, I tried to figure out what to do next. I had my phone, but no way of reaching it to call Jace. Of course, it wasn't even an option not five seconds later when Rush pulled it from the back pocket of my jeans and dropped it to the ground. A crunching sound followed.

Fear engulfed me as Rush steered me toward a waiting sedan. I knew I should scream or try to run, but the fear that Rush had someone watching Aleks had me keeping silent.

I was shoved into the sedan. The two guys with Rush flanked me in the back seat as Rush got into the front passenger seat.

We drove for a good twenty minutes before the car pulled to a stop outside what appeared to be an abandoned warehouse. Rush dragged me into the small building. One of his men followed, the other two stayed outside. There was a bunch of assembly line equipment, but I couldn't tell what it was for. Rush shoved me against a conveyor belt. He took the gun the other guy handed him and put it to my forehead. I managed to stifle my cry of fear, but I couldn't help but close my eyes.

"Where is it?"

When I didn't answer, he jammed the gun against my head. "Where is it?"

"Where's... what?" I croaked as I forced my eyes open.

It was just in time to see the blow coming.

Pain radiated out from where the side of Rush's fist had slammed into my temple. I managed to stay upright, but I couldn't keep from crying out in pain. I could feel blood start a slow slide down my face.

"Don't make me repeat myself," Rush warned.

"I swear, I don't know what you're looking for."

"I want the fucking location!"

Pain seared through my brain as he hit me again. I couldn't keep myself upright. But it didn't matter because the other man hauled me to my feet and slammed me back against the conveyor belt behind me.

"I don't know what location you're talking about," I said.

"Did you think that son of a bitch's death would be the end of things? He gave you up, Caleb. Said you had it." Rush asked.

I could only assume he was talking about Jennings or my father. I shook my head, but before I could say anything, Rush's fingers wrapped around my throat, instantly cutting off my air. I instinctively clawed at his hands, but my efforts were futile.

"Or maybe you were thinking that you could take up where he left off? That you could milk me like he did?"

Understanding dawned at his words, but it didn't matter because I couldn't say anything with Rush's hand slowly stealing my life away. My vision started to dim and spots danced before my eyes when Rush suddenly released me. I collapsed onto the ground and tried sucking in air, but I couldn't seem to manage it.

"You were a good fuck, but not worth anywhere near the amount of money that fucker was getting out of me. But guess what, I paid in full. You want even a cent out of me, it's going to cost you a lot more than a quick fuck in the dirt."

Rush yanked me to my feet and then turned me and bent me over the conveyer belt. Terror ratcheted through me as he blanketed my body with his. I could feel his dick pressing against my ass. "Maybe I ought to get a preview to see if you're even still worth it."

I dug my fingers along the underside of the edge of the conveyor belt and winced when I felt something pierce my skin.

Something sharp.

As Rush began grinding against me, I closed my fingers around the object to see if I could work it loose. I didn't make much progress because Rush chose that moment to reach for the zipper on my pants. "The phone! You're talking about Dad's phone!" I screamed, though the words came out in a strangled rasp since my throat hurt so bad from Rush choking me.

He stilled, then jerked me upright and turned me around. "So you're done playing innocent, huh? Where is it?"

I wasn't even sure if my father had kept the phone he'd used that night. The cops had confiscated his phone when he'd been arrested, but it wasn't the one he'd owned while on the camping trip. But it didn't surprise me in the least to learn he'd told Rush I had the phone. Something like that would have been sure to get Rush to come after me, even if it wasn't true.

"If I tell you where it is, will you let me go?" I asked, knowing full well what Rush's answer would be.

But he didn't actually answer me. Instead he grabbed me by the throat again, but he didn't apply enough pressure to cut off my air. "Do you know how many good men I lost because of you? I mean, there I am, minding my own business, when I get a call that you're dredging up the past."

"Did Mr. Jennings call you? Or did he call my father? That's what started it, right?"

"That faggot Richard called your father first saying we were all going down. Your father told him he better figure something out because the video on the phone only implicated him and me. The little fucker practically ordered me to fix things."

"You mean Mr. Jennings," I said. "I thought he was my father's friend and that you worked with him."

"My sister's kid went to Richard's school," Rush said. "Your father and Jennings grew up together. When your father was looking for someone to do some stuff for him – off the books – Richard sent him my way."

"Did Mr. Jennings really kill himself or was that you?"

Rush laughed. "Did you actually think he hung himself out of guilt for what happened in those woods?" He leaned in so close to me that I could smell his breath. "He may have put on a good show about not wanting to fuck you, but you should have seen his face when he sank inside that tight little body of yours. The hounds of hell couldn't have stopped him at that point."

Rush shoved me back against the belt. The second my fingers closed around the lip of it, I searched out the sharp piece of metal again and frantically tried to pry it loose.

"Where's the phone?" Rush demanded.

I knew my time had run out. There was no way for Jace to find me, so trying to hold out made no sense. But my instinct to survive was stronger than ever. I managed to straighten and stepped closer to Rush. "I don't have it, Rush," I murmured. "He lied to you. If the phone exists, it might as well be gone because I don't have any idea where he would have put it. There's no evidence to implicate you in anything."

I dared to take another step closer to him. It had our bodies almost practically touching. "I won't tell anyone what happened. You know I'm good at keeping secrets. I kept yours all those years. I... I did what you wanted me to do. I'm good at that too. My dad made sure of that."

I heard Rush draw in a breath of air and saw his jaw tick. He stepped forward, pressing me back until I hit the belt behind me. He loomed over me, but I held my ground. I quickly located the piece of metal and tore at it with my fingers.

"Are you actually trying to proposition me?" he sneered.

"I'm trying to stay alive," I responded. "I don't give a shit about the past. I'll do anything to get out of this."

Rush studied me for a moment, then looked at the other man. Several long seconds passed before Rush nodded at him. I was both glad and horrified when he left.

I thought maybe Rush would order me to my knees, but he clearly wasn't interested in playing around, because he grabbed me by the hair and yanked my head back. "Let's see how tight your ass is after all those years of your daddy plowing it."

Rush released me long enough to rip my pants open. My fingernails broke and I could feel blood spilling over my hand as I tore at the piece of metal. I stifled my cry of fear as Rush turned me around and bent me over the conveyer belt. I lay perfectly still as he slid his hand over my bare ass. Satisfied with my show of supplication, Rush's hand disappeared and I heard his zipper being drawn down, followed by the sound of him spitting, probably into his hand so he could wet his cock. I bit into my lip to keep from calling out for help. It was at the exact moment that Rush's dick bumped against my ass that I got the metal free. As Rush leaned over me and slapped his hand next to me on the belt while his other hand worked his dick between my cheeks, I eased the piece of metal from beneath the belt and got a good grip on it. The second Rush's cock pressed against my hole, I reared back hard enough to hit Rush in the nose with the back of my head. Pain blinded me for a moment as Rush let out a shout. His weight disappeared from my back and I quickly turned around. He had his hands covering his bloodied nose.

"You little—"

That was all he got out before I plunged the piece of metal into his neck as hard as I could. Blood spurted as Rush staggered backwards. He reached for the metal, his eyes wide. I tried to jerk my pants up so I could make a run for it, but a wave of dizziness passed over me and I fell to the ground. I started to crawl as the sound of gurgling filled my ears.

I was dimly aware of popping sounds coming from outside, but I couldn't make sense of why anyone would be setting off firecrackers now.

Darkness began to threaten to steal me away, but I managed to see Rush collapse to the ground. The metal was gone from his neck, but there was so much blood that I knew it didn't matter anymore.

"Caleb!"

I sobbed into my arm as Jace's terrified shout ripped through the warehouse. I tried to call out to him, but I couldn't manage it, so I had no choice but to wait until he found me.

Which was just moments later.

"Caleb, baby," Jace said frantically as he dropped to his knees next to me and eased me up onto his lap. "Talk to me," he begged.

"Willa? Aleks," I whispered, because my throat hurt.

"Safe. They're both safe. Aleks called Dante from the shop you told him to hide in."

Jace tucked me against his chest. I was still naked from the waist down. "Caleb," Jace whispered brokenly as his hand trailed down my naked hip toward my pants.

"He didn't, Jace. He didn't," I managed to say. "I'm okay."

An anguished sob tore from Jace's throat as he leaned over me. "Thank you," Jace whispered. He kept repeating the words over and over again as he rocked me back and forth on his lap. I could feel his tears on my face, but I didn't have the energy to tell him not to cry.

"Jace, let me look at him," I heard Ronan say. I could hear sirens in the distance, but I didn't know if they were for me or not.

Jace released me enough so Ronan could run his hands over me. He asked me questions, especially about my head, but I struggled to answer him.

"He'll need to be treated for a concussion, but he'll be okay," Ronan said quietly.

I felt Jace nodding against me. He tucked me back against his body. "Thank God I found you," he whispered. "Can't ever lose you."

I wanted to comfort him, because I'd never heard him sound so broken, not even when he'd learned of his sister's death, but I was having trouble keeping my eyes open. "How... how find me?" I mumbled.

I felt Jace reach down my body. He placed something in my hand, but it took me a second to figure out what it was.

It was Aleks's bracelet. His tracking bracelet.

"How?" I asked.

"He put it in your pocket," Jace explained. I remembered the moment where Aleks had grabbed a hold of my pants. I'd thought it'd been so he could stop me, but he'd been trying to give me the bracelet instead. If he hadn't managed to stick it into my pocket...

I was too tired to try to make sense of anything else. Willa was safe. Aleks was safe.

And Jace was here.

As far as I was concerned, life was fucking perfect.

EPILOGUE

JACE

SIX MONTHS LATER

"God, it's cold," I muttered.

"Watch your step," Caleb responded.

"You know this is crazy, right?" I asked. "It will still be a surprise if you take this thing off now."

"Not yet," Caleb said as he reached for the hand I was touching the blindfold with. "Just a little longer. Please?"

"Fine," I said. "But for future reference, I hate the cold. And surprises."

"Noted," Caleb said.

I listened as Caleb told me when to step. There weren't too many steps leading from the body of the plane to the ground, but it was still off-putting, since I couldn't see for shit through the piece of fabric Caleb had wrapped around my eyes.

The whole thing had started this morning when Caleb had woken me up with what he'd called my birthday morning blow job. Since he'd added the *morning* part in, I'd assumed, well, hoped, actually, that there'd be more coming throughout the day. Breakfast in bed had been next, along with a strict order for me to stay in bed while Caleb took Willa to Mav and Eli's house for the day.

I'd hoped that his return would lead to blowjob number two followed by a marathon of all-day sex, but no such luck.

As soon as he'd gotten back to our house, he'd pulled an already packed suitcase out of our closet and had told me to get dressed.

I'd been in the dark since then, both figuratively and now, literally.

No matter how much cajoling I'd done in the car, Caleb hadn't spoken a word about our destination.

Which had ended up being an airstrip just south of the city.

I hadn't had to wear the blindfold on the plane, but Caleb had closed all the window shades so I couldn't look outside, and the pilots hadn't mentioned our destination even once. However, I had gotten blowjob number two in the small bedroom at the back of the plane. I'd gotten a lot more than that, actually.

To say that Caleb had embraced his sexual awakening was an understatement. Admittedly, we'd had some rough spots as he'd recovered from Rush's attack, but we'd taken things slow and eventually Caleb had been able to put the terrifying encounter behind him.

Me, not so much.

There were still days when I didn't want to let Caleb or Willa out of the house, despite the threat to Caleb being truly gone now. Ronan, Dante, and I had killed all the men waiting outside the warehouse and Rush had bled out within a minute of Caleb stabbing him. Caleb had only had to spend one night in the hospital, but I'd kept him in bed for several days after that. Eli and Mav had returned from their honeymoon early, despite Caleb's protests. When Eli had asked Caleb if he would have been able to stay away if the situation had been reversed, Caleb had promptly shut up and hugged his brother and told him he was okay.

As the trauma had faded, Caleb and I had settled into a new normal. We'd found a house that was near Mav and Eli's that gave us some room to grow into. It was also close to the university where Caleb had enrolled for the fall semester after getting his GED. Willa had become the light of our lives and we reveled in every milestone she hit. We were eagerly awaiting her first words, which each of us were equally sure would be our respective titles.

Dada for Caleb and *Papa* for me.

The only checkbox I had left to tick off was getting my ring on Caleb's finger – something that would be a lot easier now that I'd finally found the perfect one.

And fortunately, I'd had the sense to grab it from my dresser drawer right before Caleb had dragged me out the door. Even now, I could feel the weight of it in my pocket.

"Okay, this way," Caleb said as he took my hand. The car he ushered me into was nice and warm, but when I made a move to take off the blindfold, Caleb stopped me. "Not yet."

"You do realize I'm going to get even with you for this... and your punishment will likely include this blindfold?"

I heard someone chuckle and realized it wasn't Caleb. I could feel my cheeks heating. "Caleb, baby, are we in a cab?"

"Um, maybe." He dropped his voice, presumably so only I could hear him. "And as for your other question, I'm counting on it."

With that, I stopped complaining because he'd just given me the perfect way to propose. I'd make love to him until he was begging me for release and that's when I'd slip my ring onto his finger.

At the same time that I slipped the blindfold off.

I sighed and leaned back against the seat.

"What?" Caleb asked.

"What *what?*" I responded.

I could practically feel Caleb's curious eyes on me. But before he could say anything, the cab pulled to a stop. Caleb helped me out. I expected him to lead me somewhere, but instead, he whispered in my ear, "Are you ready to see your surprise?"

"Does it include you naked?" I asked, hoping like hell the cab driver was gone. From the two distinct chuckles I heard, the answer to that was no. I listened as Caleb thanked the driver and sent him on his way. Then his fingers went to the blindfold.

"Just remember that I love you and this trip is just for you."

"Okay," I said somewhat nervously.

He pulled the blindfold off. It took my eyes a second to adjust, but when they did, my stomach dropped out.

"No way," I said. "You've got to fucking be kidding me," I said as I took in the huge snow-covered mountains. There were skiers everywhere, both on and off the massive ski runs, and the ski lift was jam-packed with people.

Oh God, he was taking me skiing.

I'd be making a fool out of myself in front of him and a million other people.

What the hell had he been thinking?

"What do you think?"

"I think you should probably make sure you're up to date on your health insurance," I said as I looked at him.

"Exactly what kind of punishment is it that you're planning?" he asked with a grin.

"Caleb," I said as I looked at the ski slopes again. "I love you, but there's just no way in hell you're going to be able to teach me to ski."

"Oh, we're not skiing," Caleb said.

"We're not?"

He shook his head. "No, that's not your surprise," he said as he pointed at the mountains. He used his fingers on my chin to turn my head slightly to the left. "That's your surprise."

It took me a moment to zero in on what he was trying to show me. My eyes went wide when I saw a woman waving at us from the opposite side of the lodge's driveway.

"Oh my God, is that…"

"It is."

"It isn't," I said in disbelief. But as the woman headed our way, I knew I was wrong. "I can't believe it," I whispered. "You got me Martha Stewart for my birthday?"

I whipped my head around to stare at Caleb in complete and utter shock. "What… how… *what*…?"

He grinned. "Turns out she and Mariana worked together on some kind of fundraiser benefiting veterans a while back. When I mentioned to Mariana that you were a fan, she said she'd make a call.

And she did. Martha has a house out here – we're in Vail, by the way. She said we could join her for dinner tonight."

"Oh my God," I repeated. I felt a sudden warmth flow through me as I remembered all the time my mother and I had spent bonding over everything Martha Stewart related.

I wanted to kiss Caleb for giving that moment to me.

So that's what I did. I brushed my lips gently over his. "Thank you," I said in all seriousness.

His eyes were bright as he smiled at me.

Because he knew what this moment was to me – it was so much more than meeting a famous person.

Caleb squeezed my hand.

"Oh, and Mav and Eli upgraded us to a luxury suite. Something about bearskin rugs – fake ones – in front of the fireplace, a mini-fridge full of strawberry milk and a private balcony with a hot tub—"

I kissed him hard. "You had me at Martha Stewart," I said.

Caleb laughed. But before I could process that I was really about to talk to *the* Martha Stewart, Caleb leaned up to whisper in my ear, "Just remember, she looks at you funny even once, I'm kicking her ass."

I let out a bark of laughter and tugged him up against me. "Got it. Do me a favor, will you?" I asked.

"Anything," Caleb said softly, and I knew he meant it.

He *would* do anything for me.

Just like I'd do anything for him.

"Whatever you do, don't let me cook in front of her. I'd never be able to live down setting Martha Stewart on fire."

Caleb laughed and leaned into me. "Okay, deal. As long as you don't tell her that Sno Balls are the best dessert in the world."

"Deal. Those will be included in your punishment, by the way."

Caleb's pretty eyes held mine as he whispered, "Promise?"

I knew what he was asking. He wanted so much more than just the promise of a fun night in bed. He wanted a lifetime of promises.

I kissed his temple. "Promise," I whispered.

And as we stepped off the curb and made our way to meet my idol,

I knew that I would gladly spend the rest of my life keeping the promises I made Caleb.

Just like I knew he'd do the same for me.

Always.

The End

Check out the next page for a sneak peek of Aleks and Vaughn's story, Unbroken

SNEAK PEEK

UNBROKEN (THE PROTECTORS, BOOK 12) (M/M)

PROLOGUE

ALEKS

"Thanks, Aleks! These are definitely getting me out of the doghouse with the missus!"

"You're welcome, Mr. Dunbar," I said as I locked the door behind the older man and flipped the *Open* sign to *Closed* and drew down the full-length blind that kept people from seeing into the flower shop after hours. I instantly felt more relaxed.

"So much for all the progress you've made, Aleks," I murmured quietly to myself.

Progress? What progress?

I told my inner voice to shut up and reached for my phone. I wasn't surprised when it rang before I could even unlock the screen. My brother Dante's name flashed on the screen, along with the picture of him, his fiancé Magnus, Magnus's grandson Matty, and Matty's best friends, Leo and Jamie. The picture had been taken during Matty's birthday party at our house – the private party.

Because I hadn't been brave enough to attend the real party he'd had with his friends or the one with the entire family. While Matty definitely hadn't minded having another party, I knew Dante and Magnus had made special arrangements with Matty's fathers to give the boy a small party that I could attend that wouldn't overwhelm me.

It had been both humiliating and a relief. Because I'd wanted to celebrate Matty's birthday with him, but it was pathetic that after two years of trying to adjust to my new life, I still couldn't do something as nonthreatening as attend a family gathering that would have more than a handful of people at it.

And not just any people, but ones who knew about my past and were always respectful of my boundaries.

"I'm leaving in a few minutes," I said before Dante could say anything.

"Let me guess, you stayed open late for Mr. Dunbar again. What did he do this time?"

I smiled. "He used one of Mrs. Dunbar's favorite vases as a hole for putting practice." I didn't actually know what that meant, but as someone who understood how much Mrs. Dunbar loved her flowers and the vases she put them in, the fact that Mr. Dunbar had even touched one of the vases, let alone used it for a purpose other than it was intended for, explained why Mr. Dunbar had been forced to go for one of the more expensive arrangements today.

"Idiot," Dante muttered. "Why don't I come get you?" Dante asked. "If I leave now, I can be there in fifteen minutes."

I was more than tempted to take my brother up on the offer, but doing so would be yet another step backward for me.

"No, it's okay. I... I want to take the bus."

I really didn't, but most of the things I did these days were less about what I *wanted* to do and more about what I *needed* to do.

Dante was silent for a moment, no doubt torn between encouraging me and trying to change my mind. I wasn't the only one who'd been rattled by the abduction of my friend, Caleb, three days earlier. I'd been with the young man when some men from his past had shown up at the small park we'd been at. Caleb and his infant daughter had come with me to support me as I'd tried to work on being around a crowd of people. I'd done pretty well at Caleb's brother's wedding a couple of weeks earlier, so I'd been feeling confident that I could somehow magically handle being around a large group of complete strangers.

I'd been a mess.

But I'd managed not to flee.

Until Caleb had spotted a man who'd been hunting him. Caleb had shoved his daughter, Willa, into my arms and had told me to go into the nearest shop and call for help. He'd then taken off to lead the men away. It had been a horrific situation, but fortunately my brother and Caleb's boyfriend, Jace, had been able to find him.

The whole thing had set me back quite a bit, and it had undoubtedly given Dante a scare too. It had all been too reminiscent of my own abduction twelve years earlier when I'd been eight and Dante had been sixteen. Dante had been with me when I'd been taken from a mall and he'd spent nearly every moment since then looking for me.

Despite knowing the reasons I'd been taken, I had no doubt that Dante had been shocked by what he'd found when he'd shown up at a mansion just outside Chicago one night to rescue me.

I could still remember the events of that night as if they'd happened yesterday, instead of a little over two years ago. Dante and Magnus had watched in horror as I'd followed the command I'd been given to strip and bend over a desk. I hadn't even hesitated to do as I'd been told.

Because it was all I'd known.

Show this man what you are...

I flinched as the voice permeated my mind. I'd worked for two long years to get Father's voice out of my head, but every time I was certain I'd managed to silence it, it would randomly appear again.

I was coming to accept that it was a part of me.

Just like I had long ago accepted that I would always refer to Marcus Parks as *Father*, despite sharing no blood with the man. Not to mention the fact that the things he'd done to me had had absolutely nothing to do with being any kind of father to me.

Even the man's death hadn't changed that.

Father's death automatically had me thinking about another man I'd tried long ago to vanquish from my thoughts, but for a whole other set of reasons.

I only knew him as Vaughn. I wasn't sure if that was his last name or first. I shouldn't have even known that much about him, because Father hadn't liked it when the guards talked to me.

But Vaughn had done more than talk to me. He'd become like the thin stream of light that had somehow managed to break through the black paint covering the little window of the first room I'd been cast into after I'd been taken.

Sometimes that stream of light had been the only thing that had kept me wanting to open my eyes each day.

"Aleks?"

Dante's soft voice broke through the memories of the dark-haired, dark-eyed man who'd been my only source of light for the longest time…

"Sorry," I said. "I'll take the bus, Dante." I was proud of how firm my voice sounded, even though my stomach was tied in knots.

"Okay, I'll see you in a bit," Dante said.

"Okay. Love you, meu melhor…"

Dante paused for a moment, and when he said, "Love you too, irmãozinho," I could tell he was choking up a bit. I was too. I always did when he called me his little brother. I'd thought him lost to me forever for so long that it was sometimes hard to accept I had my big brother watching out for me again like when we'd been kids.

I hung up the phone and tucked it into my pocket, then hurried to finish closing the store for the night. It was already starting to get dark out and I really didn't want to risk missing my bus and being forced to wait fifteen minutes for the next one. I'd lucked out that my work was on a bus line that went directly by Magnus and Dante's house. It meant not having to deal with transfers. The bus itself usually wasn't too crowded, but on the occasions it was busier than normal, I usually stood near the back exit rather than sitting and reading a book on my phone (a concept I still hadn't gotten used to).

As I worked, I found myself reaching for the bracelet on my left wrist, only to remember it wasn't there. Touching the bracelet throughout the day had become a habit that I just couldn't break myself of.

Because it wasn't an ordinary bracelet.

My brother had designed it to include some kind of tracking device so he'd always be able to find me. He'd given it to me after I'd forgotten my phone one day about two months after Dante and Magnus had rescued me. I'd been walking the four blocks from home to the library and had gotten lost. Instead of remaining calm and asking someone for directions, I'd panicked and gotten myself even more lost. I'd ended up missing for hours, and by the time Dante had found me, I'd been sitting in the middle of the sidewalk crying like a baby. A passerby had called the police, who'd managed to get enough information out of me to call Dante and Magnus.

After that, I'd been afraid to leave the house for weeks. It was only when Dante had given me the bracelet and told me it meant he'd always be able to find me that I'd ventured out again. The bracelet had become my lifeline to the outside world.

But I no longer had it. On the day Caleb had been abducted, I'd managed to stuff the bracelet into his pocket. It had allowed Dante and Jace to track Caleb's location and rescue him from the men who'd taken him. Unfortunately, the bracelet had gotten lost in the shuffle of Caleb being transported to the hospital, and Dante was still working to get me a new one. But I still had my phone. Not only had *I* made a point of remembering to grab it the past few mornings, but Dante and Magnus had both checked to make sure I had it on me before I'd left the house.

After making sure everything was locked down, I hurried out the back door. I only had a few minutes to meet the bus, so I didn't do my usual routine of scanning the alley behind the shop several times before turning my back while I locked the door.

As I began walking toward the northern end of the alley, I heard the sound of squealing tires. I looked over my shoulder just in time to see a green van come careening around the corner of the alley's southern entrance. I told myself not to panic, but instinct won out over reason and I began running. I kept looking over my shoulder as the van closed in on me. When I saw a figure step out of the back door of one of the other shops, I shouted, "Help me, please!"

I practically slammed into the guy. "Please, they're after me!" I yelled frantically as I pointed to the van. I wasn't completely sure it wasn't just some random, reckless delivery driver, but I wasn't taking any chances. The van was less than a hundred feet from me and coming fast.

When the man didn't respond, I tried to push past him, but he grabbed me by the upper arms in a painful hold.

And that was when I knew.

He hadn't been coming out of one of the shops because he worked there.

He'd been waiting for me.

"No," I whispered as pure terror ripped through me with violent force.

I opened my mouth to scream again when the man holding me punched me in the face. The blow left me reeling and I hit the ground hard. I tried to get my bearings as pure panic clawed through me, but I wasn't fast enough.

A second blow left me too stunned to do anything at all. Several pairs of rough hands grabbed me as the world spun. I was lifted and thrown onto a cold, metal floor. More hands, or the same ones – I wasn't sure – held me down as the van's door slid shut.

It's happening again.

Tears streaked down my face. "Please, don't!" I begged, but that was all I got out before a piece of fabric was jammed into my mouth and tied behind my head. I flailed my arms and legs, but they were bound with plastic ties within seconds.

"Get his phone," one of the men said.

I was quickly searched and let out a harsh sob when my phone was yanked out of my pocket.

"Toss it," I heard someone say and then I heard a window opening.

And with it went my only lifeline.

I began crying uncontrollably, but my captors didn't take any pity on me. Instead, one gruffly said, "Shut the fuck up," and then he covered my head with some kind of hood, pitching me into darkness.

They left me alone as I rolled onto my side and sobbed into my gag. My hands were bound in front of me, but the second I lifted them to try and get the hood off, I felt something sharp at my throat.

"Do it and I'll cut you. He said bring you back, but he didn't say shit about doing it in one piece."

I froze as the tip of the blade trailed down my throat. When I felt it snag on the first button of my shirt, I stiffened. Then it was popping the button off my shirt.

The second button followed.

Then the third.

I squeezed my eyes closed and let out a moan of denial.

"Knock that shit off, Spears."

"The order was to bring him back. Didn't say we couldn't have some fun along the way. It's a long drive to Chicago."

Bile rose in my throat. They were taking me to Chicago?

Despair had me folding in on myself, not caring about the knife anymore. There was only one reason they could be taking me back to Chicago. Father might be dead, but there were plenty of men who'd be happy to take his place.

I stopped listening as the men argued, and searched out that place inside my head where I wouldn't hear them anymore. There'd be no hood, no gag, no van...

Alstroemeria... friendship.

Amaryllis... splendid beauty.

Anemone... fading hope.

I let out a sob when I realized it wasn't working. From the time I'd been handed a book with stunning pictures of all kinds of flowers, along with their meaning, I'd recited the list of flowers in alphabetical order whenever I'd needed to block out what was happening to me. But I could still hear the men bickering; I could still feel the floor of the van beneath me and the rocking motion that went with the vehicle taking turn after turn. The gag was still there, as were my bindings.

I felt a keen sense of betrayal by my own mind as I lay there and tried to accept that I would never see my brother again. Because there was no way Dante was going to be able to find me a second time. It'd been sheer luck that he'd managed it the first time.

My body began to shake violently as this new reality crashed down on me. I had no idea how long we drove for, but it felt like hours.

"What the fuck?" I heard one of the guys say. "What is this asshole doing?"

The man sounded annoyed, and I felt the van slow.

"Just go around him!" one of the men sitting near me said.

"He's in the middle of the fucking road," came the response.

"Idiot probably broke down," a third man grumbled.

There was a brief moment of silence as the van slowed even more, then someone yelled, "He's got a gun!"

A split-second later came the squealing of the brakes. I rolled forward, then back as the van careened out of control. I heard a chorus of yells and curses, along with several popping sounds. One of the guys grabbed my arm as the sliding door was opened.

"Wait... wait—" I heard the guy named Spears yell, then there were another few popping sounds and then silence.

Complete and utter silence.

I lifted my hands to try and get the hood off, but froze when a hand closed around my arm. I tried to scramble back, but the hold on me was firm.

"It's okay," I heard a man say, then he was pulling me to an upright position. I could feel fingers at the base of the hood. It was removed a few seconds later and despite it being dark outside, my eyes still felt the need to adjust. There was enough light from the dome light inside the van to make out the man who was working to release the gag.

I let out a sob of relief at the familiar sight of the dark hair, brown eyes that almost appeared black, and bearded face that was just inches from mine.

Vaughn.

"It's okay, Aleks, I've got you," Vaughn murmured as he got the gag off and dropped it on the floor of the van.

The combination of terror and relief mixed in a cacophony of emotions that I couldn't control and before I could stop myself, I lifted my bound hands and looped them over Vaughn's neck. I tucked my nose against his throat and breathed him in to prove to myself he was really there.

He still had the same scent – some kind of woodsy smell mixed with musk and just a hint of butterscotch.

I wanted to laugh at that.

The brutally dangerous man loved butterscotch.

And it was how he'd gotten me to trust him when I'd first met him, because he'd shared his butterscotch candies with me.

In secret.

Because I hadn't been allowed to have candy.

Or anything else.

I couldn't form words as I clung to him. He held me against his big, warm, strong body, making me feel even safer. I could have stayed there all day, but Vaughn gently eased my arms up over his head and settled them in front of me.

And that was when I noticed the bodies.

Two in the back of the van with me, two in the front seats, and one just outside the door on the ground.

The ones whose faces I could see had their eyes open and perfectly shaped holes dead center in their foreheads. There wasn't even much blood.

I was dimly aware of Vaughn tucking the gun in his hand into his waistband and then pulling a small utility knife from his pocket. He cut through the ties at my feet, then pulled me to a standing position.

"Are you hurt?" Vaughn asked as he quickly scanned my body, then settled on my face, which was no doubt bruised from the punches I'd taken.

I shook my head and then lifted my shoulders so I could wipe my wet face on my shirt sleeves.

And that was when I realized my hands were still bound. Before I could ask Vaughn to remove the plastic ties around my wrists, he grabbed my arm and led me from the van. "We need to get moving," he said. "Someone could come along at any minute."

Wasn't that a good thing?

I felt off-balance as he steered me toward a sedan that was parked in the middle of the road. I had to lean into him to keep myself from stumbling, and I was glad when his arm went around me. He was considerably larger than me and while his bulk should have scared me, Vaughn was the exception to that general rule.

Vaughn was the exception to a lot of rules.

While I'd initially thought him to be just another one of Father's guards who'd become infatuated with me, he'd been different. He'd never once made a move on me, and when things had come to a head in Father's study the night Magnus and Dante had shown up to rescue me, it had been Vaughn who'd saved us all. I'd ended up stabbing Father in the back – literally – when he'd been preparing to shoot Dante. Dante had still gotten shot, but only in the shoulder.

But then Father had turned the gun on me.

And that was when Vaughn had appeared, and I'd watched Father's eyes go wide as a bullet had torn through his neck. Blood had spurted everywhere, and he'd collapsed onto the very desk he'd made me bend over on. Vaughn had shot the other two guards in the room before I'd even been able to process what was happening, then he'd calmly walked up to me and helped me stand from where Father had knocked me to the ground. He'd touched the spot on my face where Father had marked me, then he'd shot Father in the head.

I'd never seen Vaughn again after he'd gotten me, Magnus, and Dante out of the house.

But I'd dreamed of him often.

Almost nightly.

Strange dreams I didn't always understand.

But that I enjoyed just the same.

And now he was here, saving me again.

Vaughn led me to his car and got me settled in the passenger seat. He walked around the front of the car and climbed into the driver's seat. I turned and held out my hands as I said, "Can you... can you take me home, please? I don't want to wait for the police. Dante will be worried... he'll... he'll help us explain what happened to the police."

Vaughn got the car started, then turned to look at me. There was enough light from the touchscreen in the dashboard to see his face.

And I didn't like what I saw.

In fact, it had fear skating through me.

Fear that turned to a sensation that I could only describe as agony as a sense of betrayal hit hard and fast.

"Vaughn," I whispered as I jutted my hands toward him a bit, desperately hoping I was wrong. "Please untie me and take me home."

Tears began flowing down my cheeks long before he turned away from me and put the car in gear. Long before he set his eyes on the road ahead of us. And long before he confirmed my worst fear with seven little words that cut through me like the sharpest of blades.

"I'm sorry, Aleks, I can't do that."

ABOUT THE AUTHOR

Dear Reader,

I hope you enjoyed Jace and Caleb's story. Yes, Dalton and Silver will get a story at some point. Up next in the series are Aleks and Vaughn who you first met in Atonement, Dante and Magnus's story.

As an independent author, I am always grateful for feedback so if you have the time and desire, please leave a review, good or bad, so I can continue to find out what my readers like and don't like. You can also send me feedback via email at sloane@sloanekennedy.com

Join my Facebook Fan Group: Sloane's Secret Sinners

Connect with me:
www.sloanekennedy.com
sloane@sloanekennedy.com

RESOURCES

RAINN (Rape, Abuse & Incest National Network) has both a comprehensive website and a hotline that can assist you.
   https://www.rainn.org

As a survivor of self-injury myself, one of the most important things to remember is that you are not alone and that there are resources out there that can help you find a different way of coping with your pain. This website is a good place to start:
   http://www.mentalhealthamerica.net/self-injury

ALSO BY SLOANE KENNEDY

(Note: Not all titles will be available on all retail sites)

The Escort Series
Gabriel's Rule (M/F)
Shane's Fall (M/F)
Logan's Need (M/M)

Barretti Security Series
Loving Vin (M/F)
Redeeming Rafe (M/M)
Saving Ren (M/M/M)
Freeing Zane (M/M)

Finding Series
Finding Home (M/M/M)
Finding Trust (M/M)
Finding Peace (M/M)
Finding Forgiveness (M/M)
Finding Hope (M/M/M)

The Protectors
Absolution (M/M/M)

Salvation (M/M)

Retribution (M/M)

Forsaken (M/M)

Vengeance (M/M/M)

A Protectors Family Christmas

Atonement (M/M)

Revelation (M/M)

Redemption (M/M)

Defiance (M/M)

Unexpected (M/M/M)

Shattered (M/M)

Non-Series

Letting Go (M/F)